'What would *you* like in a husband?'

A mere twenty-four hours ago such a question would have amazed her with its impertinence. As she sat there considering his question she discovered that she had already taken the measure of this man. Captain Ross Rennie was as transparent as water—a capable man with no inclination to dither or waste his time or anyone else's. He had spent a lifetime in duty to his country so intense and harsh that it did not let go, even in a snowy village in Yorkshire. She knew it was not a casual question because he was not a casual man.

'I've never really thought about it,' she told him honestly.

He didn't believe her. 'Come, come, Miss Rennie, you're a fine-appearing Scottish lass!'

'Thank you kindly,' she said with a smile. 'I also live with my aunt and uncle, who have no particular obligation to see me wed. They're not the sort of people who exert themselves.' She thought about the matter. 'And perhaps I have not exerted myself overmuch either.'

She didn't say that in any attempt for pity, and he seemed to know it. With a smile, he touched her hand…a light touch.

THE
WEDDING RING
QUEST

Carla Kelly

First published in Great Britain 2014
by Mills & Boon, an imprint of Harlequin (UK) Limited,
Large Print edition 2014
Harlequin (UK) Limited, Eton House, 18-24 Paradise Road,
Richmond, Surrey TW9 1SR

© 2014 Carla Kelly

ISBN: 978-0-263-23980-5

Harlequin (UK) Limited's policy is to use papers that are natural,
renewable and recyclable products and made from wood grown in
sustainable forests. The logging and manufacturing processes conform
to the legal environmental regulations of the country of origin.

Printed and bound in Great Britain
by CPI Antony Rowe, Chippenham, Wiltshire

Carla Kelly started writing Regency romances because of her interest in the Napoleonic Wars, and enjoys writing about warfare at sea and the ordinary people of the British Isles rather than lords and ladies. In her spare time she reads British crime fiction and history—particularly the US Indian Wars. Carla lives in Utah, USA, and is a former park ranger, and double RITA® Award and Spur Award winner. She has five children and four grandchildren.

Novels by the same author:

BEAU CRUSOE
CHRISTMAS PROMISE
  (part of *Regency Christmas Gifts* anthology)
MARRYING THE CAPTAIN*
THE SURGEON'S LADY*
MARRYING THE ROYAL MARINE*
MARRIAGE OF MERCY
THE ADMIRAL'S PENNILESS BRIDE
HER HESITANT HEART

linked by character

My Bonnie Mary

The trumpets sound, the banners fly,
The glittering spears are ranked ready;
The shouts o' war are heard afar,
The battle closes thick and bloody;
But it's no the roar o' sea or shore
Wad mak me langer wish to tarry;
Nor shout o' war that's heard afar—
It's leaving thee, my bonnie Mary!

Robert Burns

Chapter One

This was no ordinary return to Plymouth; Captain Ross Rennie felt it in his bones. A frigate captain much wiser than he—dead now, like so many friends—had described it best during one of those chats on the far side of the world when another frigate pulled alongside to visit and hand off mail.

In the course of their conversation over beef too long in brine and green water, they described recent fights with the French or Spanish, depending on where national allegiance had swung in an endless war. The long-defunct captain had looked Ross square in the eye and said, 'Sometimes a victory is only a hair's breadth better than a defeat.'

A young captain at the time, Ross had nodded, wondering later what the devil the man meant. As his thirty-six-gun frigate *Abukir* sailed into Plymouth on a rainy day, Ross felt that hollow, sinking feeling of defeat, when he should have been over the moon with joy. The emotion had been growing since his ship had been ordered to join the convoy escorting Napoleon and his entourage to Elba after his banishment there in 1814 by the Allies. A time or two during the short voyage from France, he had stood on his own quarterdeck and observed Bonaparte on HMS *Undaunted*, Captain Tom Ussher's frigate.

Ross almost hated himself for finding the man so fascinating, but the exiled emperor seemed to demand attention. Ross noticed other telescopes trained on Napoleon.

The longer he watched Napoleon, the greater grew his personal sense of disquiet, the greater his sense of defeat. Normally a sanguine fellow, Ross felt himself grow grim about the mouth. *He's so short and stout*, Ross thought. *So ordinary.* He took his observation into dangerous territory then, the worst place any officer could take himself. *How in the world did this man rule my life for twenty-four years?* Ross found himself asking.

For he had. For more than a generation, Ross had sailed where this tyrant intended, fought French and Spanish ships, logged miserable hours twice in prisons, lost a leg, found a true love and lost her, too. Supposedly he was in the service of poor King George III, but Ross knew what all officers and men in the Royal Navy knew—had there been no Napoleon, there would have been no war. He would probably never have gone to sea in a fighting ship. Without that stout little man, Ross Rennie would probably have conned nothing more dramatic than a merchant vessel.

'You ruined my life,' he murmured one lazy afternoon as they approached the island of Elba, some twelve mere kilometres from Tuscany. The only man within earshot was the helmsman and he was used to hearing his captain mutter.

But because he *was* sanguine and normally rational, Ross had to reason with himself. Was this true? The war was over, so he did something unheard of: he leaned his elbows on the ship's rail. He looked up when he heard the sails luff, and laughed, knowing his sudden lapse of ship's discipline had caused the helmsman to stare and lose his concentration.

Embarrassed, Ross straightened up and administered the patented Rennie stare to his helmsman, who quickly corrected his error. Not one to leave a good seaman flustered, Ross nodded to the man. 'I'm going to do it again, Carter,' he said and returned to his casual pose. The *Abukir* continued on course.

True to his nature, Ross made a mental list of pros and cons. Aye, he had spent his life on board fighting ships, but that had likely proved more interesting than coasting around England and Scotland, and maybe to far-off America with a cargo of dried herring, shoes or corsets.

Had the navy not taken him to exotic Portugal, he would never have met Inez Veimira, whose love still made him smile. And he most certainly would never have fathered the boy who waited for him now in Plymouth, a boy with hair as dark as his own, but curly, with full lips instead of Scottish ones and an olive tint to his skin. Nathan's brown eyes were his mother's alone. Their beauty had given Ross pause to miss Inez Veimira, until his natural optimism turned his regrets into those little blessings a healthy son furnished.

The loss of his leg at Trafalgar in 1805 had not been without a little good fortune, as Ross chose to see it. The ship's surgeon had only needed to take his mangled leg off five inches below the knee. Difficult as it was, and too long his stay in the Plymouth hospital, the surgeon had assured Ross that an officer who still had his knee could command a quarterdeck and expect advancement. And so it had proved.

And there was this, probably his greatest blessing: Napoleon's stupid war had turned Ross Rennie into a leader of men, a rock-solid fellow whose sensible decisions made the *Abukir* a good home for men like him. The helmsman was a case in point. Once caught in Captain Rennie's firm but benevolent web, men tended to stay there through the years, knowing they were in good hands.

Seen from this light, Ross decided perhaps the war that had spanned all seven seas and ushered out one century and welcomed another had not been a total failure. By the time the *Undaunted* and her escort dropped anchor in charming Elba's harbour, Ross's heart was calm again. True, the war was over with Napoleon and, as a valued post captain, Ross knew the Royal Navy would find something for him to do. As a father, he wanted to sail to Plymouth and spend some time with his son. It remained to be seen whether he had the clout to manage both, but he thought he did.

As it turned out, he was right on both counts. True, that immediate return to base in Plymouth had dragged out until November as the *Abukir* and others like her continued to patrol the Channel.

While people in England had devoted much time rejoicing that the Beast was on Elba, the Royal Navy took a more cautious view and continued to patrol waters at least less hostile.

Hoys and lighters still made their way back and forth to victual ships like Ross's long at sea and they conveyed letters. Many a night after mess Ross read and re-read his letters from Nathan and hoped his son did the same thing with the missives he sent, accompanied by those exotic things only a Navy man could come across: oranges and lemons, a prayer rug from North Africa and Gouda cheese from the Low Countries, specifically for Maudie Pritchert, who had the raising of his boy.

If only Ben Pritchert, sailing master, had lived to see Napoleon on Elba. On that final voyage from the Channel to Plymouth, he missed Ben even more than usual. It had been his sailing master, a father in his own right, who had suggested Ross take his infant son from Portugal to his own wife in Plymouth. In 1804, the year of Nathan's birth, Oporto had suffered one of those earthquakes the coast was prone to. It was nothing as severe as the 1755 disaster, but the port merchant's home had been demolished, along with all its inhabitants except a week-old baby covered by his mother's body.

So the nuns at the nearby convent had told Ross, as he had shouted Inez's name over and over in the ruins, when he came into port a week after the quake. He knew she had borne him a child during his last voyage of seven months' duration to the Baltic. More than that, he did not know. The unexpected voyage had scuttled elaborate wedding plans, beyond quick nuptials, because their child was already underway. But that was the Royal Navy, which took no interest in the lives of its men. The good sisters had taken over the care of his little morsel and laid his son in his arms when tears still streamed down his face.

They had willingly fostered his child, named Nathan Thomas Fergusson Rennie and christened in the Holy Catholic faith because that was what the nuns did. Three months later when HMS *Fearless* was posted from Oporto to Plymouth for extensive repair, the nuns had returned Nathan to him, along with a goat.

He had known there would be a seaman or two who probably knew exactly what to do with a milking goat and they had not failed him. What had touched him to his soul was the way every man on board took an interest in his son. There had been no lack of volunteers willing to walk back and forth with a colicky baby, after Ross was ready to drop from exhaustion. His son's first English lullabies were sea ditties better left shipboard.

Maudie Pritchert had received the baby with open arms. Two years later, she wore widow's weeds. It was no wonder that as his prize money collected ashore, Ross had purchased a better house for the Widow Pritchert and her four children, plus his son. He paid her a handsome income to raise the boy he only saw at intervals. Now that the war was over and he was sailing home, Ross knew he would continue that stipend throughout that kind woman's career on earth, for she had saved his son's life.

His debt was far greater. After Ross had learned to stump around on a peg-leg and manage a quarterdeck again, Ben Pritchert saved his life during a skirmish not even worthy of inclusion in the *Naval Chronicle*. They had been coasting off France when a larger French frigate came out to play. In the middle of hot action, Ross lost his balance on his rolling deck. His sailing master rushed to steady him and took the deadly splinter in the back that would have cut Ross in two. He would owe both Pritcherts until he died.

* * *

Sailing into Plymouth harbour this time was more bittersweet than he would have imagined. For nostalgia's sake, Ross conned the *Abukir*, savouring the moment. He glanced towards the houses that marched up the gentle slopes away from the town centre, wondering if Nathan was watching. During his last visit a year ago, he had given his son a telescope. Maybe in a few years, he would give him a sextant. Maudie said the lad had an aptitude for mathematics.

On the advice of the overworked harbour master—so many ships returning—he dropped anchor, then looked around at the disorderly order on the *Abukir's* decks. His orders said the ship was to be refitted and refurbished. Two months and he would sail again—where, he had no idea. Two months of shore leave was one month and three weeks longer than any break he had enjoyed since the Peace of Amiens in 1802.

With a reluctance that surprised him, Ross turned the ship over to his number one, assuring him he would return in a day or two to settle out any complications with dry docks. He knew his officers yearned to leave the *Abukir* as much as he did. The men would go home, too, those who had homes. Others would hang around the docks, spend their money and be glad to see him in two months, if they hadn't been pressed into another vessel short of crew.

His chief bosun's mate insisted on piping him over the side himself, which was flattery, indeed. Because all eyes on deck were on him, Ross did his best to descend the ropes with dignity, never easy with a leg and a half. When he was safely settled in his launch for the pull to shore, he raised his hat and saluted his crew. *It's only two months*, he reminded himself as he felt unfamiliar tears gather behind his eyelids.

Although there were hackneys waiting to take him anywhere in Plymouth, Ross waved them off. He wanted to walk from the harbour to Maudie Pritchert's house. He knew his sorely tried leg would start to ache before he got there, but he needed the opportunity to shake off his sea legs. In parts of England far from the coast, the watch would probably be summoned to deal with men lurching and rolling down the street. Not Plymouth, a Navy town that understood what it meant for its men to remind themselves how to walk on a flat surface that didn't pitch and yaw.

A peg-leg presented its own challenges, but he

arrived in good time at the base of Flora Street, with its pretty pastel houses. As always, he stood there a long moment, wondering how much his boy had changed. Nathan was ten years old now. No one knew what his actual birth date was, because there hadn't been time to register anything before the earth moved in Oporto. A few visits back, the two of them had picked June 7th, an unexpected compliment, because that was Ross's birthday.

When he had asked his son why he wanted to share a birthday, Nathan's answer confirmed for all time that while it was possible to take a Scot far from the land of his ancestors, the economy remained. 'Simple, Da,' his son had told him. 'It's a tidy thing to do. We'll have cake but once a year, but we'll have twice as much.'

It was the perfect answer. Nathan, whose mother had been a heavy-lidded, sloe-eyed daughter of Portugal and deeply fond of cake, was a fitting combination of Dumfries and Oporto.

'Twice as much,' Ross agreed.

With the war over, he had plans this time, since a prodigal amount of leave stretched ahead that would take them through Christmas. The two of them were bound for Dumfries, where Ross's older sister lived with her surgeon husband. He hadn't seen her in years, but that was nothing because he had always been a prodigious correspondent and so was Alice Mae Gordon. She had promised them a good visit and hinted that she knew of a piece of property in need of a landlord in nearby Kirk-bean. 'In sight of open water,' Alice had written, to further entice him.

He stood a moment more, wondering at the half dread he always felt, hoping his son hadn't changed too much since the last visit, but well aware that children grow. *Will he remember me?* he always asked himself. *If he passed me on the street, would I know him?*

Ross took the customary deep breath·and continued up Flora Street, his eyes on a yellow house, where flowers still fought the good fight against late autumn. He knew that in Scotland, the flowers had long surrendered to winter, but this was lovely Devon.

He walked slower because his leg pained him and because there was always that moment when he wondered who would greet him. For the first time since Inez's death, for the first time in the terrifying and fraught years since, he wanted a wife to greet him, too. It was a heady thought and he entertained it cautiously, thinking of all the times he had assured his officers and wardroom confidants that he would find another wife when the war ended. Maybe the time was now.

Ross stopped outside Number Six Flora Street and looked up at the second-storey window that he knew was Nathan's room. His heart skipped a little beat as his dear son looked down on him. The boy disappeared from the window and Ross watched the front door. It slammed open and his son hurtled outside and into his open arms.

Ross was home from the sea.

Chapter Two

For someone without much choice in the matter, Mary Rennie had finally had her fill of relatives. Maybe it was the season; more likely it was her Cousin Dina. Maybe it was simply time for an epiphany.

Her father, long dead, had been a clergyman in the Church of Scotland. He knew a thing or two about epiphanies, especially the January 6th one involving the Christ and the Magi. Mary had a different epiphany in mind, the one where you realise something startling that probably should have happened years ago.

She blamed it on her propensity to be a late bloomer, but there she was, twenty-seven years old and tired of relatives, especially Dina. And so she told Mrs Morison, her only confidante, when they were peeling potatoes in the kitchen.

Mrs Morison was cook and not generally the peeler of potatoes, except that Betty, the scullery maid, had a toothache and Mrs Morison never seemed to mind a good chat with Mary, especially over tea and biscuits on a raw October afternoon in Edinburgh. Dinner was a long way off, and there was time to peel and chat and drink tea.

'Oh, my dearie, Dina is engaged to that prosy foreign fellow and she is blue-devilled,' the cook announced, after heaving herself up to retrieve more biscuits. 'Never trust a man from over the border.'

Mary smiled to herself. She had never been over the border, herself, but Papa had assured her years ago that Englishmen were only doing the best they could and Presbyterians could be charitable.

'Aye, Mrs M.,' she said, applying herself more diligently to the potatoes. She stuck the potato on the end of her knife and wagged it at the cook. 'But why must *I* suffer because *she* is engaged? She whines and carries on, and I don't know why. Isn't a bride-to-be supposed to be cheerful?'

Mrs Morison peered at her over the top of her spectacles. She lowered her voice and leaned closer. 'I think she is already afraid of her wedding night.'

'That's months away,' Mary whispered back. 'Besides, I would think that once you find a man to love, that wouldn't be a consideration.' She leaned back as another epiphany followed hard on the heels of the first. 'Ah. Maybe she doesn't really love Mr Page?'

Mrs Morison gave her a sage look and shook her head, tut-tutting as she peeled.

'Then why…?' Mary put down her knife. 'Oh, dear. Is she afraid she'll never get another offer?'

She considered the matter. It was probably true. Dina Rennie wasn't high on good looks. Mary couldn't help but smile, remembering the time last summer when one of the street sweepers neighed when Dina passed by. But it was wicked to joke about Dina's long face, or so Papa would have told her. Mrs Morison was saying something, so she glanced up.

'You have the family looks—all of them, I think,' Mrs Morison was saying. She shook her head and returned her attention to the root vegetable in her lap whose skin was starting to turn a little brown from lack of attention.

Maybe, but none of the money, Mary thought, knowing that the cook was too kind to mention it. Not that any of the Rennies were particularly attractive, she knew, but Papa had married a Max-well from Spring Hill and there was the difference: lips a little fuller than the Scottish norm, a trim and tidy figure, deep auburn hair—none of the Rennie carrot hue—and snapping green eyes. Mary felt the freckles were a discount, but Mama always said they were a happy sprinkle across her nose and no detriment.

'I wish I had money,' she admitted, because she knew Mrs Morison was no tattletale. 'I'm twenty-seven and something should have happened to me before now.'

When she lay in bed that night, Mary considered her age and virgin state. She smiled in the dark, remembering how carefully her Aunt Martha had skirted around matters of procreation, how it was accomplished and women's subservient role. Since they were much the same age, Dina had been party to the same conversation, her eyes wide, her mouth a perfect O. Mary had listened to Auntie's red-faced circumlocutions and kept her own counsel. Before Mama had died when Mary was fifteen, she had been more plain spoken.

There had been a quiet admonition, though, a coda to the conversation about men and women and What They Did. 'Remember this, my darling daughter: some day there will be a man who will meet all your requirements. Wait for him, because he will be worth it,' Mama had advised, making no effort to disguise that lurking Maxwell twinkle in her eyes.

Too bad Mama had died two weeks later, killed by the wasting disease. Papa had never enjoyed good health, so he took the opportunity six months later to join his wife in a better place than a Montrose rectory where the chimneys drew badly and no one was ever warm.

'And so I came to Edinburgh,' Mary informed the ceiling, that night of her epiphany. 'They are good to me here. I lack for nothing, but I have become part of the furniture.'

The matter was on her mind a week later after All Saints Day. Although Aunt Martha never would have admitted it, she was a superstitious woman. She never went below stairs with her Christmas cake recipe on All Hallows Eve, when ghosts walked. Mary and Mrs Morison were far too kind to ever tell the good woman that even ghosts weren't interested in the Rennie Christmas cake.

It always puzzled Mary that Auntie kept the

fruit-cake recipe squirrelled away in her bedchamber, as though it were a great treasure and liable to be stolen in so unprotected a place as the kitchen. Mary was the last person who would ever have told Auntie that Mrs Morison had long ago copied the recipe and kept it among her own well-used recipes in that kitchen so open to thievery and who knew what else.

'It is time,' Aunt Martha announced and handed over the much-creased paper with all the ceremony a Scot ever indulged in. 'One dozen this year, if you please.'

It was always one dozen, four of which remained at home to be consumed around Christmas, after a six-week curing. The other eight were sent to friends and family.

Mrs Morison nodded and accepted the recipe, promising to take it to bed with her and put it under her pillow, until it was safe again upstairs with Mrs Rennie. 'Lord love her,' the cook had murmured after her employer went upstairs.

The only thing that saved the cakes from rejection was the thick layer of marchpane Mrs Morison applied to two of the cakes that remained at the house on Wapping Street. Mrs Rennie had looked more thin-lipped than usual the first time

Mrs Morison applied the coating, but Uncle Samuel had nodded his approval, so that was that.

He had approved even more of the other two cakes remaining hearthside. In her desperation to make the cakes less dry—perhaps she had had her own epiphany—Mrs Morison drowned the other two cakes in rum. True, the recipe did include rum, but only a Scottish amount. 'I fear my hand slipped,' Mrs Morison had fibbed to her employer, the first time she served that particular rendition.

Uncle Sam had done more than nod his approval. He held out his plate for another slice. 'And make it thicker,' he added, his voice only slightly slurred.

So rum it was, and marchpane, for the Wapping Street cakes. The cakes to be mailed had rum, but not quite as much.

Making the cakes was a week-long event, with Monday and Tuesday taken up with endless chopping of glacé cherries, candied peel, sultanas and currants. Almonds generally were halved. Mrs Morison baked the homebound cakes on Wednesday, giving them ample time to cure or ferment in a dark space. The cook had been gradually adding more and more rum to the marchpane cakes, as well, which wouldn't get their mantle of thick icing until closer to Christmas.

For the entire week, Mary had joined Mrs Morison and the scullery maid, now minus a tooth, in the ordeal of Christmas cakes. Dina hadn't the patience for all the chopping and dicing, which Mary found a relief. She loved her cousin, but a few hours of non-stop talking gave Mary a headache. Dina's conversation had taken a decidedly querulous turn, now that she was engaged, and was even whinier than usual.

Perhaps I am envious, Mary thought, as she diced candied cherries and candied peel to Mrs Morison's exacting specifications. *I would like a husband because that would mean children and I do enjoy wee ones.*

Thursday had seen the construction of four more cakes, also baked, doused and sent to a dark corner to rest and lick their wounds.

The last four of the yearly cakes were in process on Friday, when Dina stormed into the kitchen and upset everything. Mary had finished cracking the eggs into the soft butter and caster sugar. As she stirred and Mrs Morison gradually added flour, Dina strode around the kitchen, fire in her eyes.

She was waving a small object. Mary wished her cousin would go away. Mixing the batter was her favorite part of the whole process. She wanted to enjoy, without drama, the smoothness of the batter and the buttery fragrance as it competed with vanilla bean.

But Dina needed an audience. With a pang, Mary realised she had for too long unwillingly furnished that audience. *I am too complacent*, she told herself, as Dina wound herself up like a top. *What would she do if I walked away?*

Mary was fated never to know. By now, Dina had tears in her eyes.

'I ask you, has there ever been a stingier husband-to-be than Algernon Page?' she fumed.

'What is it, my dear?' Mary said at last, because it was required of her. She continued swiping down the sugar crystals in her mixing bowl, thinking Dina might get the hint.

Not Dina. Her cousin stuck a small ring in Mary's face. 'That…that cheapskate sent me this paltry bauble for Christmas! He thinks I'm going to wear it.'

Mary looked closer. It *was* a small ring, very thin gold with what looked like little scratches. She squinted. No, they were leaves or twigs. 'Hmmm. Perhaps it has some family meaning,' she ventured. 'Only that the whole family consists of clutch purses,' Dina shot back. 'Would *you* wear such a thing?'

I would if I loved my future husband, Mary thought, even though she knew she would never say it. She decided Dina wanted some comment, so she mumbled something that seemed to fill the silence.

'I won't wear it,' Dina said, making her long face suddenly longer. She stared at the cake batter, as though daring it to contradict her. Her eyes narrowed and she tossed the spurned ring into the batter. 'There! Send it to someone.'

She stormed out of the room without a backward glance. Mary stared at the batter, then at Mrs Morison. 'She can't be serious.'

'Poor Mr Page,' the cook said with a shake of her head. 'He's in for a merry dance.' She chuckled and picked up the wooden spoon that Mary had leaned against the side of the bowl when Dina demanded everyone's attention. She gave the spoon a few turns, then sent Mary into the scullery for the tin of glacé cherries and orange peel.

'Fold them in, my dear,' she told Mary.

'Really?' Mary asked, amazed at Mrs Morison's audacity.

The cook nodded. 'It's not much of a ring.' She laughed a little louder. 'Let's hope no one bites down hard!'

Mary joined in the laughter. 'I don't think anyone really eats these cakes, do you?'

'I wouldn't know and I would certainly never admit such a thing to your aunt.'

After everything was added, Mrs Morison exercised the power of her culinary office and spooned the batter into the four weathered and venerable tins that the Rennies had probably used since Emperor Hadrian built his wall. Mary hesitated when Mrs Morison opened the Rumford.

'You're certain?'

The cook shrugged as Mary slid in the pans. 'I'll put these cakes in a separate place. If Miss Flibbertigibbet changes her mind, we can find the ring.'

'But that's…'

'A waste? I think I will call it a diversion.' Mrs Morison narrowed her eyes and glared at the ceiling above. 'Your cousin owes us one.' She put her hands on her hips. 'Do you realise we will have to listen to Dina up to and including the wedding in March?'

* * *

Mary thought about the ring later that night after she put on her nightcap and padded down the hall to see if her cousin needed anything. *I wonder why I do this?* she asked herself and nearly turned around. She remembered Mrs Morison's words in the kitchen and reminded herself to keep the peace. It was a long time to March.

'I'm not interested,' her cousin said when Mary suggested there was still time to retrieve the ring. 'Hand me that coverlet, Mary.'

Mary did, wondering when it was that Dina had stopped saying thank you for little services rendered. Funny she hadn't thought of that before her epiphany. She waited a moment, but Dina only waved her hand in a peremptory gesture. 'You're welcome,' Mary said softly. After that, she did not ask about the ring again.

After two weeks' incubation, the cakes for home consumption were boxed and stacked in the scullery. The next batch went to the postal office on the Royal Mile, taken there in all ceremony by the newest footmen. Mary worried over the last batch of four, asking Dina if she had changed her mind. Her cousin only gave her ringless hand an airy wave as she went out the door with Aunt Martha for a dress fitting. The plan was to announce the Rennie-Page engagement at a Hogmanay party, which required a new gown.

'Very well, Dina,' Mary muttered as she handed the footman the last four rum-soaked cakes, wrapped in gauze, boxed and addressed, along with exact change. She went upstairs to her room to frown over her paltry wardrobe and wonder what she could refurbish for the Hogmanay party. She knew Aunt Martha would allow her to have a new dress, too, but it would be even nicer if her aunt suggested it first.

She looked out the window as the footman walked towards the postal office. 'And that is that,' she said, thinking of the ring.

But that wasn't that, not by a long chalk.

When she was seated on the mail coach one day later, Mary decided that Thursday, December the 1st, 1814, would be long remembered on Wapping Street. More and more, she had taken to eating breakfast below stairs with Mrs Morison, because she liked the cook's company. Her breakfast partner upstairs was only Uncle Samuel—all he liked to do was peer at her over his newspaper, give her a slight nod, then dive back into the pages. Dina never rose before ten, when the mail was delivered.

Below stairs, Mrs Morison usually had some pithy reflection on the state of affairs in the Rennie household. Failing that, she sat with Mary to look over the day's meals and assign some useful task that kept Mary from boredom upstairs, where life was comfortable, but not much was required of her.

Since Christmas approached, Mrs Morison had assigned her to the agreeable chore of inventorying the spice cabinet. Since her arrival in the Rennie household twelve years ago, it had been Mary's duty to open each aromatic little drawer in the spice cupboard, take a good whiff and decide which spices had run their course and which could hang around another year.

Mary had just opened the cloves drawer when there came an unearthly shriek from the upstairs bedchambers. The note quavered on the edge of hysteria as it rose higher and higher. Alarmed, Mary watched with big eyes as a crystal vase shivered on its base.

'My God,' she said, closing the drawer and running into the kitchen, where Mrs Morison stared at the ceiling.

Above stairs, a door slammed, another door

opened and slammed, a few moments passed, then another scream of anguish shattered the calm of Wapping Street. Mrs Morison crossed herself and she wasn't even Catholic.

'We…we…could go upstairs,' Mary suggested, but it was a feeble suggestion, much like the chirping of the last cricket on the hearth before winter.

By unspoken consent, they remained where they were. Another door slammed, then there was a great tumult on the stairs as the sound of disaster came closer and closer to the kitchen.

Mary and Mrs Morison looked at each other, mystified. 'What did we do?' Mary asked.

They held hands as the racket reached the stairs to the kitchen. Mary took a deep breath as the door slammed open and Aunt Martha and Dina squeezed through the door at the same time, Aunt Martha with fire in her eyes and Dina more pale than parchment.

If she hadn't been so mystified, Mary would have chuckled to see that Aunt Martha had a tight handful of Dina's already thinning hair. She gave her daughter a shake.

When Mary just stared, open-mouthed, Aunt Martha said something that didn't usually pass her lips and thrust a letter into her niece's hand.

Holding it out to Mrs Morison as well, Mary read the letter, a stilted bit of prose from Dina's fiancé, not designed to tickle any woman's fancy or much else. Her eyes widened and she felt her own face grow pale. As imaginary buzzards seemed to flap about and roost in the kitchen, Mary read it again.

"'My choice and chosen one, that little bauble I sent you was given to my great-great-great-who-knows-how-many-greats grandfather by Queen Elizabeth herself. It is the dearest wish of my heart—and a Page family tradition—to see it on your finger when we announce our engagement on December the thirty-first.'"

'Oh, my,' Mary whispered. She stared at her aunt.

Aunt Martha gave her daughter another shake. 'Dina just told me quite a tale. I am here for you to dispute and deny it.'

'I fear we cannot,' Mary said finally, when no one else seemed prepared to speak.

'Then we are ruined,' Aunt Martha said as she sank on to a chair that Mary quickly thrust behind her.

Dina began to wail, until she was shut up sharply by a resounding slap from her mother. 'You are a foolish, foolish lassie,' Aunt Martha hissed. 'What are we to do?'

More silence, until Mrs Morison cleared her throat.

'Simple. We send Mary to find those four cakes and retrieve the ring. She will start tomorrow.'

Aghast, Mary stared at the cook. Mrs Morison just smiled and patted her hand.

'My dear, you are overdue for an adventure. Wouldn't you agree?'

Chapter Three

Trust a little boy to find travel by the Royal Mail adventurous. Captain Rennie knew he would have preferred post chaise, but Mrs Pritchert informed him that Nathan longed to ride the mail coach. 'When we're in the Barbican, he always has his ears on the swivel to listen for the coachman's blast and eyes in the back of his head to watch the horses,' Mrs Pritchert explained. 'And the uniforms! He pined for one when he was five.'

As if Ross needed an explanation. He used to do that in Dumfries a century ago, when the world was peaceful and he was a little boy. He could barely remember such a time; thank God he had a son to remind him.

'Aye, Nathan, we'll take the Royal Mail,' he said, which practically made his boy wriggle with delight.

Still, it was hard travel for a man wanting nothing but comfort for the first time in more than a decade. Captain Rennie was starting to feel every single one of his thirty-eight hard-lived years when the mail coach pulled into Carlisle on December the sixth. By contrast, Nathan was as bright-eyed as on the morning they set out from Plymouth, with Mrs Pritchert's tears and blessings.

'That's how women are,' Ross had assured his son, as the child watched Plymouth recede in the distance. 'They cry and fuss and let you go finally.'

'But she's not really my mother,' Nathan said, looking around for his handkerchief. 'I have a cold.'

Ross was wise enough to overlook his little sniffles. With a pang, he knew his son was close to the kind Mrs Pritchert; he knew no other mother. He put his hand on Nathan's neck and gave him a little shake. 'Laddie boy, we'll be back in Plymouth in a month and she'll be waiting for you, mark my words.'

As the miles passed, he had also realised with another pang that he didn't like to see the ocean disappear from view. He said as much to Nathan, who gave him a look like the one he had given his son when Mrs Pritchert disappeared from view.

'We'll have a good time,' Nathan assured him in turn and they were content with each other.

The first day with Nathan was always tentative. When his son was still a baby, there had been several days of reacquaintance, with lots of shy glances from both of them and maybe sentences started and stopped or half-finished. Now that he was ten, Nathan required only a few hours to remember his father. By the end of the first day's travel north, he was laughing and telling Ross a year's worth of school stories, memorising scriptures under duress and watching the harbour with his telescope. When he grew tired, Nathan leaned against Ross's arm with a sigh of contentment. Or maybe that was his own sigh.

They had struck a bargain before leaving Plymouth. Nathan might want to travel by the Royal Mail, but, by God, they were going to stop every night in a respectable inn. As much as he loved his sister, Ross wasn't in so much hurry to get to Dumfries that they needed to travel all night, too. He had taken this route before and knew where the good meals and soft beds were found. But more than that, he had a list this time. Not just a list: *the* list.

December the sixth found them in Carlisle, the

last stop of any consequence before Scotland. He had given Nathan a map of England and Scotland, because ten years was the right age to begin charting a course. He was not surprised at the look his son gave him when he informed him they were stopping at the Guardian.

'But Da, if we continue tonight, we'll be in...'

'Dumfries before midnight,' he finished. 'This is true.' He leaned closer to his boy. 'This also is true: for years, I have been dreaming about Cumberland sausage—an entire four-foot length—and whig bread served with Cumberland rum butter.'

'Four feet of sausage?' Natham repeated, his eyes wide.

'I will share,' Ross told him, the soul of generosity. He ruffled his son's hair. 'Would you deny a captain such a meal, after weevily ship's biscuit and thick water?'

'Never, Da.'

'And if we can find sticky toffee pudding...'

The Royal Mail stopped at the Borderers, and after making sure when the morning coach to Dumfries was due, he directed Nathan down the High Street to the Guardian, home of the best Cumberland sausage he had even eaten.

If he were to try to explain to Nathan just how

badly he wanted this moment, he knew a ten-year-old would never understand. There were times on the tedious blockade, or in the middle of the heaving Pacific, when he had stared into the distance, willing Cumberland sausage to appear. It embarrassed him to think of that weird obsession now, but such it was. He knew he was not alone in longings far removed from war. That was the nature of the beast: to wish yourself away from it.

They walked down the High Street, before turning on to a side street. For a tiny moment, Ross feared that the Guardian had closed its doors, or no longer served sausage. He smiled to see the venerable building, probably looking the same as when Caesar's legions had bellied up to the bar, getting courage to attack the Picts.

He remembered to remove his tall fore-and-aft hat, because the entrance was low. He probably would have removed it anyway, out of reverence for the Cumberland sausage, which he could already smell.

'We would like a room and a parlour for the night,' he asked the landlord, who looked vaguely familiar. 'And dinner, of course.'

Apparently the innkeeper was also impressed to see such splendour, if one could call a boat cloak splendid, in his little lobby. He stared at Ross's hat on his counter.

Ross tried to keep his question casual. 'There is Cumberland sausage cooking, eh?'

'Indeed there is, Admiral.'

'Just captain.'

Just. Just. No one this far north and inland would ever imagine how hard he had worked to get the title of post captain and the right to wear two epaulettes, instead of just one. Ross's cynical side took over. One of his fellow captains, dead since the blockade, had remarked once over blackstrap in the wardroom, 'With two epaulettes, the lads'll at least slide another cannonball into your coffin so you'll sink faster.'

The transaction completed, the innkeeper turned around the register and held out the quill. Ross dipped it, then signed his name.

He stared closer at the register, noticing the name above his.

'Mary Rennie?'

A question in his eyes, the landlord looked at the register, too. 'Oh! Beg pardon, sir. She did mention that a fellow was stopping by later. You're earlier than I reckoned. You'll want to share that parlour,

I am certain.' He beamed at Nathan. 'And this is your little boy?'

'Aye.'

Perhaps the same last name gave the innkeeper leave to attempt familiarity. 'I wouldn't say he favours either of you.'

'Sir, I...' Ross began, then closed his mouth, because the innkeeper was already intent on getting his guests together.

'You'd probably rather share that bedchamber, too.'

'No, I...'

The innkeeper was already starting down the hall. Ross looked at his son and shrugged. He knew he had the force of personality and years of command to stop the man short with a single barked expletive—God knows he had terrified lieutenants for years—but suddenly, he didn't want to.

'Let's find out who this Mary Rennie is,' he whispered to Nathan, who grinned back, a partner in crime. 'Maybe we'll like her.'

The innkeep stopped before a closed door and gestured grandly. 'I'll serve your dinner in here, Captain,' he said, then snapped his heels together and executed a sharp about face, marred only by the way his rotundity kept swinging, even after he stopped. Ross knew better than to make eye contact with Nathan.

When he just stood there, indecisive, Nathan tapped on the door.

'Mr Barraclough? You're early,' he heard from the other side of the door, followed by quick footsteps.

At least he thought that was what she said, since her accent was so thick and rich. A glance at his son told him that Nathan hadn't understood any of it.

Mary Rennie opened the door. Ross found himself gazing at considerable loveliness, which made him say, 'Ahh', involuntarily.

He only took a quick look; to ogle would have been the worst of manners. Life at sea had trained him to make rapid assessments. In a tiny space of time, that moment between 'Fire!' and 'Reload!', he took in magnificent auburn hair and green eyes that reminded him of a particular bay near Naples. Mary Rennie's gaze was clear eyed, straight on and not suspicious. What most captivated him were the freckles on her nose.

He knew better than to look down at her bosom. That little glance at her face suggested that other parts would be just as pleasant.

Nathan was elbowing him as discreetly as a young boy did anything, which made her smile deepen, as she gazed from one to the other. 'Mr Barraclough, I had no idea you had a bairn.' God bless the wee bairn. Nathan sketched a bow and declared, 'I am Nathan and I don't know what's the matter with my da.'

That's all it took; Ross remembered himself. He tucked his hat more firmly under his arm, which made Mary Rennie smile, for some reason. She leaned forwards, her eyes lively.

'There's no strong wind in the corridor,' she said, then indicated they were to enter the sitting room. 'Let's sort this out inside.'

He did as she said, putting his hat where she directed and taking off his cloak. In another minute he was seated at the table and she was pouring tea for him and tea with a lot of cream for Nathan. He didn't see any other teacups, so he knew this was for Mr Barraclough, whoever he was.

'I am Captain Ross Rennie and my son has already introduced himself,' he began. 'Quite possibly you have confused me with someone else.'

'Rennie?' Her expression went from puzzled to understanding. 'Oh! I suppose the innkeep thinks we are related.'

'I rather think he believes we are man and wife,' Ross said, then could have bitten his tongue, because she blushed furiously. He kept going doggedly, because all he knew to do was press forwards, full and bye, no matter the venture. 'He said Nathan didn't really resemble either of us.'

Mary Rennie laughed, a full-hearted sound that smacked the tension right across its snout and chased it out of the room. 'Captain, if you are from Scotland...'

'Dumfries...'

'Then he is probably correct. I am from Edinburgh in recent years, but Montrose before that. My father was rector there.' She stood up and went to the door. 'I'll ask the keep for more cups.' She turned a friendly eye on Nathan. 'And toffee pudding for you?'

Ross couldn't help the moan that escaped his lips. Nathan giggled.

'For my da, rather,' his son said. 'He's been long at sea and gets silly about food, I think.'

'For your da, *too*,' she amended, 'and enough for all of us, because I like toffee pudding.'

She left the parlour. Ross looked at his son. 'Am I embarrassing you, laddie?' he asked.

'Not yet,' Nathan replied, obviously a man to hedge his bets. 'She's pretty, isn't she?'

Oh, Lord God Almighty, he's already a son of the guns, Ross thought, impressed. He wondered for a brief moment what Mrs Pritchert would think.

The toffee pudding appeared with Mary, who carried it on a tray, along with plates, forks and tea cups.

'You went right to the kitchen?' he asked. Maybe Mary Rennie knew something of full and bye.

'Certainly. And what is Mr MacDonald doing but preparing a monster dinner of sausage, neeps and taties, whig bread and Cumberland butter. Captain, I told him to serve it in here, because you're starting to interest me.'

Chapter Four

Mary Rennie, he'll think you're the most outrageous flirt in the history of Scotland, she scolded herself, amazed, as she set the pudding on the table. 'I mean…' she started, then stopped, honest to her heart's core, because that was how she was raised. 'No, I mean just that. I've met a rascally army officer or two, but never a sea captain. And could we be cousins?'

The sea captain laughed out loud, which surprised her, considering stories she had heard of the solemn and stoic men of that profession.

'A rascally army officer or two? That is all?' he teased in turn. 'There are many more, Miss Rennie. Just ask any inmate of the Royal Navy. As for cousins, dessert first. Genealogy can wait.'

He accepted the bowl of pudding after she poured a little clotted cream on top. He must have known they were both watching him, but he dug into the dessert with a single-minded zeal that told her worlds about him. The first bite must have been a little bit of heaven, because he rolled his eyes. She couldn't help observing his face, with its sharp features and weather wrinkles. He looked forty-five at least, but it was entirely possible that he was younger.

'Twelve years, madam,' he said, gesturing with the spoon, but so careful not to drop a scrap. 'I have wanted this for twelve years.'

Mary looked at his son, already seeing a co-conspirator there. 'What do you think? Should we let him eat the whole lot?'

Nathan shook his head. 'I want some, too, and besides, Mrs Pritchert would scold him for eating dessert first.'

She glanced at the captain, already knowing he would supply the details, even though the pudding beckoned.

'Mrs Pritchert is an estimable female and the widow of my best sailing master. She is rearing Nathan, because his mother died in an earthquake in Oporto. We think he was a week old.'

He spoke with a matter-of-fact tone that she found beguiling, considering that she was weary of her aunt's circumlocutions and the tragedy that was Cousin Dina's life. She liked the look of him, too. Most of the men she knew were men of business and finance like her uncle, with white, indoor skin and soft hands. None of them had an interesting scar like the one that ran from Captain Rennie's left eye to his hairline. And absolutely no one had a peg-leg.

'How on earth did you get Nathan home?' she asked, intrigued by two lives that were far more interesting than hers.

'By the grace of God, a goat and a frigate with willing nursemaids,' he said, and there was no overlooking the fun in his eyes. She could only imagine at the desperate sadness, but that had probably been about ten years ago, if Nathan was as young as he looked. She knew how time could smooth away jagged edges; oh, my, she did.

It *was* good toffee pudding. She ate a smallish portion and left the rest to the captain. Nathan did the same thing, which touched her heart. Captain Rennie worked his way steadily through the dessert and appeared none the worse for wear when he finished. She could have laughed out loud as he eyed the residue around the rim of the bowl. Probably aboard his ship and dining alone, he would have run his finger around that rim; maybe even licked the bowl.

Mary hoped he would feel inclined to tell her more, before he and his son found their own private parlour. Her own day of travel had been boring in the extreme, without a single person of interest on the mail coach to talk to—not that she would have addressed a man she did not know, at least not one younger than sixty.

'There now,' he said, putting his empty bowl back on the tray. 'After that restorative, let me think about my Rennie family tree. Feel free to jump in, Miss Rennie, if someone sounds familiar. My great-grandfather, Thomas Rennie, from Castle Douglas, had five sons. There was Angus, Max, Andrew, Douglas and Gerard. Ring any bells with you?'

'Andrew,' she replied promptly. 'Named after the saint, but wasn't, or so my father said. Papa was a rector, though, so few measured high on his scale. Papa's grandfather was Gerard.'

He smiled at that. 'Douglas was mine. I met Great-Uncle Andrew once.' He leaned closer and there was no mistaking the twinkle in his eyes.

'I also remember that Da counted the silverware when he left.'

Mary gasped and laughed out loud. 'My father tells me similar stories. I think we are cousins of some stripe or other, Captain.'

She had not been raised to pry, but Mary knew she did not want either of them to leave her orbit so soon. Nearly a week on the road, tracking down Christmas cake, had shown her the dismal side of travel: there was no one to talk to. It was easy enough to bury her nose in a book on the mail coach during the day, or exchange pleasantries with respectable-looking females, but the evenings did drag.

'I shouldn't pry...'

'Pardon me for asking...'

Nathan laughed at them both. 'Mrs Pritchert always says to take turns in conversation.'

'I always defer to rank. You first, Captain Cousin.'

'*I* defer to the ladies, Cousin Mary,' he said in turn. 'May I guess your question?'

'It's not a difficult one. Where are you going?'

'We're heading to my sister's home in Dumfries for Christmas.' The glance he gave his son was a fond one. 'Nathan has a chart and assures me we could have been there late this evening, but I wanted to eat here. My turn now: Where are *you* going?'

She opened her mouth to reply, but there was a knock on the door. 'Come in.'

His face red from the heat of the kitchen, the innkeep struggled under the load of a massive tray. He was followed by a small boy with a smaller tray. She looked at the captain, and he was watching her, a smile in his eyes that spread to his whole face as she watched, contradicting everything she had heard about the dour members of the sailing fraternity. Aunt Martha would probably have questioned the propriety, even if he was a Rennie, but Aunt Martha was nowhere in sight.

'Right here, sir,' she told the keep. 'We'll dine together.'

The keep gave her a puzzled look, as though wondering why there was any question about the man and boy dining with her. Hadn't the captain already informed her that the keep thought them to be husband and wife? She looked to her new-found cousin to explain the situation, but his eyes were on the food. He would have to speak to the innkeeper later.

She could have closed the door and walked away

and her cousin never would have noticed, which amused her. Captain Rennie liked to eat. She could also have stripped off her clothes and he wouldn't have noticed. She couldn't help her laughter at the roguish thought.

He looked up and surprised her. 'Come, come, Cousin Mary,' he chided. 'Food has its place in my universe, but not to the exclusion of good company.' He eyed the sausage with real appreciation, when, with a modest amount of Scottish fanfare, Mr McDonald lifted of the domed lid. 'Mary, you may have…how many inches of this?'

She looked at the coiled sausage, moist and sweating and giving off the most heavenly aroma. Her mouth watered. It looked far more adventurous than the bowl of vegetable soup she had considered. 'Six inches, Captain.'

'Cousin Ross,' he amended and nodded to Mr McDonald. 'You heard the lady, sir. Six inches. Reminds me of a scurrilous joke I shall never tell. The same for you, laddie?'

Nathan nodded, his eyes wide. 'Do…d'ye plan to eat the rest, Da?'

Mary watched with delight as the captain pursed his lips, squinted and eyed the monstrous sausage.

Even after the keep and cook severed two portions, the remaining bulk was formidable.

'Probably not, Son, if I plan to sleep tonight and not spend the wee hours of morning in the head. Maybe when I was younger, I could have.' He eyed Mary without a single repentant look. 'Plain speaking, ma'am. We Rennies specialise in it. Do you?'

'I suppose I'd better,' she told him, determined not to be embarrassed because she found father and son so fascinating. 'Go easy on the neeps and taties, then.'

Mr McDonald served them and stood there. Mary suspected his sedate little inn seldom sheltered visitors as interesting as the Rennies.

Captain Rennie dismissed the keep with a slight nod, the kind of gesture that would have meant next to nothing if she had attempted it. Coming from a post captain, the nod sent McDonald to the door immediately. *Too bad I cannot give a nod like that and send Dina scurrying*, Mary thought. *I'll have to watch how he does that.*

The whig bread smelled divine. She wasn't sure about the rum butter until she tried a dollop on a scrap of bread. She couldn't help her exclamation of pleasure. The captain took a break from his mouthful of sausage and buttered a larger slice for her, as though she were a child.

'You're used to looking after people, aren't you?' she asked.

'A shipful, Cousin,' he said around that mouthful of sausage. 'Two hundred and fifty when we have a full complement, which is seldom.'

She savoured every bite of the bread and sausage, wishing she had loosened her stays before the Rennies knocked on her door and changed the course of her trip for one night. The errant thought crossed her sausage-soaked brain that she was going to miss them tomorrow.

Mary stopped eating just after Nathan pushed his plate away and staggered to the sofa to flop down. The captain showed no signs of quitting. The four-foot length of sausage had been greatly diminished and she wondered if he had a hollow leg as well as a peg-leg. She glanced at it, curious to know how he kept the thing on, then glanced away. She had never sat so close to someone with a wooden leg before, but it didn't follow that she had lost all her manners.

She sat back and tried to hide a discreet belch behind her napkin. 'That was amazing, Captain.'

'Ross,' he repeated, a man most patient. He set

down his fork, but only long enough to add more potatoes to his plate. 'Are you finished?'

Mary nodded. 'I should have done that fifteen minutes ago.' She chuckled. 'Cap—Ross, I was going to have a bowl of vegetable soup and a hard roll.'

He just rolled his eyes at that dismal news and continued his tour through the Guardian's cuisine. 'Tell me, if I am not prying overmuch, what has brought a lady out on the road? I would think you should have a chaperon stashed somewhere.'

Mary shook her head, touched at his concern. *I suppose you have added me to your stewardship of two-hundred-and-fifty men,* she thought. *And one small boy.* 'I'm past the age of needing a chaperon.'

'I doubt that. You can't be a year over twenty-four.'

'Try almost four years over.' She leaned closer. 'Since you are being impertinent, so shall I be. How old are *you*?'

'What do you reckon, Cuz?' he asked. 'I probably look fifty, but I blame the wind and general stress.'

'I was going to say forty-five,' she told him.

'You're off by seven or so. I am thirty-nine in January.'

'Antique, indeed,' she murmured. 'Well, now, we are both getting on in years, but this is my first adventure. Care to hear about it?'

Ross did, surprising himself. He had spent so many years dining alone with charts and logs that the prospect of an evening with a pretty lady beguiled him. He glanced at Nathan, whose eyes were starting to close from the effects of such a meal.

Mary observed him, following his gaze. Without a word, she got up and took a light blanket off the back of the sofa. As he watched, she covered his son, then placed the back of her hand lightly against his cheek. Nathan opened his eyes, smiled at her, and made himself comfortable in that way of adaptable little boys.

She sat down again. 'I am supposed to be having an adventure, all because of Christmas cake. Perhaps you call it fruitcake.'

'I don't call it anything.' He chuckled. 'I suppose I would have eaten nearly anything in my Turkish prison, but fruitcake?'

She widened her eyes, and he enjoyed the effect because her face could be so animated, he was rapidly discovering. 'Turkish prison?'

'A story for another day. It's your turn now,' he reminded her.

He kept eating while she told him a tale of Cousin Dina, a valuable ring and a cook named Mrs Morison who had volunteered her to retrieve four fruitcakes. Her tale was so homely and simple it took a moment to soak into his brain, because he was used to bad news, and storms and broadsides and noise.

'You have commandeered three cakes already?'

She nodded, then laughed softly, careful not to disturb Nathan. He appreciated that nicety in her. Or maybe she was just a quiet woman. Whatever the truth, he found her air of peace almost as soothing as the Cumberland sausage. 'I am suspecting that no one likes to eat my aunt Martha's Christmas cake. P'raps not even Turks! You should have seen their eagerness when I said I needed them back!'

'Did you tell them why?'

Mary shook her head. 'That would only embarrass Dina, my cousin—our cousin?' She seemed to gauge his expression. 'Aye, she's foolish, but I can be kind. I have concocted a taradiddle that the ingredients are a bit off and shouldn't be served.'

You are kind, he thought. 'And?' he prompted.

'No ring in those three cakes.'

She trilled her *r*s so beautifully. Ross enjoyed the sound, as well as the thickness of her accent. He found it almost a balm to his soul because it reminded him of earlier years, before Napoleon had decided to rule the known world. Ross thought of his mother suddenly and her well-nigh impenetrable brogue. Mam had died while he languished in a Spanish prison on the other side of the world in Caracas, Venezuela. He would have given the earth to hear her lovely voice one more time.

'Captain?' Her voice was soft and she looked concerned.

'Just woolgathering,' he told her. 'I've been a long time away from a good brogue with no bark on it. The Royal Navy tends to smooth out most Scotsmen.'

'You, included.' She smiled at him, then glanced at his sleeping son. 'I'm not so certain your wee bairn can understand much of what I said. Ah, well. I'll be hopefully travelling back to Edinburgh tomorrow, triumphant with a ring, and you'll be on your way to Dumfries.'

'Aye.' Funny that he wasn't so pleased to think of that. Silence settled on them both, and he teased his vanity with the notion that Cousin Mary might miss him a little. He was done with dinner—or at least all he dared cram down his gullet—but he didn't want to leave her orbit just yet. Time to snatch at a straw. 'This fourth Christmas cake. Who has it here in Carlisle?'

She seemed not to mind his temporising. 'Miss Ella Bruce, a chum of my auntie's from their younger days at the Lorna McKay's Select Academy for Females,' she said with a straight face. 'Don't laugh! Aunt Martha learned to create any number of improving samplers.'

He laughed anyway, leaning back in his chair, still mystified by peacetime conversation. 'Would it surprise you to know that there is someone on nearly every frigate, ship of the line and tender who has a sampler reading, "Great Britain expects every man to do his duty"?'

'Do you?' she teased.

'Of course! My sister Alice Mae in Dumfries has two daughters.' He sat back, thinking of the samplers, and Trafalgar, and Lord Nelson dead on HMS *Victory*. They were all in the employ of Napoleon, the grand puppeteer of Europe who pulled his strings so everyone would dance and caper about to his tune. But Cousin Mary didn't know what that felt like.

Or did she? To his surprise, she leaned forwards and touched his hand, just the smallest touch. And here he thought he had trained his face to show no expression, especially not when things were going wrong and everyone looked at him to save them. Why in the world was he letting down his guard to this sweet lady intent on collecting Christmas cakes? Maybe he shouldn't have eaten so much Cumberland sausage.

'Do you know these people with the fruitcake?' he asked, wanting to change the subject.

'Not one of them,' she said as quickly, maybe wanting to change it, too. 'Only last week, my auntie asked herself why on earth she is still send-ing Christmas cakes to people she hasn't heard from in decades. I suppose that is what people do at Christmas; ergo, Ella Bruce gets a fruitcake.' She laughed. 'Don't look for logic, Captain; it's Christmas.'

Ross couldn't think of anyone, except his son, that he had ever sent anything to at Christmas. He opened his mouth to admit it when someone knocked on the door.

Mary gave the door a frown that hinted she wished they had not been interrupted, or so he wanted to think. As she got up to open the door, her hand just brushed his shoulder—again, the lightest touch. He had probably imagined this one, because he didn't think she was a forward woman at all.

'This will be Miss Bruce's emissary,' she whispered.

'Eh?'

'I sent a note to her home, explaining the situation, and he responded at length, but managed to impart amazingly little.' Her voice dropped to a conspiratorial whisper. 'D'ye think he's a solicitor? Let's hope *he* has the cake.'

Let's hope he doesn't, Ross thought suddenly as she opened the door. *Maybe you could use a chaperon, if the cake has strayed. Pray God it has crawled away to die somewhere else.*

Chapter Five

His name was Malcolm Barraclough, and he was the bearer of bad news. He was also prissy and overly dramatic, making Mary supremely grateful he was unknown to her. Let Miss Ella Bruce have the pleasure of his stultifying company once Mary quitted Carlisle.

After ten endless minutes of listening to Mr Barraclough explain who he was, Mary made a fearsome mistake—she glanced at Captain Rennie and witnessed an amazing eye roll. Maybe the Rennies truly were inclined more to plain speaking, as he had said. She doubted that the captain had wasted a word in his entire life. This led to her second epiphany: she needn't suffer bores gladly.

Mary staunched Malcolm Barraclough's haemorrhage of words. 'Sir, please take a seat. You are

Miss Bruce's nephew and she has taken herself off to Stirling? Is that the gist of it?'

The man nodded, surprised, and obviously unused to interruption. 'She will be back e'er long, but gone just long enough for your little errand to—ahem—save my bacon.' He put his hand to his forehead. 'I did a rash thing.' He hung his head in manufactured shame. 'I'm not certain what I was thinking.'

Captain Rennie laughed, but was rewarded with a fishy stare. 'Were you foxed? Three sheets to the wind?'

The estimable Mr Barraclough drew himself up, which was amusing enough, because he was even shorter than Mary. 'Captain, I am an elder in the Kirk!'

'Ooh, no vices allowed?' the captain asked in an innocence as manufactured as Barraclough's humility.

'None whatsoever.'

You have a playful streak, Mary thought, giving the captain her own fishy stare. She returned her attention to her sitting-room guest. 'I was hoping you would just bring me the Christmas cake, Mr Barraclough. The ingredients were a wee bit off and my auntie wanted me to retrieve them. I explained this in my note to you this afternoon.'

'I cannot return it, for I have sent the Christmas cake to another,' Mr Barraclough confessed. His head hung lower. 'My Aunt Ella has no idea.' He struck a little pose. 'I lay the blame at Cupid's door.'

The captain turned away and his shoulders started to shake. *Don't look at him*, Mary warned herself. She had to ask. 'Cupid's door? But this is Christmas, sir, not Valentine's Day.'

'Cousin Mary, people can fall in love at Christmastime, too,' the captain said, his expression bland, except for a lurking twinkle. 'Surely it happens all the time.'

Mary looked from one man to the other, one a tease and the other a prig, and fell back on her remedy for all ills. 'Gentlemen, shall we have tea?'

Mr Barraclough agreed to tea, settling himself at the table with the air of a man prepared to stay all evening. Mary poured, wondering if tea had been a tactical error. She knew better than to look at the captain, who had seated himself on the sofa beside his sleeping child. She wanted to laugh when he crossed his legs and the peg rested atop his knee. He waggled it once or twice; Mr Barraclough stared, then coughed and looked away.

The sight of the peg-leg seemed to have deprived him of speech, which gave Mary the opening for her questions. 'Sir, did Miss Bruce know about the cake?'

'No. It arrived after she left to visit her sister, my mother. She gets one every year.'

'A sister? How amazingly profligate,' Captain Rennie said.

'Sir! A fruitcake! From someone in Edinburgh I have never met!'

The peg-leg waggled again and Mr Barraclough stared at it. *I'm going to thrash a post captain in the Royal Navy, once this bore leaves*, Mary thought.

'What did you do with the cake?' she asked.

After another look at the wooden leg, Mr Barraclough dragged his eyes away and told a tale of Miss Bruce's unrequited love for a solicitor and the thirty years she had pined for him. It was the stuff of Highland legend, if Mr Barraclough was to be believed. 'Mr Maxfield was too shy to declare himself, so my mother tells me, and my aunt too much a shrinking violet to nudge him.' He paused for breath finally, casting sidelong glances at the peg-leg, which had mercifully settled down, to Mary's relief.

'And?' Mary prompted. 'My aunt has never mentioned such a tale.'

'Aunt Ella falls into severe melancholia at Christmas, because Mr Maxfield wasn't ever brave enough to kiss her under the mistletoe positioned so strategically at the Select Female Academy.' He sipped his tea noisily. 'For thirty years, she has pined, cried and taken to her bed at this time of year, when most Christians rejoice. I have witnessed this annual agony and it is not a pretty sight! Then she goes to Stirling and pines and cries there, too.' He gave a gusty sigh. 'Such is the fate of the spinster, I suppose.'

Lord, I hope not, Mary thought, then tried to remember the last time anyone had kissed her under mistletoe, much less a kissing ball. To her dismay, nothing came to mind.

'But what does this have to do with the missing cake?' Captain Rennie asked. To Mary's surprise, he sounded interested.

'I, sir, am a romantic,' Mr Barraclough announced, with a click of the teacup on the saucer. In his tight, shiny suit, he looked more like the counting-house clerk he probably was, and no solicitor. Mary felt her heart soften as she began to understand this little man, probably no more acquainted with adventure than she was.

'After ten years of listening to my aunt suffer this annual torment, I decided to mail the fruitcake to Tavish Maxfield, along with a note declaring her steadfast love and a proposal of marriage. I signed it Ella Bruce.'

Silence, then the captain applauded. 'Well done, Mr Barraclough!' he declared.

'D'ye think so?' the man asked, blushing like a maiden. He tweaked the few hairs forming a fringe around his head, smoothing them with nervous fingers.

Mary stared at them both, the captain's admiration seemingly genuine, and Mr Barraclough's pleased expression told Mary worlds about his own quiet life, shared with a spinster aunt. *Almost like my life*, she thought reluctantly.

'Sir, it takes a bold stroke to conquer the heart! Rather like war at sea,' Captain Rennie said. 'If Mr Maxfield follows through and goes to Carlisle, your auntie will be so pleased. If he does nothing, she'll at least be none the wiser.' Rennie clapped the man on the shoulder. 'Brilliant!'

Mr Barraclough beamed at Mary. 'Maybe I

shouldn't have fretted and worried so much,' he said. 'I am not ordinarily so impulsive.'

'Maybe you should not fret,' she agreed, in charity with him because Captain Rennie was. She glanced at the captain, who now sat calling no attention to his peg-leg. 'More tea, Mr Barraclough?'

While Nathan slumbered on, Mr Barraclough stayed another hour, drinking tea, eating some of the rapidly congealing Cumberland sausage and telling them about his life in the counting house of Mackey and Wilde. It was as boring and dry as toast, but the captain seemed to take an interest in each dull detail. Mary listened in growing admiration of her cousin as Ross Rennie teased out little scraps of information about Mr Barraclough's own pining for Jennie Lynch, a rector's daughter. As her cousin made affable conversation with a man probably as lonely as his maiden aunt, Mary had the smallest glimmer what sort of captain he was and felt her own heart grow warm at his effortless kindness. She amended that mentally—his kindness once he had got past his teasing nature.

Just as kindly, Captain Rennie found a way to end the evening's interview. He took out his watch and shook his head sadly. 'Sir, all good things must come to an end, and look you here, my son is sound asleep.'

The two men shook hands, then Barraclough bowed gallantly over Mary's hand. It was a self-conscious attempt, but it touched her heart. Maybe she could take a page from her cousin's book.

'Mr Barraclough, perhaps it is time you gave Jennie Lynch a kiss under the mistletoe,' she suggested, pinking up as much as her parlour guest at her presumption.

'Aye to that,' the captain said. 'Remember the bold stroke.'

The counting-house clerk nodded thoughtfully. He bowed to them both and started for the door.

'Oh, wait!' Mary said, hurrying to his side. 'You didn't tell us where you sent the fruitcake.'

'I forgot.' Mr Barraclough giggled. 'I directed it to Tavish Maxfield, Esquire, Number Fifteen Apollo Street, York.' He beamed at them. 'Mrs Rennie, you must be so happy to have your captain home from the wars.'

'My…' She glanced at the captain, then looked away, suddenly as shy as Miss Ella Bruce, who was probably sobbing out her heart in Stirling right now.

'She certainly is happy to see my waterlogged

carcase,' the captain said to Mr Barraclough's retreating figure. 'And I am glad to be here.' He closed the door and leaned against it.

'You could have told him the truth,' Mary said, her face on fire.

'We'll never see him again. If I had corrected him, he would have been embarrassed. What would be served?' He sat down by his sleeping son again, his hand going naturally to Nathan's leg in a caress. 'He was a little fellow in need of an audience. I hope to goodness he does kiss Miss Lynch under the mistletoe. Hope he gives her a really loud smack.'

Mary wasn't certain she should say what was on her mind, but now her cousin was giving her that same interested look he had given to their late guest. She saw no subterfuge in his expression and it gave her courage. Or maybe it aroused her lately submerged sense of humour, because no one on Wapping Street in Edinburgh seemed to tease or joke.

'Don't deny that you started out to discommode the man,' she chided. 'I thought he was going to climb the wallpaper when you started waving about your...your peg.'

He crossed his leg again and gave it another waggle, which made her laugh softly, so as not to wake Nathan.

'Dear Cousin, you'd be amazed how *San Agustin* can disturb the pompous. Yes, my crew named it after the Spanish ship o' the line that gave it to me at Trafalgar!' He put his hands behind his head then, regarding her. 'Eventually, they just called it Gus,' he added, when she laughed. 'Of course, they never dared to tell *me* what they called it, but word gets about in close quarters.'

His expression became serious, almost wistful. 'D'ye know, when Mr Barraclough started to talk about the counting house and his little life, I was reminded all over again what a large stage I have been playing on. Would I change places with him? Sometimes.' He gave her a wry smile. 'During this leave of mine, I must accustom myself to life among people who have never worked for Napoleon, as I did.'

She looked at him, startled, then understood what he meant. 'The grand wizard of Europe?'

'Aye, lass. Puppermaster, grand wizard, what you will. The Admiralty pays my salary, but Napoleon employs me. We all dance to his tune.'

So did I, Mary reminded herself, unwilling to say it out loud. She hadn't thought of Lieutenant Reginald MacDowell in five years at least, but for just a moment, she was seventeen again and in love.

'You, too?' he asked.

You surprise me, she thought, wondering at his ability to delve deep without appearing to. She nodded, too shy to say more. No reason for this man soon to leave her life, once they said goodnight, to know how her heart broke when the lieutenant informed her of his need to marry a lady with money. Rather than yielding to bitterness, she had pined in sorrow, then suffered in more silence when she learned of his death at Salamanca two years later. By then, Lieutenant MacDowell had his own widow and a son who would never know him. Funny that she had never thought to blame Bonaparte.

'It appears Boney has meddled in all our lives.'

Captain Rennie said it softly. Mary opened her mouth to tell him about Reginald, then closed it, choosing not to become as pathetic as Malcolm Barraclough. She decided he looked a little disappointed and wondered how many midshipmen and lieutenants he had counselled through the years. The captain had been kind to take an interest, but the hour was late and the Cumberland sausage had well and truly adhered to the serving platter.

'How did he meddle in your life, Mary? Call me nosy—I want to know.'

'I nearly became engaged to a lieutenant in the light artillery, until he decided he needed a wife with an income of her own,' she said. 'I gather that uniforms are expensive.'

'Cad,' he said. 'And?'

'He found someone else rather quickly, so I do not think he was truly invested in me,' she said, finding it less difficult to talk about than she would have thought. 'Perhaps it was for the best.'

'I trust he died on some battlefield,' Ross told her. 'Serve him right.'

'Actually, he did, but he left a wife and infant. Don't be so flippant, Captain.' She hadn't meant for that to come out with real force, but it did. Maybe she had cared more than she knew. Maybe she should have talked about Lieutenant MacDowell to another human being and not kept it all inside her.

'I *am* sorry,' he replied. 'Callous of me. No one is unscathed, I shouldn't wonder.'

'Captain, I think…' she began, then stopped, wanting to change the subject. She was silent a moment, and the enormity of Mr Barraclough's parting words sank in. 'Dear me, York.'

* * *

Ross hadn't known his cousin long, but her sudden frown told him the obvious: this little lady bent on finding a ring in a fruitcake had probably never ventured any farther south than Carlisle. And for God's sake, had someone *bullied* her into traipsing around for fruitcake? She was a lady alone on the Royal Mail. He smiled inside. At the mercy of bores like Malcolm Barraclough? The smile left. And maybe a sea captain? Did she have enough money? Was he ever going to feel free of responsibility that had descended like a sodden mantle around his shoulders when he strode his first quarterdeck? Perhaps not. Perhaps he didn't want that peculiar sense of stewardship to vanish now.

'Cousin Mary, it appears you have to go to York. Could you use some company?'

Chapter Six

Mary frowned. She knew where York was on her uncle's atlas. For years she had considered it high adventure to flop on the sofa when no one was using the sitting room, prop open the atlas on her stomach and imagine herself in exotic locales like London and Brighton. The prospect of actually venturing farther south from Carlisle into England was something she had not considered when she let Mrs Morison and Aunt Martha cajole her into retrieving the dratted Christmas cakes.

It'll be simple, she thought with some chagrin, remembering Mrs Morison's words. *You'll probably find the ring in the first cake you pick up. You'll be home in no time.*

'Hmm, from the look on your face, Cousin, I think you hadn't planned on voyaging in foreign waters,' her cousin told her.

'No, indeed.' *You must think me a complete ninny*, she thought, considering the obvious competence of the man looking at her with such a pleasant expression. *Might as well admit it.* 'I can imagine what your opinion of me is,' she said, eager now for him to quit her sitting room, because she felt like a fool. 'You've sailed into real danger for more than twenty years and I'm frightened of the prospect of York!'

Mary couldn't even look at him. He startled her by touching her chin until she had no choice but to look into his eyes. And quite blue eyes they were.

'My opinion of you is merely that you have never been to York and it *is* a large city.'

He said it so kindly that her embarrassment vanished and her charity returned. 'I suppose it is a little odd for someone to be canvassing the countryside for fruitcake,' Mary said, then laughed out loud. '*I* think it's odd!'

'No more strange than a post captain traipsing about for Cumberland sausage.' He glanced at his son and lowered his voice when the boy muttered something in his sleep. 'Personally, I could have stayed another day in York when we passed through earlier this week. My current sailing master told me about a shop in York that makes excellent blood pudding.'

'You're hopeless!'

'I know.' He didn't touch her hand, but he stood closer. 'Let us accompany you to York and retrieve that pesky cake.'

She wavered, then decided, with a shake of her head. 'You have just been there. I'm no navigator and I expect you are, so you know better than to backtrack to York. You're so thoughtful, Captain Rennie, but I can find York, Apollo Street and this old gent pining for love of Miss Bruce.'

'It's no hardsh—'

'Yes, it is,' she interrupted. 'You tell me this is your first actual holiday—'

'Shore leave.'

'—in twelve years.' She glanced at the Cumberland sausage, supine in its solidified juices. 'You've obviously been planning this...shore leave for eons.' She held out her hand to him. 'Cousin, don't worry about me. I hope you have a happy Christmas on land. Goodbye.'

The look of disappointment in his eyes surprised her, she who never elicited much response from her own relatives, much less one on such a distant branch of her family tree as the captain. She also knew he would recover, because that was what men did.

Captain Rennie shrugged. When he turned to pick up his son, he took a side step to get his balance. Mary shot her hand out automatically to steady him, her hand firm against the small of his back.

'Thank you,' he told her with no embarrassment. 'Sometimes I still overset myself.' He picked up Nathan.

Mary released her grip on the captain, deciding not to be embarrassed by her quick reaction if he wasn't. She touched Nathan's hair, brushing it back from his forehead. When he opened his eyes and blinked, she touched his cheek. 'I hope you have a lovely Christmas, too,' she said softly. 'Don't let your papa eat too much sausage all at once.' She gave it a thought, then shrugged and kissed Nathan's forehead.

Mary held the door open for the captain, watching as he carried the child from her room. He stood there a moment, then shook his head and turned around.

'Cousin Mary, I never told the innkeep that I needed a separate room. He's thinking we're slinging our hammocks in here with you, because we are all Rennies.'

'My goodness.' She gestured to the sofa. 'Put Nathan down in here again and make your arrangements.'

He did as she said, then grinned and knuckled his forehead like a common sailor as he backed out. 'Suppose there are no spare rooms?' He winked at her and it took years off his weather-blasted face. 'Come, come, Cousin, it's nearly Christmas, and we know how troublesome landlords are at that season!'

'You, sir, are a rascal,' she said firmly. 'Find a room at this inn.'

He did, returning quickly with a key in hand. He stood by the sofa, looking down at his son. 'You know, Mary, I have it on good authority that parents will often stand as we happen to be standing and just gaze at their sleeping children. That has never been my luxury. Pardon me, but I am savouring this moment.'

'Savour all you want, Captain,' she replied, her voice as soft as his. 'I've never had this luxury, either.' She couldn't help herself. She brushed the hair from Nathan's forehead. 'His mother must have been a beautiful woman.'

'She was. I never saw a bonnier lady.'

He must have thought such a comment was a bit cavalier, since she was a woman, too. He touched her nose with his finger, just a light touch. 'But I do like freckles, something a man never sees in the Iberian Peninsula. 'Night, Mary, and goodbye, I suppose.'

He picked up his sleeping child again and, key in hand, went a few doors down the hall. She almost went to help him when he fumbled with the key and kept Nathan from waking up, but he managed. He closed the door and that was that.

But it wasn't. Hours later, Mary was still wide awake and staring at the ceiling. She worried about money first, then reminded herself that she was excellent at economising and York wasn't so far. Besides, if she needed more funds, Uncle Samuel would send them.

Thank goodness that the forlorn Miss Bruce didn't pine for a man in Bath. York likely had modest establishments for careful travellers. Mary worried next about her fellow travellers, then reminded herself that since Aunt Martha had never felt inclined to send a servant to accompany her on trips about Edinburgh, she had long ago perfected her stern, leave-me-alone face that could quell all but the most relentless bores and roués. No one would bother her on the Royal Mail, not even in England.

She had no remedy for the loneliness that was beginning to plague her, even though she had only been a little more than a week on her quest for the Christmas cake. The days were lively enough, because there was usually a woman or two on the Royal Mail of sufficient gentility to share a nod with and then a polite conversation. And she always carried a book in her reticule. The nights were troublesome, cooped up in one inn or another with no one to speak to, once she had tracked down, acquired, sifted through and then discarded the Christmas cakes.

Until she had begun this impromptu journey, Mary hadn't realised how much she enjoyed popping down to the kitchen for a chin-wag with Mrs Morison, or even listening to her Aunt Martha complain about this or that, or Uncle Sam speak to her until he retreated behind his morning newspaper. Cousin Dina hadn't been any fun at all, since she had agreed to marry Mr Page.

'It's only a few more days to be lonely and then

you will be home in Edinburgh, Mary,' she told the ceiling. 'Buck up a wee bit.'

That should have been enough, but she took her thoughts a step further tonight. Maybe she could blame it on Mr Barraclough and his little hopes, dreams and flights of fancy. He was a man living with a maiden aunt, perhaps for years, and he was fussy and silly already. All good wishes aside, Mary doubted supremely that Miss Jennie Lynch would ever stand with him under the kissing bough.

She lay in bed and realised that the saddest specimen of humankind in the world must be a ridiculous spinster or bachelor. *Spinster I may be, but please God, not a ridiculous one*, she thought as she fluffed her pillow, then pounded it and tried to sleep.

Nothing worked, so she thought about Captain Rennie, wondering how a man did what he did, taking the punishment of broadsides at close range or typhoons in the South China Sea without wanting to run screaming into a dark corner, as she thought she might. And how in the world did he maintain his balance on a slanting or pitching deck? She wanted to ask him, but the opportunity was gone.

Besides the obvious differences, Mary suspected that men were different in other ways, too. Her urge had always been to stay as far away from trouble as she could. Possibly if women ran the world, no one would fight. Although still not married to her, perhaps Lieutenant MacDowell would at least be alive to know his son, instead of dead on a Spanish battlefield he had probably never heard of, before it became his final resting place.

Mary wondered when her ever-so-distant cousin Ross had last spent Christmas ashore. It was too late to ask him. She knew the mail coach to Dumfries left before the sun was up. He and his son would be long gone before the York Mail left. She only knew that because she had overheard some of the other passengers talking about York. She would have to trust his sister to make his holiday—his shore leave—a good one. On that note, she finally slept.

Ross knew his son would go back to sleep as soon as he was in his nightshirt, but he didn't. Instead, Nathan put his hands behind his head, wriggled into a comfortable spot and frowned.

'What?' Ross asked. 'I know that look.'

He couldn't quite bring himself to tell his boy

that Inez had given him that same look a time or two, when he wasn't quite measuring up. A pity his son never knew his own mother.

Nathan didn't question his comment. 'It's this, Da,' he began. 'I don't think we should let Cousin Mary travel by herself on the Royal Mail. I mean, the common coach is fine for us, but she's a lady.'

'Aye to that. You know, I've been having the same thought. What can we do, though, outside of kidnapping her?'

'Oh, Da!'

They laughed together. Ross lay down beside his son, assuming the same position, hands behind his head. After a moment's thought, he leaned on his elbow. 'Are you expecting me to think of something?' he asked.

Nathan nodded. 'You're the man here.'

'Very well. I'll think about it.' He leaned over and kissed his son, then rose to put on his own nightshirt. 'Now go to sleep.'

'We really don't have much time,' Nathan pointed out. He closed his eyes, his expression blissful. 'Da, she touched me and I liked it.'

She touched me, too, and I liked it, Ross thought, surprised. 'All right. I'll devise a plan. Will that do? Will you go to sleep now?'

* * *

When Mary woke up, dawn struggled in the east. She must have been roused by the sound of the Royal Mail, departing for Scotland. She yearned to be on it, even if she found herself squashed between ordinary folk headed to early markets, as she had found on other early mornings. Well, Captain Rennie and Nathan would only be crowded for a few hours themselves, since Dumfries was not far. Her destination was York, which made her sigh, turn her face to the wall and snuggle deeper into her blankets, eager to put it far from her mind for another hour.

When she woke again, the room was light and she could not ignore the day. She sat up, not pleased with herself and even more cross with Mrs Morison, who had so calmly enlisted her for this trip. No matter; Mary could put on her quelling face and no one on the Royal Mail would trouble her with conversation.

She washed and dressed, then went into the sitting room, looking with real distaste on the Cumberland sausage and wishing she had directed the innkeep to remove it after the Rennies had left. She would do that when she went into the commons room to request breakfast, a prospect that didn't thrill her. The commons rooms were usually peopled by farmers resting after taking produce to market and she did dislike being ogled.

She stopped at the door and looked down at a folded square of paper pushed into the room, her name on it. She smiled to see 'Cousin Mary' and picked it up, curious. She read the note and her eyes opened wider. She read it through again out loud, thinking she might comprehend better what Captain Rennie had wrought.

"'The Lords of the Admiralty wish to inform Miss Mary Rennie that Captain Ross Rennie, post, requests and requires her permission to serve as an escort during times of war, and all trips into enemy territory—York,'" she read, shaking her head in amazement. She laughed out loud to read smaller printed words in parenthesis. "Aye, we are at peace now, but I know my employer pretty well and do not trust him to stay on that little island so close to France." You would know,' she murmured.

The note was close-written, but easy to read. Perhaps the economy of space came because he was used to writing in a ship's log. She scanned the remaining paragraph, gasped at his impertinence, laughed at its conclusion, then reread it, touched.

'"Because the Royal Mail is reliable, but uncomfortable, and Captain Rennie likes to travel in comfort when he can—which hasn't been often in the past twelve years—he has already engaged a post chaise for the journey to York,"' she read, amazed at his effrontery, which Aunt Martha probably would have called it. Mary wasn't so sure. '"Besides, he is determined to stop at Skowcroft for excellent dessert and the mail coach would not oblige him. Cousin Mary, do not disappoint this peg-leg warrior of the Royal Navy."'

'So you will stoop to the sympathy card, sir?' She laughed out loud and read the postscript. '"He also knows of some excellent shepherd's pie in York proper."'

Mary stood still for a long moment, tapping her finger against the note. She read it again, wondering about a man who had already engaged a post chaise to take her to York, because he knew she felt nervous about travelling alone. She couldn't think of a time when anyone had been so generous to her on such short notice.

A reminder of the timid Mr Barraclough made up her mind. 'I will do it, Captain Rennie,' she said out loud. She took a deep breath and opened the door.

There they stood in the corridor, father and son, both looking at her with a hopeful air. She burst out laughing.

'Oh, you two! What can I do but accept your kind offer?' she told them.

'Wise of you, since we weren't going to take no for an answer,' the captain said. 'Would you be willing to break your fast with us in the commons room?'

She was, sitting down to another excellent sausage, considerably shorter than four feet, eggs and coffee. If she had felt shy, the emotion didn't last long, not with Nathan needing a little attention tucking his napkin under his chin and then a better alignment of the buttons on his shirt when he finished. Perhaps he had dressed in the dark; possibly fathers didn't notice such details of dress.

When Nathan was tidy and the dishes withdrawn, the captain pulled a sheet of paper from his pocket. He spread it on the table. 'I have here a list of inns along our route,' he told her. 'Through the years, this sheet has graced the wardroom table on occasion, as I solicited information about good food in all corners of Britain.'

She looked at the list, seeing different handwriting. 'This is what passes for entertainment on a frigate at war?'

'Aye, miss, especially on the far side of the world, when we are drifting along in the doldrums and it's hotter than Dutch love.'

Mary blushed. 'Really, Cousin.'

Ross Rennie looked not a bit dismayed. 'I confess to a salty tongue. You'll get used to it.' His expression turned nostalgic. 'When you're down to bad beef, weevily bread and thick water, and the wine has run out, a list like this is surprisingly comforting.'

He jabbed a line. 'Look you here. If we leave now, we'll be in Skowcroft for luncheon, and that is where...' He stopped and looked at the barely legible line. He ran his finger gently across the words now. 'I had a midshipman, name of Everett from Skowcroft, who swore by the lemon-curd pudding at the Begging Hound.'

'I trust he has been back to enjoy it,' Mary said.

'Alas, no. He died in the Pacific. He was but fifteen.' The captain leaned back, his eyes troubled now. 'I...I suppose I want to have a dish of pudding for Dale Everett.'

She took the list from the table and scanned it.

'Brown bread with quince jelly? I do like quince jelly.'

'My former purser told me about a public house in Ovenshine.' He shook his head. 'A true scoundrel he was.' He correctly interpreted her expression and took the list from her. 'Here now, blood pudding in Wamsley, according to a pharmacist's mate who lives in Wamsley as we speak. They're not all dead, Mary, or rascals.'

Could it be that you need this little side trip to York even more than I do? she thought. The idea beguiled her far more than the prospect of fruitcake.

'Isn't your sister going to wonder where you are?' she asked, making one more attempt to call the man to reason.

'I sent her a letter before the sun was up, telling her we had to go to York on business.' He grinned, and it threw years off his weather-thrashed face. 'Hopefully, she will never ask what the business is. When do you need to report back to Edinburgh?'

She sipped her coffee and thought a moment. 'For certain by Christmas Eve. I believe that is when Dina's fiancé will arrive in Edinburgh and expect to see that little ring on her finger. And you?'

'Probably about the same time. That gives us

about a week, which will give me another week after to return my son to Plymouth and school, and get me back to sea.'

'We can be in York by tonight.'

The captain shook his head, then raised his finger for the innkeeper's attention. 'Weren't you listening, Mary? It's Skowcroft for lemon-curd pudding and Skowcroft ain't exactly on the beaten path.'

Chapter Seven

Skowcroft was far from the beaten path, but the thought of lemon-curd pudding set Mary's mouth tingling, even so soon after breakfast. How kind of Captain Rennie to concern himself with her welfare and how kind to have a list of places to stop along the way. She made one last half-hearted attempt to dissuade him, assuring him that the Royal Mail was good enough for her, but he wasn't buying it.

'Cousin, I'm not used to an argument,' he said firmly as he let the postilion open the door and pull down the step. 'Up you get,' he said to his son and boosted him inside. He looked at Mary. 'Do I need to boost you inside?'

Alarmed, she shook her head, then noticed the humour in his eyes. 'I suppose I must go to York in style,' she told him as he helped her into the chaise.

'I believe you must,' he agreed.

She made herself comfortable while the post boy put her satchel in the boot. She glanced out the window, where the captain was acquainting the older postilion with his list and probably explaining the need for Scowcroft, off the regular route. They were travelling in style, with four horses to pull their chaise and a postilion seated on each near horse.

'Papa likes to have his own way,' Nathan told her.

'I believe most of us do, but seldom get it,' she said with a laugh. 'Perhaps another requirement is being a post captain. People probably do what he says.'

Nathan nodded. 'I do.' He smiled at his father when the captain came inside the chaise and settled next to him. 'Papa, I have been carrying on a creditable conversation.'

Mary laughed out loud. 'A most creditable conversation, Cousin!' she declared. 'Nathan tells me that you are used to getting your way.'

'I expect it, madam,' he assured her.

His arm just naturally seemed to curve around his son's shoulders, and Nathan leaned close with a small sigh that went to Mary's heart. *How sel-*

dom they must see each other, she thought, *but how close they are. I see nothing of command here.*

'Well, I *usually* expect my own way,' the captain amended and exchanged an amused glance with his son. 'It was Nathan's idea that we ride the Royal Mail. He likes it when the coachman blows his yard of tin. How could I say nay?'

'Does this coachman have a yard of tin?' the boy asked.

'No. Postilions do not announce themselves. By the way, his name is Tom Preston and his son is mounted on the horse closest to the chaise.'

Nathan absorbed that fact. Mary could practically see the gears turning in his brain. 'I doubt your father will let you do that, too,' she told him. 'It's cold out there. I hope they can keep warm.'

The boy nodded, his expression thoughtful. 'Da takes care of me.'

Mary glanced at the captain, then looked away, startled to see tears in his eyes. *My goodness, how hard it must be to say goodbye to a child and sail into danger*, she thought. *Thank God the war is over.*

'I have the distinct impression that you take care of many people and now you have added one more to that number,' Mary said, her voice soft. Impulsively, she leaned forwards across the small space and touched his hand.

He looked up from his contemplation of the floor boards and grinned at her. His eyes were still shiny with tears, but he didn't seem to mind that she saw them. 'I have broad shoulders, Cousin,' he assured her.

She nodded, unsure what to say, because his words touched her heart. She sat back, thinking of all those anonymous members of the Royal Navy who took care of her and everyone else in the British Isles. She thought of them when news came of a sea battle, but ordinarily not otherwise. Still, they patrolled the oceans and English Channel, and had stood blockade duty for dreary years, keeping her safe. And here was this nice man, a far-distant cousin, seeing her to York. Mary smiled to herself, thinking she would have to write a quick note to Mrs Morison, telling her that maybe she was having an adventure after all.

She wanted to chat, but there was Nathan, his eyes drooping already. In a few moments, his head rested against his father's thigh. In another minute, his eyes closed.

'He didn't get much sleep last night,' the captain

whispered. 'He was so afraid that you wouldn't let us escort you to York.'

Mary had her own struggle. 'Happen he inherited your broad shoulders.'

'Happen he did.'

He was silent then, looking out the window, where snow began to fall. Mary watched his eyes begin to close, too, which made her wonder if both of the Rennies had stayed awake too late, worrying if she would agree to this decidedly ramshackle scheme.

Mary watched the captain. He did have broad shoulders and the peg-leg wasn't intrusive; she had already become accustomed to it. Still, how did a man function with such a thing? What did his leg actually look like? How did he stay upright in a storm? She had a hundred questions, not one of which she would ever ask.

'Suction and straps, Cousin.'

Startled, she glanced at the captain, obviously no longer asleep, as he watched the trajectory of her gaze, a twinkle in his eyes.

Mary felt her face flame. She could have uttered a half-dozen apologies, but what was the point? He had caught her staring at his wooden leg. She recognised the moment for what it was. *Yea or nay?* she asked herself and decided yea would do.

'I *had* wondered. How did you know?'

'I've seen that glance a time or two and generally from the female sex,' he told her, as calm as could be. 'The peg itself is padded inside. I ease in my stump and then fasten the two leather straps to a belt around my waist under my clothes. You're the first lady I've ever explained it to.'

Another ripe moment. She knew she could nod, apologise a little, then say no more, except that she wanted to know more. 'Does it ever hurt?'

Bless his heart, Captain Rennie seemed to understand. 'If I stand too long, or walk great distances.' He chuckled. 'That's not generally a problem on your average frigate.'

'Oh. But aren't there periods when you are on deck for hours?'

'Most days, Cousin, so, aye, it does hurt,' he said. He shifted Nathan a bit and settled himself more comfortably. 'Look you here.' He raised his trouser leg until she saw the bucketlike contraption and the beginning of a strap.

'It was amputated mid-calf?'

'Aye. I'm lucky. I still have my knee. We have a cook on board my frigate who lost his leg to the hip, almost.' He shook his head, but Mary saw admiration in his expression. 'He stumps around with a crutch and cooks amazing victuals.'

'Still, you probably could have left the sea.'

'Never, Cousin,' he said, his voice firm. 'I am at home on the ocean and have somehow convinced the Sea Lords that I am valuable.'

Mary nodded. She had more questions. The captain must have known it, because he extended both hands and curled his fingers, as though trying to coax the words from her. She smiled at that. 'You make a peg-leg sound simple, but I doubt it is,' she ventured.

'On board, I wear a peg that is slightly broader than this one.' He laughed out loud. 'This is my gentlemanly town peg! It's easier to stand on a wider hunk of wood and maintain my balance. And if the sea is really rough, I secure myself to the ship and let it hold me up. There's no end of rope located conveniently.'

'Goodness. I can't imagine trying to maintain balance on a slanting deck.'

'Like everything, Cousin, practice. We usually stand loose with legs wide apart, maybe one foot behind the other.'

He looked down at his sleeping child and gave

the boy a look so fond that she couldn't help a moment of envy, wishing someone would look at her that way.

'I was nearly a month in Plymouth for some rapid refitting when Nathan was three. I used to take him in the tin tub with me. He cried when he couldn't take off his leg, too, when we bathed.'

His comment was so matter of fact and disingenuous that Mary was completely disarmed. 'Feeling sorry for you would be pointless,' she stated.

'Completely.' He crossed his legs and waggled his peg at her, as he had discomfited Mr Barraclough only last night.

Mary put her hands to her mouth so she would not laugh too loud and wake up Nathan. 'You're a rascal *and* a scoundrel,' she told him.

'I'm a navy man. It's one and the same.' He looked out the window again, where the snow fell faster. 'I wouldn't be a postilion on a day like this. Poor Preston and son. I wonder, Mary: should we stop for the day at Scowcroft? What is today, by the way?'

'December the seventh. I'll still have time to wrest that fruitcake from Miss Bruce's long-lost lover, provided he hasn't died of apoplexy from the shock of Mr Barraclough's love note. There's probably even time for a few side trips for victuals, as you call them,' she added.

'Then let's do it. I know I'd rather ride out a typhoon on a quarterdeck than sit on a cold horse with snow pelting down. I'll tell Preston when we stop.'

Ross Rennie seemed disinclined to doze, and Mary had found her tatting shuttle. She tucked her legs under her and made herself comfortable on her side of the post chaise as they continued the journey, slower now, as the snow grew heavier. When she shivered, the captain removed his boat cloak and draped it across her lap. She smiled her thanks and didn't bother to insist he keep it for himself. Not even twenty-four hours in his company, Mary knew he would overrule any paltry objection she thought up. And he did have broad shoulders.

'How did you lose your leg?' she asked when she was comfortable again and tatting.

'Trafalgar, on the deck of the *Sirius*, a thirty-six-gun frigate. I was first luff to Captain William Prowse, the best tarpaulin who ever sailed.'

'Tarpaulin?'

'Up from the ranks or a grizzled old veteran; Will Prowse is both. I vow Captain Billy has forgotten more about the management of a ship than

I will ever know.' He looked down at his wooden leg and gave it a hard knock, which made Nathan stir and then resettle himself on his father's thigh. 'Sorry, Nate. Frigates are the eyes of the fleet, Cousin. Our task at Trafalgar was to lie upwind of the *Victory* and pass on her flag signals to the rest of the ships. It was lively, but not particularly dangerous.'

He tapped his wooden leg a little kinder this time, almost a caress. 'Wouldn't you know, I was the only serious injury on board during the battle.' His leaned back and his voice took on the quality of reminiscence. 'There I was, standing on the quarterdeck by Captain Billy, writing down a signal from *Victory*, when, blam! A splinter from a cannonball misfired from the *San Agustin* took off my leg as slick as be-damned. One second I'm standing there and the next second I'm lying on the deck, slippery in my own blood and wondering what the hell happened.'

'A splinter?' she asked, her eyes wide.

'Not the little kind you get under a fingernail.' He gestured. 'About a yard long and wicked.' He smiled. 'The auxiliary helmsman slung me over his shoulder and carried me below deck to the surgeon. I left quite a trail, I am told. Bones tidied me up and left me a good flap and I have my knee. Piece of cake, Mary Rennie.'

She frowned at him, and he just gazed back, as pleasant as could be.

'I'll never understand sailors,' she said finally.

'You weren't meant to. Didn't your mother warn you about seamen?'

'She died when I was fifteen. I doubt Mama ever met a mariner of any sort.'

Mary was silent then, looking out the window in her turn. *I have lived such an ordinary life*, she thought, as the snow pelted down. The post chaise moved slower and slower.

You damned fool, scare your cousin to death, Ross chided himself as he watched his cousin return her attention to her tatting, her expression thoughtful. She had such a pretty face, framed with dark red hair pulled back into a low chignon. No one would ever mistake her for a diamond of the first water, but he relished her quiet air and the sense of calm he felt around her. In a fraught life of noise, terror and bedlam, alternating with weeks on end of stupefying boredom, there was something so restful about her. He thought again of Nathan's comment: 'She touched me.'

He liked the way her hair curled out from under her bonnet, as though unwilling to be wrangled and confined in that chignon. There was nothing memorable about her face, except its calm. She had a charming way of giving him her undivided attention that he found flattering. Maybe that was what Nathan had noticed, too.

Funny thing about Mary; she looked absolutely nothing like the woman on a different wardroom list—the one he had composed mid-ocean in the horse latitudes when not a breath of wind stirred so much as a hair follicle for a long and dreary month. The heat and monotony were stupefying and no one wanted to even talk about food. Wardroom chat turned to women, as it frequently did on any ocean. He was a first luff then, young and with blood so hot he'd have willingly sacrificed two or three years off his likely short existence to drop anchor in Otaiheite with its island full of obliging women. While they sweated and his captain swore at them and drank deeper, his young officers had each compiled a list of absolute necessities in female companionship.

Some of those necessities he blushed even now to remember, but he never forgot the gist. His wife of choice some day would be tall and blonde, with a low, seductive laugh—why that mattered, he couldn't have said then or now—and just the faintest French-Caribbean accent. As much as he hated the Frogs, he remembered a memorable night in Martinique with just such a woman, the wife of a Frenchman way too long at sea. His ward-room mates had been forced to practically peel him off that fetching *madame* before the frigate sailed without him. Ross never forgot that accent.

That was twenty years ago. He'd kept that par-ticular list for years, until it sank with the HMS *Marlborough* and he'd ended up in that Turkish prison. By then, he didn't need the list, but his tall, blonde beauty with the French accent remained his measuring stick for a future Mrs Rennie. He glanced at Mary, wishing for a fraction of a second that she possessed even one of the requirements. Alas, not one. He smiled to think about her thick accent, quite far removed from sibilant and seduc-tive French. True, her dark red hair was attractive. Ah, well. He knew the war wasn't over yet; there was still time to find the woman of that long-gone but never-forgotten list. Maybe, just maybe, this as-yet-unknown Mrs Rennie would have Mary's innate kindness with children.

The chaise moved slower and slower. At one

point, the postilion stopped and dismounted, tromping back to the chaise to shake his head over worsening conditions. There was no denying the relief in his eyes when Ross said they would be staying the night at Skowcroft. That was the nice thing about travel on land, Ross decided, as they started up again, slower still. On land, it was possible to just call it off for a day until conditions improved. At sea, there was always the wind, or lack of it, to dictate and demand. No matter how the wind blew or the snow fell, Skowcroft lay dead ahead and required no great effort to locate. He looked out the window and there was a village already. Hopefully, the Begging Hound wasn't boarded and shuttered.

'Please be open,' he said out loud.

Mary looked up, a question in her eyes.

He felt his face grow warm, knowing he must have sounded like the veriest fool. He didn't know what to say.

She did an amazing thing, one that convinced him that helping his cousin might turn out to be the smartest act he had performed since marrying Inez Veimira.

'It will be open, Captain,' she said, all the assurance in the world in her voice. 'And there will be lemon-curd pudding, just as Mr Everett said there would be. Just you wait.'

Strangely calmed, he nodded and returned his gaze to the white world. Another fifteen minutes, and they came to a stop in front of a stone building that looked as though it had been hunkering down against snow and wind since at least the reign of Good Queen Bess. The hound in question was a painted dog with drooping eyes and ears that swung rhythmically to and fro with a creak. It was a hound of dubious origins, but exactly as Midshipman Everett had described it, there on the far side of the world, somewhere by Otaihete, with its bare-breasted women who would spread their legs for the payment of a nail, but who didn't know how to make lemon-curd pudding.

Mary didn't need to know that, he decided, with a little smile. The smile left his face as he thought of Dale Everett, such a talented young lad with chronometer and sextant, dying so far from this white world. Unlike the French, the Royal Navy buried its men at sea, not stacking them belowdeck to rot, swell and burst on the return trip. Ross had written his usual letter of condolence and passed it off later to a frigate heading home. He hoped it had arrived eventually, but he had never enquired, never visited. There was always the excuse of no time, but even had there been opportunity, he doubted he would visit.

Until now. He took a deep breath as the post chaise slowed and stopped. Nathan woke up and rubbed his eyes, looking around. In five more years his son would be as old as Dale Everett, when that talented midshipman, drenched in sweat, drew his last breath and let it out slowly and finally, so far from home.

The sea is my home, Ross reminded himself. *This is the alien world.* He glanced at Mary, who was watching Nathan. She reached out to straighten his son's jacket and run her fingers through his wild hair. Maybe it wasn't going to prove as alien as he had feared, at least until they came to York, found the Christmas cake and parted company. He had no idea where he belonged, but he was like all men of the sea, willing to be flexible, because that was what the service demanded. Call it the price of Admiralty.

He looked at his son and his cousin, already considering them his crew. 'Here we are, mates,' he said, which made Mary smile. 'I'm almost afraid to ask if the Begging Hound still serves the best lemon-curd pudding in Yorkshire. I have it on good authority that was the case in 1803, but that was eleven years ago. Shall we?'

They did. He had to duck and remove his hat to negotiate the low ceiling, but his crew passed inside with no difficulty. Before he closed the door, he looked back at his postilion with some sympathy. Preston helped his son down from the near horse. He stood a moment in the doorway, watching the Prestons shiver and slap gloved hands on each other. In another moment, the ostler and a young boy joined them to lead the team to shelter, grain and hay. He closed the door and turned to face what must be the innkeep, his face red from the heat of the kitchen.

'Welcome, sir,' the man exclaimed, wiping floury hands on an apron of dubious cleanliness. 'You're a long way from home.'

You have no idea, Ross thought. He nodded to his host. 'We were planning to travel on, but my postilion assures me that is not wise. Do you have a room or two?'

'Aye, Captain.'

'We'd like rooms, but before that, we would like your lemon-curd pudding.'

Ah, the moment of truth. Was Midshipman Everett right, or was lemon-curd pudding a figment of a homesick boy's imagination? Ross glanced around. The public room was bare, hardly surprising, considering the storm. Maybe the innkeep had decided not to make pudding, knowing that few customers would venture far from their own hearths today. He almost feared to look the man in the eye because he did not want to be disappointed, not after years of longing.

He turned to his host to see the man all smiles, as though he knew a crew from the frigate HMS *Abukir* would be arriving on schedule for luncheon.

The keep gestured around him, giving them leave to try any or all tables, maybe even rearrange them, so happy he was to have customers. 'I'll have it to you almost before you can decide where to sit!' He looked at Mary, then at Nathan. 'Madam, do you want your boy to eat sweets before beef and bread?'

Mary blushed so becomingly, opened her mouth to make some explanation or other, caught Ross's eye and merely nodded. 'We'd all like to try the pudding, but do serve the captain first. He's waited a long time for this rare treat.'

God bless the ladies. Ross pulled out a chair for her, and she sat down. He took his courage in his hands and whispered close to her ear, 'Decided not to bore the man with details, eh?' he teased.

'I'm old enough to be Nathan's mother. It's a logical mistake,' she whispered back. 'Don't try me, Cousin.'

'I would never.' The look she gave him curled all five of his toes.

If a stout man who hadn't shaved yet, and with flour on his fingers, could present lemon-curd pudding with something approaching a flourish, then the proprietor of the Begging Hound could be judged and found not wanting.

With solemn step and slow, as though he bore in a haggis to a piping tune, he came into the commons room carrying a bowl with steam rising from it. He was followed by an equally serious little girl holding spoons and bowls. Ross's mouth watered as he smelt the tang of lemon and the warm comfort of wheat. He remembered that little wardroom in the middle of the South Pacific crowded with officers as hungry and homesick as he was, all of them listening to Dale Everett describe the pudding.

He didn't think his expression had turned melancholy, but Mary's hand rested firmly on his arm.

'A generous helping for the captain,' she said, because he could not speak.

And there it was before him, tangy and hot and quivering a little. He lifted his spoon with a hand that trembled and sank it deep into the yellow goodness in front of him. First to his nose for a deep whiff worthy of a connoisseur of fine port and then to his mouth.

Great God of battle, he thought, in all reverence. *Dale, you were right. I wish to heaven above that you were here.* He swallowed the pudding around an enormous boulder in his throat. He set down the spoon, unable to take another bite. Damn his eyes, he was about to cry.

Chapter Eight

Mary's heart went out to Captain Rennie as he bowed his head over the pudding, unable to eat because he was in tears. The publican stared at them both, shocked.

'It's…it's most generally reckoned to be good pudding,' he stammered.

'You're completely right,' she told the man. 'Captain Rennie has been thinking about this pudding during long, long years at sea, keeping all of us safe from Napoleon. Please understand his emotions. Your pudding is wonderful.'

The keep nodded and gave the captain a kindly glance. With a nod to Mary, he left them alone. She calmly fished in her reticule and found a handkerchief, which she handed to her cousin. Nathan's eyes began to well with tears as his father pressed the handkerchief to his face and took several deep breaths.

Mary gestured to Nathan. He came to her side, and she took his hand. She led him outdoors where the snow was beginning to let up. 'Let's just stand here a moment, breathing in and out, and give your father a solitary moment.' She made no mention of Nathan's tears, but his empathy touched her heart.

Mary took her own advice until she was in control again. The air was brisk, but the wind had stopped, along with the snow. So the captain expected them to just hunker down at the Begging Hound until morning? She realised suddenly that there was more work to do in Skowcroft.

Nathan tugged at her hand, and she leaned down. 'Why did Da start to cry? I've never seen him cry, and it scares me.'

Leaning wouldn't do. Mary crouched in the snow, her hands on Nathan's shoulder now. 'I think he is remembering Midshipman Everett, and maybe other crew members like him who are no longer with us.'

The boy nodded, but his eyes were still troubled. He swallowed and leaned into Mary. 'Sometimes when she thinks we are all asleep, Mrs Pritchert cries.'

'She's missing her husband, Nathan.'

'Do you think Da cried when he found me and then discovered my mama was dead?'

Nathan was in control of his own emotions now, discussing his mother calmly because he had never known her. Mary took a deep breath of her own. She imagined all the sorrow of sailing into Oporto after a long voyage—who knew *how* dangerous— looking forward to a baby her cousin knew would be born during his absence and finding rubble instead of a home.

'I suspect he did.' She hugged him, then got to her feet. 'But what a relief it must have been to find you alive.'

Nathan nodded, becoming again the practical, matter-of-fact child she was coming to appreciate after less than a day in his company. He tugged her hand. 'I want more of that pudding and we don't know that Da won't eat it all, once he feels better.'

Mary laughed. 'We'd better hurry!'

Cousin Ross hadn't touched another bite of the pudding he had yearned for and travelled out of his way to find. He sat there, tears dry on his face, just staring at the wall at a painting of dogs much darkened by years and tobacco and chimney smoke. Mary doubted he even knew the painting was there.

This situation was new to her; maybe Mrs Morison hadn't even reckoned on such dealing when she assured Mary she was overdue for an adventure. Mary had never dealt with a man in pain before, or a little boy in need of reassurance or travel in foreign lands. She stood a moment in silence of her own, thinking what her father, late Church of Scotland minister, would do in her place. He would quote some scripture or other, she told herself. She thought a moment. The only one that sprang immediately into her brain was Psalm 37, which began 'Fret not'.

She looked down at the captain to see that he was looking at her now. So much for what her father would have said or done. She knew what her mother would have done so she did it. Without a word, Mary kissed the top of his head and sat down beside him. Without losing a beat, she spooned the pudding into a bowl for Nathan, who sat on her other side. She dished up another for herself.

'We weren't about to let you steal a march on us and eat the whole thing,' she said after several bites, each more delicious than the one before. 'I think Midshipman Everett was entirely right. What was his first name again?'

'Dale,' Ross said and picked up his spoon again. He ate another spoonful and then closed his eyes, this time in obvious pleasure. It was the same expression she had noted last night when he dug into the Cumberland sausage. 'His father was vicar in this parish, so his origins were similar to mine.'

It was normal, ordinary conversation, and she had begun it. 'Mine, too, then. My father was a minister in the Kirk of Scotland.' She cast caution to the wind and nudged his shoulder. 'So you are a minister's son.'

'Aye, miss.' He dipped into the bowl for another serving. 'You and I are obviously from the righteous branch of the Rennies. Well, you more righteous than I, I shouldn't wonder.' He gave a private chuckle at that, which she had no intention of quizzing him about, then looked around her to see his son. 'What do you think of this pudding?'

'Da, we should begin every meal with a sweet.'

Ross gave his boy a look almost as mournful as the one on the Begging Hound. 'We daren't. Mrs Pritchert would set my leg on fire.'

Mary put her hand to her mouth to stifle what she knew was going to be an unladylike guffaw.

As calmly as she had kissed his head, the captain took her hand away from her face. 'We need a good laugh, my dear.'

She obliged, which somehow gave permission for the innkeep to peer around the door leading to the kitchen. The captain gestured to him. 'Now we'll have the rest of our meal.'

They decided on mutton stew, which made Nathan look mutinous until his father promised more lemon-curd pudding, since they had finished the bowl. Dark bread and marmalade rounded out a meal that Mrs Pritchert would have approved, sparing the captain's leg, as Nathan reminded him. 'D'ye think your peg would really burn, Da?'

'I'd piss it out before that happened,' the captain joked.

'Stop it, you two!' Mary exclaimed.

'Have you no brothers?' the captain asked.

'Not one. Is this the kind of humour I would have been subjected to?'

'Constantly. More pudding, please,' Ross asked the proprietor when he came to clear the table.

'Sir, could you tell me if a vicar by the name of Everett still presides in this parish?' Mary asked when he returned.

The innkeeper looked at her for a long moment and she realised, with some embarrassment, that her accent was too thick for the Englishman. 'Vicar name of Everett still here?' she said slowly and louder, thinking that might help.

The keep nodded, to her relief, because she knew her face was flame-red. He pointed. 'Go to edge of Skowcroft. Big house, red shutters,' he said, just as distinctly, as though she spoke some rare language from Africa's interior and the fewer words, the better.

Nathan grinned at the odd conversation, but Ross Rennie's face lost its animation.

'It's stopped snowing, but we were just going to stay right here,' he said quickly.

'We are not,' Mary told him, her voice gentle now. 'The postilion and his son are half-frozen. Lemon-curd pudding is only part of what you need to do here.'

The captain was silent for a long moment, pressing his fingers against the bridge of his nose, while Nathan continued happily through another bowl of pudding.

'I hadn't planned on this,' he said, but Mary chose to hear it as a feeble protest.

'I think you did, Captain Rennie, on some level

or other,' she contradicted. Where her courage was coming from, she didn't know, but she suddenly understood this man.

He tried one more time. 'The Christmas cake...'

'Can wait.' She turned to Nathan, who had finished another bowl and sat there, looking dazed. 'We're going to visit the vicar, then we'll be back here to stay the night.'

Nathan nodded, obviously content to do what she said, although she had not a particle of authority to command.

'Well, Captain Rennie?' Mary stood up and held out her hand. If he didn't grasp it, she would leave her cousins alone and take the next conveyance to York, probably branded forever as a meddler by a distant relative she would never see again. *You've been sent to find a stupid fruitcake and that's it,* she reminded herself. *These cousins are so remote a relationship as to belong in another country.*

Maybe the captain was right. Maybe she *was* trying to complicate a simple list of foods put together by homesick, hungry men during a long war. Like one of those sea birds that flew huge distances with elegant wings, but were clumsy on land, Doubt stumbled into the commons room of the Begging Hound and plopped down at her feet.

She was prepared to lower her hand and turn away when Captain Rennie snapped out of the doldrums he had sunk into and gave her a resolute look. He took her hand and she hauled him to his feet, using both of hers.

'I believe you are right, Cousin,' he told her. He pressed her hand tighter. 'Don't give up on me just yet.'

It was a quixotic thing to say, but after all, here she was in Skowcroft, not precisely snowbound, but with no mail coach nearby. 'I won't give up on either of you,' she assured them both.

After settling the luncheon bill, Captain Rennie spent a moment outside with the postilions, who seemed content to spend the night in Skowcroft. The ostler had room for them in the barn and Preston declared their wants were few. The captain sent them indoors to find their own meal. With an expression lodged somewhere between resignation and pique, he gestured for Mary and Nathan to join him.

Shop owners were already at work on the snow in front of their establishments. With Mary on one side of him and Nathan on the other, Captain Rennie began a slow progress through the village.

'I'm not too confident about my leg on snow, you two,' he warned them. 'If we all go down in a heap, you can both walk away and pretend you don't know me.'

Nathan laughed. 'Da, you're quizzing us.'

'Not for the world,' his father said, the humour back in his voice. 'I'll be upended like a Galapagos turtle.'

By the end of the street, he seemed more sure of his footing. After another few yards, there was the church with big house, red shutters next to it. He stopped and took a deep breath. Mary had linked her arm through his. She nudged him forwards, and he pressed her arm against his side, keeping her close, as though he needed her, which she found flattering. No one had really needed her since Papa took sick and died.

'Suppose they swoon or rage and rail at me?' he asked her in a low voice, so Nathan could not hear.

'How long ago was...?'

'Before Trafalgar.' His expression turned from uncertain to wishful. 'It seems so long ago. Dale would be twenty-three now if...' His voice became purposeful. 'Nathan, you go ahead and knock on that door.'

His son raced ahead, surefooted on the snowy

path. Obviously the vicar didn't have servants eager to shovel walks, or any young boys at home, Mary decided.

'What do I say to them?' he asked her suddenly.

She didn't know what to tell him, because the door opened just then. A small, grey-haired woman stood there, smiling at Nathan. She looked up at Mary, and the captain came closer. The smile left her face when she saw his boat cloak and tall bicorn hat, visible signs of his profession.

Oh, please, Mary thought.

They hadn't reached the steps yet and the captain had stopped. Gently, he untwined his arm from Mary's, took off his hat, and made a sweeping gesture and bow.

'Madam, are you Mrs Everett?' he asked. 'I am Captain Rennie. I…I believe you had a letter from me.'

Eyes wide, the woman's hand went to her throat. She watched him calmly for a long moment, then came down the snowy steps and directly into his arms. Mary turned away because tears threatened her vision. Nathan crowded close to her, and her arms went around the little boy as he stood in front of her.

Bereft mother and post captain stood close together, arms around each other, consoling each other without a word spoken. Mary swallowed and blinked back her tears as a man in priest's garb came towards them from the church so close by. In another moment the circle of two had become three.

It was never about lemon-curd pudding, Mary thought. A greater epiphany struck her, far more startling than the earlier one in Edinburgh, when she decided she was weary of relatives. *And you didn't know it until I told you, Cousin.*

After a moment of silent mourning, the three separated. The vicar, smiling now, to Mary's astonishment, gestured towards the wide-open front door.

'What a bunch of loobies we are!' he chided gently. 'The Church of England has no provisions for heating the great outdoors at your average vicarage.'

Captain Rennie laughed, and Mrs Everett patted his chest, as though comforting him.

Nathan looked up at Mary. 'Is everything all right, do you think?' he asked, keeping his voice low.

Mrs Everett heard him anyway. She touched his head. 'Everything is quite fine, my dear,' she assured him, then looked at Mary. 'I should apologise for grabbing your husband! Do come in, Mrs Rennie. And what is *your* name, young man?'

'Nathan,' he told her. 'That's my father,' he informed her, in case there might be any doubt. 'This is Cousin Mary, not my mother, although I like her a lot.'

The vicar ushered them up the front steps while Mrs Everett apologised again. *I'm not so certain I would have corrected you*, Mary thought, which brought colour to her cheeks. *It seems like a waste of words, explanation and more apology, and I will never see you after today, dear lady.* Mary decided that once the lost fruitcake was found and she was home in Edinburgh, she would have to ask herself why she wanted to be so casual about her association with Captain Rennie. It pained her to think that proper manners vanished by close association with members of the Royal Navy. Maybe she was getting old and careless.

The vicarage was warm, simple and welcoming, with samplers bearing admonitory Bible verses crowding the walls, silent testimony to many daughters or a single, zealous one. A maid appeared and soon found herself staggering under a boat cloak, tall hat, Nathan's overcoat and Mary's ordinary grey cloak. A few whispered words to the same maid resulted in tea and biscuits in a few minutes. A quiet word from Captain Rennie to his son sent Nathan seeking a shovel. Soon the scrape of shovel on walkway was heard, which made Mrs Everett smile.

'How kind you are, Captain,' she said, passing him the plate of biscuits. 'Our youngest son is even now at St Stephen's and our yardman is a little old for snow.'

'He's happy to oblige, ma'am,' Ross replied. 'He lives in Plymouth and seldom sees snow.'

They all sipped tea in silence, as though no one knew quite what to say. Since Mary was seated so close to the captain, she leaned against his arm. 'I believe you should show the Everetts your list, Ross.'

He gave her a sudden smile, and she realised she had used his Christian name without coaxing. 'It's a good place to begin,' he said simply and took the much-creased paper out of his inside pocket. He handed it to the vicar and pointed to the name he had underlined.

Mr Everett nodded and smiled, even as he dabbed at his eyes. 'Look, Lavinia. Dale never could resist the lemon-curd pudding.'

She took the sheet from him and lovingly ran her finger across her son's name. She read through the entire list, then looked at the captain, her eyes bright with unshed tears. 'What is this, Captain?'

'The wishes and dreams of homesick men, my dear,' he told her, taking the paper from her. 'It made the rounds in many a wardroom. Everyone added his favourite food, and where to find it.' He ran his finger down the list. 'You'll notice that some of the boys and men put their own homes.' He took several deep breaths. 'When did you receive the letter I sent? In 1803, not long after your son died of the fever near Otaheite, I handed it off to a passing frigate bound for Portsmouth.'

'We received it in December of 1805,' the vicar said, when his wife could not speak. He leaned forwards, his eyes earnest. 'Did he serve king and country well?'

'As well as any man I commanded,' Captain Rennie replied. 'Dale had an aptitude for mathematics.' He leaned back, his shoulder touching Mary's now. 'Let me paint a picture for you of deep-blue water in the middle of the Pacific, a calm day and the sun high overhead. I had five earnest midshipmen on the quarterdeck gathered around my sailing master, Ben Pritchert, as he instructed them in the finer points of longitude and latitude. Mr Everett never made a mistake.'

Mrs Everett sighed and looked out the window at the snowy scene. 'He was a long way from home.'

'The HMS *Militant* was his home.' Ross Rennie swallowed. 'He was one of my sons. I mourned his passing. I suppose I still do.'

Again there was silence, except for the scrape of the shovel outside as Nathan worked his way towards the street.

'Will you send your son to sea, Captain?' Mrs Everett asked.

'If he chooses to go, just as your son chose,' he reminded her. He took a small book from his pocket, thumbed through it and held it out to the vicar. 'October 15, 1803. And here are the co-ordinates of where your son lies. Do you have a marker for him in your graveyard?'

The Everetts clutched each other's hands. 'We do.'

'Then copy this and carve it on his stone. I would have given the earth to have seen him safely home, but it was beyond my power. We have all been ruled by a monster, but thank God he is on Elba now,' Ross said. 'Excuse me, please.'

Without another word, he got up and left the

room. Mary held her breath as she heard the front door close. They all looked out the window to see him take the shovel from Nathan and continue to the street.

The vicar took a sheet of paper from the escritoire and a pencil and copied the co-ordinates. 'Close to Otaheite,' he murmured, then handed the little book to Mary. 'A place we will never see, Lavinia.'

Mary looked at the book in her hand, realising with a start that she held a meticulous record of all the dead on Captain Rennie's ships, probably from the time he first commanded. The number shocked her, but as she looked at it, she began to suspect why he had insisted on accompanying her to York. *You just wanted to have some fun, didn't you?* she asked herself. *How can a man carry around such a book? Should I have insisted you come to the vicarage?*

'We miss Dale,' Mrs Everett said simply when the silence seemed too large for the room. 'Time has passed and smoothed some of the rough edges.' She went to the window. 'We remember the lovely times and now we know exactly where he was buried. I can't begin to express my gratitude to Captain Rennie.'

Chapter Nine

I'm a coward, Ross thought after he finished the walkway and stood with Nathan, who admired their work. *I don't want to go back in that house, except that I left Mary there.*

He thought he could walk away with his son right now and Mary would not follow him. She owed him nothing, really. Possibly she was even feeling some guilt at forcing his hand, however gently, with the Everetts. He knew enough of her in their brief acquaintance to be certain she would continue to York in search of a silly fruit-cake, achieve her objective and return to Edinburgh. He and Nathan could return right now to the Begging Hound and chivvy the postilion into driving on. They would be at his sister's home in a day or two, as he had been planning for months.

Beyond something to chuckle about with Nathan in years to come, that was the end of the story.

He had left his hat and cloak inside and his little book, the pernicious butcher's bill he had kept through the years. He could send Nathan inside for those and Mary would not follow him.

Ross opened his mouth to ask his son to do precisely that, but stopped. The door opened and there was Mary, coming towards them now. He could not then have explained the relief that swept through his body like small arms' fire. She was not about to abandon him. He could have fallen to his knees in gratitude, because he had two knees still.

I told you that a man can do anything with two knees, he thought irrationally, as she walked towards them. As she approached, he wondered if she would find half a leg repugnant to look at. Good thing he would never know, because he decided he didn't want to be abandoned by her just yet.

She came right up to him with no hesitation and something militant in her eyes, as though she expected an objection. He vaguely remembered her expression from a similar one his wife used to direct at him when she knew she had a better idea than he did. Generally, Inez was right. He waited, probably aware, as Mary couldn't be, that her expression was entirely wifely. He wondered about that as the thought idly flitted through his brain that it was a pity she was not tall, willowy and blonde.

She was kind, but firm. 'Cousin, the Everetts have invited us to stay the night, and I have accepted.'

He knew better than to argue. A smile played around his lips as he thought of legions of midshipmen and lieutenants who had regarded him with fear and trembling. They would never in an eon of time ever have thought a woman would tell Captain Rennie what to do. He decided he rather liked it, even though the prospect of an entire evening with the Everetts terrified him. He nodded.

God bless the ladies. She touched his arm. 'They look on your visit as a gift from heaven, Ross.'

'You're not bamming me?'

'I would never.' A smile played around her lips. 'Well, I might, but not about this.'

'Very well, Mary. If you insist.'

'I do.' She did not seem startled at his immediate acquiescence, which delighted him on some level that he hadn't visited in years. Mary turned to Nathan. 'Do you like to sing? Mr Everett said that he

is taking his young parishioners carolling tonight.'
She glanced at Ross and gleefully he noticed a bit
of uncertainty in her expression now. 'Adults are
welcome, too, but I don't know...'

'Can't you sing, Cousin?' he asked.

'I can, but there's a lot of walking.'

'We'll only go as far as you want,' he teased.
'After all, if you get cold, we can set my leg on
fire to keep us warm.'

'Didn't you just tell me how you could p...put
out a fire?'

'I have you there,' he said softly, delighted when
she blushed.

They could joke, but he still hesitated to go back
inside. She must have seen it, because she crooked
out her arm for his son. 'Come, Nathan, *we* have
enough sense to go inside where it's warm.'

Nathan put his arm through hers and looked at
Ross. 'Da?'

'Just a minute.' Mary handed Ross the little book
he had left inside, her face suddenly solemn.

He pocketed it, then took her other arm and let
her escort them inside. He knew he was a brave
man at sea. Maybe he could be a brave man on
land, as long as his cousin didn't stray too far in
Skowcroft. An epiphany: cousins had their uses.

* * *

Dinner at the vicarage was an unalloyed delight, to Ross's amazement. He gave all credit to Mr Everett, who, with a few questions, drew him out about life at sea. He couldn't bring himself to ask why this topic wasn't painful to them, but Mrs Everett seemed to understand his unasked query.

'Dale used to send us the most marvellous letters, full of little drawings and stories of life below deck. He found his new world interesting, so we did, too. Please tell us more,' she asked as they ate.

It was easier than he would have thought to reminisce until he felt a little like an antiquarian, reliving old glories to a bored audience. Except that it was obvious no one found his stories dull. He could tell they yearned to know every detail of their son's life and he obliged them. It gave him true pleasure to tell the Everetts that their son was the only cully he knew who plotted true courses without fail from Mr Pritchert's quarterdeck classroom.

'Never once did his navigational directions land our frigate in the middle of St. Peter's behind the high altar, or in Ohio, United States,' he informed them. 'I have since wished for second lieutenants as accurate as Dale Everett.'

They laughed and the conversation moved in other directions. Mr Everett apologised for keeping him talking until his food turned chilly, but Ross assured them he did not mind. He looked around at the kindness that surrounded him and felt boulders sliding from those broad shoulders he had boasted of.

Mary gave him a broad smile as she helped Nathan with the correct fork. It pleased him to see her hand on the back of his son's chair as she gave him her gentle attention. She had a sure touch with children and he wondered how she acquired it, considering that she was a spinster, as she had announced earlier. Briefly, he wondered how Inez would have mothered their son, then had his own epiphany: it was time to tuck Inez into a corner of his heart, instead of letting her wander through it. He wasn't certain who or what should fill up other parts of his heart not inhabited by his son, his ship and crew, but he did like his cousin's sure touch. And maybe some day, when he was certain the war was really over, he would find a wife like Mary.

Ross couldn't help an inward smile, wondering if she would laugh or look askance at him if he ever told her about his tall, blonde, willowy woman with the French-Caribbean accent. He decided she would laugh and wish him good luck.

He shouldn't have feared that conversation might dwindle and leave them with awkward silences. In her matter-of-fact way, Mary kept the table chat moving along. She asked them about Dale's interests when he was home and their favourite memories. Centring the conversation on Dale startled him at first, until it dawned on him that the Everetts were starving to talk about their son. The vicar said as much, as they rose from the dinner table.

'Even after all these years, people still tiptoe so carefully around us, my dear,' he confided to Mary. 'They fear it would make us sad to speak his name.' He shook his head. 'To say nothing makes us feel like he never existed and we do not want that.'

'How do you know to do this?' Ross whispered to Mary, when the Everetts went to answer the doorbell and usher in what sounded like a legion of children.

Mary blushed, which he found so beguiling, he who laboured among hard men who never blushed. 'Didn't you notice how Mrs Everett's eyes brightened when you told her about her boy's navigational skills?' She stopped and her blush deepened, which made him smile at her, making her confusion worse. 'Cousin Ross, everyone likes to be thought well of. We all want to be special to someone.'

'Do you?' he asked, teasing her.

'I would like to be,' she said, her voice so soft he wasn't certain he had heard her, not above the tumult from the hallway now.

The parish children made conversation difficult, as the vicar moved his younger parishioners into the sitting room. With unholy glee, Mary smiled inside to see their awe of Captain Rennie and his own reddening cheeks. Their unbridled interest made her suspect that post captains in the Royal Navy didn't make their way so far inshore too often.

She took a moment to admire her cousin, too. He was tall and sturdy, filling his uniform nicely, but there was a starved look about his face, where weather lines had taken a lengthy toll. She couldn't explain it, but he had the appearance of a man who would always be hungry, even if he sat at a banquet table every night. In an era of full-fleshed men, his face was lean, carved that way by relentless warfare. She didn't find it unpleasant, but she wondered what would make such a man as her cousin happy.

True, she had her own sorrows and misgivings about the somewhat stingy hand life had dealt her. Her parents were dead, her aunt and uncle kind but indifferent once her wants were provided. And Dina? She was spoiled and wilful and the author of Mary's current circumstances, sent on a silly expedition for fruitcake. For that expedition, Mary suddenly decided she could forgive Dina her slights, condescension and supreme silliness. Mary's own epiphany told her she was having fun for the first time in years.

In the way of vicars Mary remembered from her own father, Mr Everett soon had his Christmas singers sorted out and ready for the challenge ahead. With a flourish, he introduced Nathan to the horde, which quickly absorbed him into the pack. Coats and mufflers came on and the open door beckoned again. The vicar looked at the Rennies.

'You may come with us if you choose,' he offered. 'We aren't very good and we don't stay out too long.'

'I'll join you,' the captain said. 'I can't even remember the last Christmas I spent on shore, and I certainly have not heard carolling in years. Mary?'

'Several ladies will be helping me with refreshments, so I can spare you,' Mrs Everett said.

Mary looked from the captain, who appeared neutral about the matter, to her kind hostess. 'I believe I can use a walk after all the lemon-curd pudding I consumed at the Begging Hound, even before dinner here. Excuse me, please, Mrs Everett?'

'Certainly, my dear.'

The night air was brisk and the stars huge. When the captain offered his arm again, she accepted, but shyly. Somehow, it was different in the dark, with Nathan far ahead and already singing with children his own age at the first house in the village. There were other parents accompanying their broods, but the captain seemed content to stay with her alone.

His tread was regular and unremarkable, testifying to her of his utter comfort in his own skin, even with a wooden leg. After only a few stops at houses with him, she couldn't help but feel a certain pride at such a distinguished escort. She also decided that the Royal Navy had it all over the other services, when it came to uniforms. The army and the Royal Marines could peacock all about, but there was something understated and elegant about a man in navy blue. All he lacked was a sword.

'You don't wear your cutlass off the ship?' she asked.

'I barely wear my hanger *on* the ship,' he replied. 'Only when I need to use it for boarding an enemy vessel.'

'Hmmm.' Somehow, it hadn't occurred to her that it was for more than ceremonial dash.

He nudged her shoulder and leaned down. 'Didn't think I'd have to repel any boarders in Scotland, or in God-help-us England.'

She laughed out loud. 'I'm a looby.'

'No, you're my cousin,' he replied, which warmed her as much as if he had said something that made sense.

They stayed with the rowdy pack for a few houses, happy to dawdle. From the captain's obvious enjoyment of that simple act, Mary suspected that dawdling wasn't on his daily roster. He had a pleasant enough singing voice, remarkable for the loudness of it. When the others looked around, surprised, at his strengthier than usual conclusion to 'O Come, O Come, Emanuel', Ross merely gazed back in all innocence. 'I put it to you, ladies and gentlemen: how would *you* get a topman's attention to reef t'gallants in a gale?'

The parents chuckled, and the vicar threw back his head and laughed. From the look of surprise on the faces of his parishioners, Mary didn't think they heard such laughter from him often. It touched her heart.

Gradually, the captain slowed down, and she slowed her steps accordingly. Kind man that he was, he decided to give her the credit for the vicar's good humour. 'Mary, I would have just eaten the lemon-curd pudding and never visited, but for your insistence.'

'I don't believe that for a minute,' she chided gently, even though she couldn't help feeling flattered.

He walked slower, and she began to notice a pronounced limp. She stopped walking and turned around. 'Back to the vicarage, sir.'

'Getting tired?' he teased but he had no objections. 'I do start to wear out,' he admitted. 'One-and-a-half legs are only part of the problem. The other problem is that while I do considerable standing on deck, I seldom walk for miles. I leave that to Wellington's army.'

The vicarage was soon in sight, but her cousin held back. He inclined his head towards the church across the yard and she let him steer the course. A branch of candles lit the interior just enough, aided by a full moon. Mary sniffed the greenery decorating the nave. The hanging of the greens was nearly two weeks ago. She thought about the last fruitcake and weighed it against the importance of this new journey with her Cousin Ross. Maybe Mr Tavish Maxfield of Apollo Street, York, hadn't yet sliced up the Christmas cake.

'You're thinking about that damned fruitcake,' Captain Rennie told her when they sat down in the last pew.

Since he hadn't tried to hide his sigh of relief to be off his feet, Mary knew they hadn't turned back a moment too soon. Funny that he could read her mind about the cake.

'I have to admit that my resolve to see the business done is weakening,' she admitted in turn. 'If I had a fiancé, I certainly would never throw away a gift he had sent, no matter how paltry.'

'I have the feeling that this Dina I do not know doesn't care much for her future husband, whom I also do not know,' he said, after pulling down the kneeling bench and resting his wooden leg on it.

'I suppose she wants a more exciting man. Mr Page will probably just nod over his newspaper after dinner, go to sleep and have to be wakened to get to bed.'

'Oh, ouch! That is your opinion of new husbands?'

Mary refused to be embarrassed. 'No, silly. That is my opinion of Mr Page.'

'What would *you* like in a husband?'

A mere twenty-four hours ago, such a question would have amazed her with its impertinence. As she sat there considering his question, she discovered that she had already taken the measure of this man. Captain Ross Rennie was as transparent as water, a capable man with no inclination to dither or waste his time or anyone else's. He had spent a lifetime in duty to his country so intense and harsh that it did not let go, even in a snowy village in Yorkshire. She knew it was not a casual question because he was not a casual man.

'I've never really thought about it,' she told him honestly.

He didn't believe her. 'Come, come, Miss Rennie,' he chided in turn. 'You're a fine-appearing Scottish lass!'

'Thank you kindly, Cousin,' she said with a smile. 'I also live with my aunt and uncle, who have no particular obligation to see me wed. They never said as much, but this is surely so. They are kind enough, to be sure, but they're not the sort of people who exert themselves.' She thought about the matter. 'And perhaps I have not exerted myself overmuch either.'

She didn't say that in any attempt for pity, and he seemed to know it. With a smile, he touched her hand, a light touch.

'Sometimes I think we of the Royal Navy take all the hard knocks.'

'I would say you do,' she said quietly.

He shook his head. 'We do it with big guns and blood and battle and noise. Your hard knocks come quietly, but I will wager they are no less painful.' His expression was self-deprecating. 'Well, certainly they are. I should remember your Lieutenant MacDowell and apologise again for my rudeness.'

She couldn't help her sigh. Watching Nathan, watching the parents accompanying their children, walking along slowly, shoulders bumping, smiling those private smiles of husbands and wives, had taken its own toll that evening. Maybe the whole, foolish trip had done that, too. When she lived so quietly in Wapping Street in Edinburgh, she lived cushioned off from others of her age. Somehow, Dina, in her great self-absorption, didn't count.

Seeing women in the mail coach, generally paired with husbands, or in the public houses and inns, Mary began to sense the world passing her by. And so there were tears in her eyes; she suddenly couldn't help it.

Chapter Ten

Captain Rennie put his arm around her shoulders and drew her close to him. His boat cloak enveloped them both, which she found comforting, not because she was cold, but because it felt like protection she hadn't known since her parents died. Her aunt and uncle were busy leading their own lives and she understood that. Here was this man she could barely call a relative, going out of his way to care a little. It was unexpected and altogether gratifying.

She couldn't help but lean into that pleasant hollow between a man's shoulder and chest that she remembered on one occasion from her late lamented lieutenant, before he'd pleaded poverty—her poverty—and cried off. She didn't want Captain Rennie's pity, though, and she sat upright to tell him that.

Before she got a word out of her mouth, he gently pushed her head back against his shoulder and tightened his grip on her.

'Suffice it to say we have both missed out on many things, thanks to Boney,' he told her. 'I will probably hate the man until I die, this employer of mine.'

'You probably shouldn't call him that. Someone might take it the wrong way.'

'And declare me a spy?' He laughed at that and the pleasant sound carried some distance in the empty church. 'Here we are at peace, Cousin—although I would not wager even a groat on that. I have a month of unbridled leisure...'

'Which you are squandering by helping me search for a fruitcake,' Mary couldn't help but remind him. 'I own to some guilt in the matter.'

'Please don't excoriate yourself overmuch,' he told her. He loosened his grip, but he did not release her. 'Between you and me, I'm dreading the visit to my sister just a little.'

'Why, sir?' Mary asked, surprised.

'Alice plans to show me a gentleman's estate for sale not far from Dumfries. She also claims I can see the ocean from the upper floor, but it will take more than a postage-stamp view to satisfy me.'

He paused, and when he spoke again Mary heard something resembling embarrassment in his voice. 'You'll think me a great fool, but I feel uneasy so far from the ocean. Don't laugh now.'

'I would never!' she declared.

'Thank you,' he said quite formally. 'I have spent most of the past twenty-four years at sea. My ship, however noisome it gets after a long voyage, is my home. The ocean is my estate.' He sighed. 'The longer I can avoid Alice's insistence that I move inshore, now that peace has broken out, the happier it makes me.'

'But Nathan? I can tell you do not wish to be away from him,' she said, thinking of the many looks he gave his son during their post-chaise journey.

'That is my dilemma. I would rather be with him always, but I still miss the sea.' He shifted, and she could tell the subject made him uncomfortable.

Then it was her turn to be uncomfortable, as he turned the conversation back to her. 'Come, Cousin, you have not answered my question. What is it you are looking for in a husband, should one materialise?'

'I told you I hadn't considered the matter,' she

said again. She was certain she could have sat up, if he hadn't been so pleasant to lean against.

He looked around elaborately, and she could not help but chuckle. 'No one needs us right now, the hour is not late and the choir is still tormenting some household or other. Think about it.'

'There's only one thing,' she said, after considerable thought. 'I just want a husband who will love me until I die.'

Captain Rennie made a sound as though someone had punched the air out of him. He took his arm out from around her and stood up. As Mary watched in surprise, he took precisely twelve steps forwards and then twelve steps back. As she watched, it dawned on her that he was probably pacing off the space on his quarterdeck.

'I didn't mean to upset you,' she said as he started his second circuit. 'I rather feel I have upset you enough today.'

When he didn't say anything, she quietly left the church and returned to the vicarage, determined to leave by herself in the morning. *All he wanted was a bowl of lemon-curd pudding and I forced him to visit grieving parents*, she thought in remorse. *I should be ashamed of myself.*

Once inside, she wanted to go upstairs, but she

had no idea which room was hers for the night. As she stood in the front entrance, dissatisfied with herself, Mrs Everett joined her. She took one look at Mary's face and frowned.

'My dear, whatever is wrong?'

Miserable, Mary shook her head. She wanted to cry, but her hostess didn't need that kind of distress.

Apparently, Mrs Everett was made from a sterner mould. She took Mary's hand, led her to the stairs and sat her down. 'I can spare a moment from the kitchen. I saw you and the captain go into the church and here you are. What is troubling you? And him?'

I'm not going to cry, Mary told herself, and she didn't. Sitting there on the stairs, she told Mrs Everett the whole silly business with the fruitcake, and her adventure, and how she met the captain and his son. 'He's planning to take me all the way to York, so I needn't travel alone in this foreign country,' she said, choosing to overlook Mrs Everett's smile at that, because she already felt foolish enough. 'I bullied him into coming to see you. I don't think he was going to. I mean, your son's death couldn't possibly be harder on him than you. Could it?'

She couldn't help her tears then. Mrs Everett dabbed at them with her apron, her expression so kind, suggesting to Mary that this vicar's wife was much the same as her own mother had been—willing to bear other's burdens.

Mary took out her handkerchief and blew her nose with some vehemence. 'I'm making a botch of this.'

'No, my dear, you are not,' Mrs Everett said firmly. 'That little book that Captain Rennie has. Did you see a lot of names in it?'

Mary swallowed, because her mouth was so suddenly dry. 'Many hundreds.'

'If I were a wagering woman, I would wager that Captain Rennie feels the pain of each death, not just one, such as we feel for our son.' She caressed Mary's cheek with her hand. 'My dear Miss Rennie, the vicar and I have four other children, three of them with families of their own. Do we miss Dale? Certainly we do and always will.'

'Please forgive me, I…'

Mrs Everett stopped Mary with a kiss to her forehead. 'There now! I think the cost to him is higher than you or I will ever know, but today, Captain Rennie gave us an indelible portrait of our son. Now I will always see him fifteen years old, sitting barefoot on a deck on the Pacific Ocean, learning how to navigate. Dale enjoyed what he was doing.' She dabbed her eyes. 'I can live with that, Mary. It was the kindest of Christmas gifts and I believe I owe it to you.' She kissed Mary again. 'Don't argue with me! Acknowledge your own kindness.'

She patted Mary's knee and stood up, holding out her hand. 'Up you get, missy! Some of the ladies and I are finishing the refreshments for the returning choir. Help us, please. We'll trust the captain to come indoors when he feels ready.'

Twelve paces up and twelve back. Ross was hardly aware when Mary left. Two more twelves, twenty-four and thirty-six. He stopped, embarrassed that he had startled Mary. He had asked a question and she had answered it so innocently. Inez had told him the same thing. On the morning of his last day in port, his Portuguese wife had held him close, pressed his hand to her abdomen, where their baby kicked, and told him, 'I will love you until I die.'

And she had. The damned shame was that she had died only four months later in an earthquake. When he returned to port, knowing that their baby would be perhaps a week or two old, he had stared in disbelief at the ruins of her father's house.

A few servants had survived the vicious contortions of the earth that had buried and killed outright Inez's parents and slowly suffocated his wife, trapped under the rubble with their son. They had met his frigate to give him the terrible news, leading him by the hand to a nearby cloister, partially damaged, too, where the Sisters of the Blessed Mary tended his son. It was enough of a shock to see his little one with a gash on his cheek that had nearly healed.

If only Inez's maidservant had stopped there. But no, she had told Ross how they had found Inez three days after *el temblor*, locating her by the faint cries of their infant, near death from starvation. Before she died, his lovely wife, the woman so proper and with never a hair out of place, had written with her own blood on the piece of roof tile that had gouged her stomach, *I will love you for ever.*

He could have done without that information. Really, he could have.

And now he had driven off his sweet cousin, who was only trying to do the right thing. Tired, his stump paining him, he sat down again at the back of the church, breathing in the fragrance of pine boughs, letting the scent so alien to a seafarer work its Christmas magic. He could apologise to Mary and take her to York the next day. Mr Maxfield would probably relinquish the fruitcake happily enough and they could both be on separate mail coaches, Mary to Edinburgh and he and Nathan to Dumfries. It didn't seem right to him, but this little jaunt *was* eating into his shore leave, after all.

He decided he owed his cousin a prompt apology, but when he left the church, here came the carollers, chilled and hungry, but triumphant as one of the leaders rattled the collection box. Feeling guiltier than usual for his own raft of sins, Ross dug into his purse and extracted several coins, the kind large enough to make the boy's eyes widen. He handed them over with what he knew was a hypocritical flourish and only laughed when the vicar assured him that they really weren't proficient carollers.

His cheeks ruddy with cold, Nathan took his hand next. 'Da, I had such fun! We never carol in Plymouth!'

'Perhaps you should,' Ross declared, getting into his son's Christmas mood. 'Heaven knows a seafaring town could use a Christian message.'

That only earned him a puzzled stare and re-minded him that Mrs Pritchert, Nathan's keeper, was a careful woman. He shook his head at his own folly. Nathan ran ahead to join his new friends, and Ross found himself in tow by the vicar.

'I vow, Captain, this has been a fine day all around.'

Ross kept up his own pretence at good humour because Mr Everett was so obviously sincere. Mary was right; the Everetts had been starved for what he, and he alone, could tell him about their son at sea.

'I agree, Mr Everett,' he said, walking with the vicar. It touched him that the man slowed down a bit, to accommodate his obvious limp. He *had* been on his peg too long.

Once inside, he had no chance to speak to Mary. The ladies hurried around, pouring hot chocolate for the young singers. There were several varieties of biscuit circulating, as well as fruitcake. He couldn't help a glance at Mary when he saw the fruitcake and was rewarded with a wry look from her that made him think she had not entirely cast him off for his rudeness in the chapel, if that's what it was.

Even after everyone left with their children, there

was still no opportunity for privacy. Mary had already disappeared, and Mrs Everett took him upstairs with Nathan, who was yawning and trying not to show it.

'I'm putting your son in Dale's room and you next door. Mary is across the hall. Come in here.'

His reluctance to enter the room where his late middie had slept was quickly overcome. He looked around in delight at the maps and charts on the walls, then a row of what appeared to be well-thumbed books about the sea. He couldn't help smiling.

'My midshipman seemed to have the ocean on his mind for many years before I acquired him.'

'He did! I can't tell you how many times he and I read *Robinson Crusoe* to each other.'

'Is it not a little unusual, madam, considering how far we are from the ocean here?'

'We took our children to Scarborough one year and that fixed the ocean in his mind for ever.' She touched his arm. 'You probably usually do the honours, but let me tuck your son in bed tonight.' Her face took on a wistful expression. 'It will bring back lovely memories.'

'Aye, then.'

'I think you'll find the vicar in the bookroom.'

He took her hint, even if he did want to work up his courage, knock on Mary's door and apologise to her. The vicar was waiting for him with two more mugs of the wonderful wassail. They sat in comfort before a declining fire. Between the wassail, and the vicar's persuasive air, Ross found himself refighting any number of engagements, from fleet action at Trafalgar, to the little ship-to-ship affairs that only made dry and dusty news in the *Naval Chronicle*.

Ross knew better than to drink any more of the wassail, not if he didn't want to endure Cousin Mary's scrutiny in the morning. He held up his hand and declared enough. 'I need a clear head to get to York tomorrow.'

'Yes, indeed, Captain,' Mr Everett said with considerable good cheer. 'She distinctly said something about brown bread and quince jelly in Ovenshine. York must wait.'

Ross laughed. 'Quince jelly in Ovenshine. My God, but that sounds like a spy's password!'

'It *is* a small village, but no spies there,' the vicar joked.

Arm in arm, they helped each other towards the stairs. Mrs Everett met them at the top of the stairs, lending her husband a hand when he appeared to waver on the top step.

'Hush now, you two!' she whispered. 'Everyone else is abed. Captain, Nathan is in here as you probably don't even remember.' She smiled into her hand, her eyes lively. 'Mary is across the hall and you are next door to Nathan. Do you have that?'

He did, ready to assure his kind hostess that he was sober...well, nearly sober. From habit, he planted his legs a little wider for balance. 'Aye, madam. Your husband makes a wicked brew, but I am more or less immune to wassail.'

The three of them laughed, arms around each other, maybe for balance, maybe because it just felt good. Ross was struck by the realisation that the only person who touched him was Nathan. No, not true. Mary had given him a push in the back in Carlisle, unbidden, but aware of his slight stagger. Good woman, his cousin.

Mrs Everett opened the door to his room, but he shook his head and looked in on Nathan first, pleased to see him sleeping so soundly in the unused room of one of the vicar's sons. He closed the door, a smile on his face, but an odd lump in his throat. Blame the wassail.

He said goodnight to his kind hosts, who went down the hall. He looked around his room, surprised to see his own luggage ready for him and the bedcovers turned down. The Everetts must have sent their man to the Begging Hound for the Rennie trappings when they were carolling.

Ross stretched and took off his uniform coat, glad to get out of it. Maybe when he felt more sure of peace and he was a post captain cast ashore living on half-pay, he could indulge in a civilian wardrobe. It could wait, because he wasn't at all convinced that his employer would be content to be emperor of Elba, after ruling the world. Instead of following his appetite from village to village, perhaps he should return to London and impress upon his superiors that Napoleon wasn't done yet. Ross doubted they wanted to hear his glad tidings, but he was nearly convinced.

With a sigh, he unbuttoned his trousers, balancing himself precariously and wishing for his servant, a hard-bitten old seaman who decided to stay on *Abukir* during drydock because he had no love of land. Hardly mattered; he could do this. The wassail didn't hold a candle to rum.

He shifted his trousers down to his hips, backed up to the bed to sit down and missed. With a thump, he landed on the floor, bruising his dignity more than his ass. Blame it on a strange room, late at night. He laughed.

The door opened. His cousin peered inside, her eyes wide. As he watched, wondering what she would do, his little prayer was answered, the little prayer he didn't even have a name for.

'Cousin, you could use some help.'

Chapter Eleven

'I believe you're right, Mary. Give me a hand up.'

Mary pulled her robe tighter. All was quiet at the Everetts' end of the hall, so she stepped inside and closed the door.

There sat the captain on the floor. The light from the fireplace lit him quite well. He sat there, his trousers around his knees now, his shirt out. He squinted, as though wondering who she was, so she came closer. He held out his hand to her.

She did her best, but he was a big man. She wrapped her arms around his waist and tugged at him until he got his good leg under him. They both sank on to his bed, and he started to laugh. It *was* funny; she joined in.

'Oh, Mary, I'm *not* three sheets to the wind. Just a bit cheerful.'

'Aye, Cousin. I'll believe you, even though thousands wouldn't.'

It must have struck him as witty beyond words, because he started to laugh again.

'Hush!' she whispered and put her hand over his mouth. To her amazement, he kissed her palm. To her further amazement, she liked it. She took her hand away, but stayed next to him.

'Now what?' she asked.

'Are you a game goer?'

'Of course I am,' she assured him a trifle tartly. 'Do you know anyone else who would travel miles and miles to track down fruitcake?'

In for a penny, in for a pound, Mary thought. She stood up and straightened his legs. It was short work to remove his trousers. Thank goodness he wore smallclothes underneath. She draped his trousers over a chair after smoothing out the wrinkles.

'Hmm.' Mary looked at the brown-leather straps that bound his peg-leg to his waist. They were attached to an iron brace clamped tight to the top of the wooden peg. Simple enough. She glanced at the captain and his eyes were closed. After a moment's hesitation, she pulled up his long shirt tail and unbuckled the strap at his waist.

He wasn't asleep. When he felt the motion he raised his hips so she could manoeuvre the strap from around his waist. It was an easy matter to pull out the strap and then gently tug away the device.

'Ahh.'

It was involuntary and made her a little sad, wondering how hard it must be every day to rig out in this uncomfortable leg and balance on a heaving deck. Mary wasn't certain she would love the ocean enough to do that. Maybe it was duty that drove him.

The stump of his leg was wrapped in sturdy cloth. Curious, she felt the end, which seemed to be padded with cotton wadding.

'Do you want me to remove this, too?' she asked.

'If you wouldn't mind too greatly. I've been on it so long today and walking more than usual.'

He spoke quite calmly, not sounding in the least tiddly or luffy or shot in the neck, or any of those slangy terms she heard from some of the servants belowstairs at Wapping Street. *I believe you are just tired down to your toenails*, she thought. Tears came to her eyes as she unwrapped his stump. She feared what she would see, but did as he asked. When she removed the cloth, she looked down at a fine knee and part of a fine leg that ended abruptly with a fold of skin. Even in the low light, she could see a tidy scar with evidence of where the stitches had gone in and come out. The end of the stump looked a little red. Still curious, she touched it lightly and felt the heat.

'You have gentle hands, Mary. Better than my servant. I can take care of myself now.'

She nodded and turned to go, but he took her hand. 'Don't leave. I need to apologise to you. Wait a minute more.'

Unsure of herself, she sat down on the chair by the bed. He sat up with another sigh and removed his shirt, then tugged up the bedcovers. 'Better,' he murmured. 'I'm not drunk.'

She smiled at that. 'I believe you, actually. I know you're tired, though.'

'Aye, Mary, aye,' he said, and it went to her heart. 'Come a bit closer.'

She stood up and pushed the chair closer to his bed. He raised up on one elbow. 'May I tell you why I was so rude in the chapel?'

Mary nodded, because she knew he would tell her anyway, and she was curious now that she could tell he wasn't angry with her.

He spoke softly, but she heard all the emotion as he told her about returning to Oporto and finding the ruins of his wife's parental home. She couldn't help her own sigh as he described seeing his baby for the first time. She had wondered a little about the small scar on Nathan's cheek. And she couldn't help her tears as he told her what Inez had written with a bloody finger on the roof tile that had pierced her abdomen.

He took her hand. 'When you said what you did, I suppose I wasn't quite prepared for that. Is that *all* women want from the man they love?'

'I'm no authority, but I think it must be,' Mary said as she gently pulled back her hand. 'I hope men want the same thing from the women they love.'

'I believe they do.' He settled into bed in that way of someone getting ready to sleep. 'It's been a difficult day and I have had many difficult days. Perhaps too many.' He closed his eyes.

'Tell me, Cousin, before you sleep: how did you get Nathan home to England?'

He opened his eyes, pleased that she was interested, from the look on his face. 'The nuns gave me a goat, which I shipped aboard.'

'No one questioned a goat?'

'Not if you're the captain, m'dear,' he said with a reminiscent chuckle. 'Or any officer or master, I suppose. You should see the average frigate before she puts to sea—goats, cows, some chickens.

Of course, we were just going from Portugal to England this time.'

'Did they question a baby?'

He shook his head. 'Again, not if you're the captain and therefore Lord God Almighty Himself on the quarterdeck. He slept, well, like a baby, in my swinging cot. When Nathan fussed, I strapped him to my chest, put my uniform jacket over us both and took our turn on deck.'

'You were bound to each other.'

'Aye, lass, in so many ways. I've sat in many a wardroom in all seven seas, discussing home and family with my peers. One common complaint— well, no, one regret—is that men and officers seldom get to really know the children they beget on land. Instead, we go to sea and don't meet until years pass, sometimes. It is the price of Admiralty.'

'You have an easy camaraderie with Nathan.'

'We have to work at it, but I did have a head start, if I can count Oporto to Plymouth. We correspond regularly, even though it might be months between the writing and the receiving.' He touched her arm. 'That's one reason I didn't object when Nathan wanted to take the Royal Mail. Sitting squished together for a long trip is a fine way to become reacquainted. It's difficult life, Mary, but it is my life. I know no other.'

Mary nodded. She hesitated only a moment, then put her hand on his chest. 'You did a good thing today, as hard as it was, Cousin, but maybe that's enough for now.' She took a deep breath. 'Tomorrow, I insist that you to take me to the nearest town with a mail-coach stop. I'll go on to York and you can take Nathan to Dumfries and your own Christmas. It's better that way. All I am doing is eating up your precious shore leave.'

He nodded, which pleased her and displeased her at the same time. She sat back and made herself calm. She had been disappointed before and she knew it would pass. Probably the captain knew that, too.

She rose and left his room quietly. Before she went into her own room, she looked in on Nathan, suddenly feeling as though her heart was going to break to leave him. She reminded herself that it really wasn't possible, except perhaps in overwrought novels, to become so fond of people in such a short time. Maybe it was the season. When she returned to Edinburgh, she would admonish Mrs Morison never to volunteer her for adventures again.

With her own sigh, she removed her robe and crawled into bed. As her eyes closed, she wondered how she could thank the Everetts for all they had done for Captain Rennie.

She was almost asleep when her door opened. No one had knocked. She sat up, suddenly hoping with all her heart and soul that it was Captain Rennie. To her infinite delight, it was.

He leaned on a cane and he was clumsy, taking a little hopping step. Without even a by-your-leave, he sank down on her bed. She moved her legs to accommodate him.

'I keep a cane for late-night trips to the place of ease in my cabin,' he told her, conversational about something her mother would have blushed and fanned herself to hear. 'I used to use a bottle, but that seemed a trifle gauche, after I started feeling better. D'ye mind?'

He lay down next to her and she discovered that she did not mind in the least. 'It's this way, Mary: I was lying across the hall, thinking how tired I am of sleeping by myself.'

'I told you you were tired,' she said, amazed at her complacency with such a liberty.

'I wouldn't have done this brazen thing, but I heard you look in on Nathan. Raise up your head.'

She did. He had a way of command without commanding that must have made him a good captain to sail and die for, she decided. His arm went under her neck and she settled in again, more easily finding that pleasant hollow where she had rested before, in the chapel.

'Thank you,' he said so simply. 'I like the ladies, but Napoleon has made any congress with them nearly impossible. Sometimes just the homely pleasure of lying with someone like this is pure heaven. Damned cheeky of me, I know. I don't expect you to understand me, but it's true.'

'I think I like it, too,' she whispered to him. Like most people, he had his own fragrance, in his case, a bit of brine. But that might just have been her imagination. Mama had told her once, a bit censoriously, that she was prone to flights of fancy. Whatever it was, she felt her eyes closing. It had been a difficult day for her, as well, rendered almost heavenly by this final bit of sweetness before she slept. She knew in her heart that he would never interfere with her.

'I promise I won't stay long. Imagine what the Everetts would think.'

Strange. She hadn't thought of the vicar and his wife since she went to his room to help him.

Aunt Martha would have been shocked, but Aunt Martha was across the border.

She heard the hesitation in his voice when he spoke; it may even have been embarrassment. 'The hardest time is before I sleep. I swing back and forth in my cot and review every battle, every broadside, every bad decision—'

'Oh, please tell me that you do not,' Mary interrupted. She put her arm under his head, which meant he had to turn closer to her.

'I do. I think of men who might have lived, had circumstances been different. I stew and I fret until I wear myself out. What do you think of?'

She wasn't going to tell him, because it was intimate and trivial at the same time, considering his own fraught life of constant war. He gave her head a little shake, as she had seen him do to Nathan.

'Come on, Mary.'

'I have a few disappointed hopes and I revisit them, if it's been a difficult day, which in my case means Dina has whined about something, or my aunt has been heaving great gusty sighs which suggest I am somehow a drain on the family.'

He gave a small groan. 'Shame on them.'

'As I said, these would be difficult days. Generally I count a few blessings and close my eyes.'

It was true. There were many women in her circumstances who could only wish for the comfort she lived in.

He was silent a long while, but she knew he was wide awake. She wondered idly if he ever snored. 'I came in here tonight because today has been a hard one and I just don't want to revisit it. I discovered when I fell in love with Inez that just lying beside a fine woman made those dreams go away. You're a fine woman, Cousin, and I don't want bad dreams tonight.' He ruffled her hair again and laughed. 'I'll be away in an hour or so. I'll sleep better and I'll owe it to you. Do excuse such impertinence.'

'Well, then, close your eyes,' Mary said.

'Aye, aye, sir,' he teased, then laughed. 'I have to tell you something: I have—or had—another list.'

'I'm afraid to ask!'

'Years ago—I think I was a second luff—we all compiled lists of what we wanted in a wife some day.'

Mary laughed out loud. 'A whole wardroom full of rascals did this?'

'Aye. My blushes, Mary, we each had our own list!'

She made a face at him, her eyes lively.

'My paragon was a tall, willowy lady with blonde ringlets. Oh, and a French-Caribbean accent, too. A low laugh, quite a ladylike one.' He jostled her shoulder. 'That rules you out on all counts, Cousin.'

She put her hand to her mouth to hide a distinctly unladylike guffaw. 'Heavens, Ross! I think Nathan barely understands me. He'll fare better with a French-Caribbean accent.'

'I lost the list in some ocean or other. When the war ends, I'll start looking for such a paragon.'

She'll be a most fortunate lady, Mary thought, amused. *I wonder if all men are this silly.*

'One thing more, Cuz. I took a look at my *other* list before I hobbled in here. We're only a reasonable day's journey from Ovenshine and brown bread and quince jelly at the Weeping Willow there. Are you game?'

'Only if that list maker is still alive,' she said, drowsy now and resigned to more travel with her captain. Funny how the matter didn't bother her.

'He is. I heard from him only a year ago. His letter was a bit garbled—he speaks in hyperboles and parabolas—but I think he even bought the Weeping Willow after he left the Navy.' He grunted.

'Probably bought it with all the monies he siphoned off from the Board of Revictualling.'

'Brown bread and quince jelly sounds so ordinary,' she said. She pulled her arm out from under his head, but turned her face into his shoulder.

He took a deep breath then, and Mary wondered if maybe she should not be so comfortable. Never mind; her eyes were closing and she did something no mother would ever have sanctioned for her daughter—she trusted a Navy man.

Chapter Twelve

Captain Rennie was true to his word and gone in an hour. He tried to be quiet, but his cane fell over. With an oath so salty that Mary gasped out loud, he went to his hands and knees, searching for the stick in the gloom of her bedroom.

'You're supposed to be asleep and not listening to a good round oath, Miss Rennie,' he whispered, still managing to inject a measure of command.

'How can I help it when you are so emphatic?' she scolded, then put the sheet to her mouth so she could laugh.

When he found his cane, he leaned on it, a hand on one hip, and glared at her until he started to smile. She couldn't help but notice how nice he looked with a bit of moonlight shining through the fabric, even with just a leg and three-quarters. If this was what Mrs Morison meant by an adventure, Mary was finding it more and more agreeable. When Ross left her room, she only heard one more strangled oath when he startled the cat, who had come upstairs to investigate. Thank goodness the Everetts appeared to be prodigiously sound sleepers.

As for herself, it was easy to return to sleep. Mary moved into the warm spot her cousin had created, grateful for it, as well as the pleasant tang of whatever was the man's personal fragrance. *If such a thing never happens to me again*, she told herself just before she slept, *I have enjoyed this*.

To Mary's relief, the Everetts made no comment about any strange sounds during the night. If anything, there was a wistful look in Mrs Everett's eyes, as though she did not want them to leave.

Captain Rennie said all that was proper, thanking the Everetts again for their many kindnesses. He excused himself from the breakfast table and, with Nathan, walked back to the Begging Hound to alert the postilion and his son. No snow had fallen during the night and it looked like a fair day for travel. Mrs Everett watched them from the breakfast-parlour window as she sipped her tea.

'I think it must be hard for them to be apart,' she

commented to Mary. The vicar had already wandered down the hall to the book room.

Mary joined her at the window, her eyes on father and son. They hadn't even left Skowcroft yet and she was already wishing York were days away. While the women stood together, shoulders touching in a way that charmed Mary, she told her hostess about the captain's desperately sad voyage to Plymouth from Oporto, his infant son strapped to his body.

'We live sheltered, quiet lives, because of men like your cousin,' was Mrs Everett's observation. She straightened her shoulders. 'And men like my son.'

The post chaise was at the circle drive too soon to please Mary. With a tip of his cap to her, the postilion's son took their luggage to the vehicle and then stood by the open door, expectant.

Captain Rennie and Nathan came indoors for farewells, taking both Everetts by their hands. 'Your kindness to us was unparalleled,' he said simply.

'Come back and see us again,' the vicar told him.

'We shall see,' the captain said, his words offering much sympathy but no assurance. He put on his hat again and bowed to them both. Nathan let Mrs Everett embrace him and smiled when she kissed the top of his head. They returned to the chaise.

'I think the captain won't be back,' Mary said when it was her turn for a hug from her hostess.

Mrs Everett held her off a moment, the gratitude in her eyes unmistakable. 'I think he will not, either.' She touched her forehead to Mary's. 'Thank you for insisting he visit us. Will *you* return?'

'Quite possibly,' Mary told her and the vicar. She laughed. 'Especially now that I am not such a ninny about England.'

She left them with smiles all around and walked towards the carriage. Mrs Everett followed her a step and touched her arm. Mary turned around.

'Perhaps you can exert a positive influence on your cousin so he will not swear at the cat in the middle of the night.'

Mary laughed in surprise, then blushed at the implication. 'What must you think of me?' she murmured.

'I think you two might be good for each other,' Mrs Everett said. 'I trust he is not too close of a cousinly connection?'

'Not at all. But we are only going to York and

then our separate ways.' *And he has this other list,* Mary wanted to say, but changed her mind.

Her eyes merry, Mrs Everett blew her a kiss and closed the front door. There was a look on her face that suggested to Mary that the vicar's wife didn't quite believe her. *I wonder if I believe myself,* Mary thought as she accepted the captain's hand to help her into the post chaise.

She sat opposite the two of them, arranging her skirts so she did not have to look at either father or son for a moment. She finally plumped her hands in her lap and glared at the Rennie men. 'Ovenshine, and that is all! This is enough adventure for me. I'm off for York after Ovenshine and you are bound for Dumfries, where you are even more overdue.'

'I thought she might say that, Da,' Nathan told the captain, who nodded. 'Do you think she is tired of our company already?'

Mary suppressed her smile as Ross shook his head. 'How could that possibly be, when we are so charming?'

The glance father and son exchanged with each other had a loveliness to it that touched her heart. 'Oh, you two!' she said. 'I refuse to indulge you, but surely you must see the value of Christmas in Dumfries with family.'

'Are you so anxious to return to Edinburgh?' the captain asked her after Nathan turned his attention to a little ball and cup with string attached.

Was she? It was a good question. Likely Dina would be moping. Uncle Samuel usually stayed longer and longer hours at the counting house during the festivities, blaming business. Mary understood his reluctance to come home early and be forced to endure endless boring details of new clothes and parties to suffer through that Aunt Martha always plagued him with from Advent to Hogmanay. *And I am usually trying to placate everyone*, Mary reminded herself. *Every year it becomes more difficult.*

'No, I am not so anxious,' she replied honestly. 'It appears to be my lot, however.'

'Why?'

'Ladies cannot really career about the countryside from public house to public house,' she said, after giving the matter more thought. It sounded feeble to her, but she had no real answer. 'Even for brown bread and quince jelly,' she concluded, which was apparently whimsical enough to destroy her attempt at reason, because Ross laughed. Only a little, but he laughed.

'They can, if accompanied by respectable gentlemen such as you find in this post chaise,' he said with the lurking good humour that was a pleasant contrast to his anguish last night, remembering Inez and fraught days.

She smiled. 'All the same, Captain, we both have places to be, and you know it.'

He nodded, gave her a philosophical look and opened the book beside him. Mary took the hint and turned her attention to the contents of her reticule, which yielded nothing more exciting than her tatting. Resigned, she started to take it out, when Nathan's little toy hit the floor. She looked up to see him sleeping against his father, who wasn't reading.

'I'll read and you tat,' she teased. 'Neither of us seems to be succeeding.'

'He told me he didn't sleep well last night,' the captain said, putting the book beside him and swinging his son's feet on to the seat. 'He was afraid you would not continue with us. I suppose I was, too.'

Mary was silent a long moment, thinking about the comfort of his arms last night. 'I gather I cannot resist brown bread and quince jelly.' The tatting went back into her reticule. 'What happened when you arrived in Plymouth with Nathan?'

'There was some crucial bit of refitting that had to be done in drydock—I won't bore you with it—and we were told we had only until the tide's turning and not one second more. Ben Pritchert and I walked to his home. Maudie opened the door and I held out my son to her.' He swallowed and tears filled his eyes. 'She opened her arms and gathered him in.'

'Was it hard to leave him?'

'You'll never know how hard.'

What is it about women? Ross asked himself as he watched an entire raft of emotions float by on Mary Rennie's expressive face. By her own admission she was a spinster, but something deep inside assured him that Mary Rennie would have done precisely the same thing, had he given his child to her. He wanted to tell her more; she looked at him so kindly, her eyes pools of sympathy, but no pity. When she cocked her head a little to one side, it was as though she had given him permission to speak.

'That was the beginning of 1804. I lost my leg

at Trafalgar in 1805, and my sailing master died saving my life when I lost my balance on a slanting deck a year later. I wish I could tell you it was a desperate battle, but it was just a little rumble when the dons and frogs came out to play at Cadiz. Hardly worth a poor sailor's life and certainly not my sailing master's.'

He didn't mean to sound so wistful. He hoped his cousin wouldn't think he was getting soft or foolish; he had never been either.

'You did what you could, didn't you?'

Again, she charmed him. He hadn't known her more than a few days and Mary Rennie was already certain he had only a good side.

'Aye, miss. After all these years fighting Napoleon, I have lots of prize money. I bought Maudie Pritchert a lovely house farther away from the docks and provided a more generous annual stipend than the Navy Board.' There he went again, feeling wistful. 'The only thing I cannot give her is the sailing master.'

Suddenly the chaise was too small. Or maybe Mary was too close. He banged on the chaise wall and got the attention of the postilion. 'I'll be back,' he muttered to her when the chaise came to a stop.

Disappointed with himself, he walked to the

edge of the road. The wind blew and he was glad of it, because he needed the wind on his face to give him some sense of where he was. He looked, but all he could see was snow and trees. Again that uneasy feeling struck him. He realised with some sorrow that maybe he was only home at sea.

He walked towards the little copse that edged the road, moving carefully because his peg sank into the snow. A little farther and he was in the trees. He heard the chaise door slam, and he felt his face go red, hoping Mary didn't think he needed rescuing. He didn't *think* he needed rescuing, but if he had to be honest, matters had changed since he had looked at her name above his in the inn at Carlisle.

'Da, this is a good idea.'

He smiled and looked back to see his son approach, hopping through the snow, because it came up to his knees. *I wish I could hop like that*, Ross thought, amused now.

'Well, now,' he said as Nathan stood beside him. He grinned as his son unbuttoned his trousers and let fly. Not one to hang back—he *had* drunk more at breakfast than usual—Ross did the same. The companionable sound was the only noise in the copse, the homeliest sound in the world of men. As he buttoned up, Ross decided that men must be the simplest of creatures, if something that mundane could restore his good humour. Of course, he was approaching the age when even a half-full bladder meant some discomfort. *My kidneys are growing old in the service of my nation*, he thought, and laughed out loud.

'I feel better, too,' Nathan confided. 'Mary thought I might.'

Oh, shudder. Nothing is sacred on a questing journey for fruitcake and brown bread. He turned towards the road again, Nathan close by, and then hand in hand.

When he opened the chaise door, Mary was looking relentlessly in the other direction. Still, he detected spots of colour on her cheeks when she turned her head. My Lord, what an attractive woman she was.

When they were moving again, and Nathan on his back now with his head against his father's leg, Ross conquered his own embarrassment. 'You know that wasn't why I left,' he said, wanting to explain it to her, but not certain why.

'I know,' she said, complacent. 'You needed some company.'

More than you know, he thought suddenly and resumed staring at a book which could have been written in Russian, for all he knew. With all his heart he blessed the unknown Mrs Morison for sending Mary Rennie on an adventure. He hoped the brown bread in Ovenshine would not disappoint.

Chapter Thirteen

The brown bread and quince jelly at the Weeping Willow, renamed Bloody Swash by the new owner, was all Ross could have asked for. Unfortunately, the purser had not improved. Since separating from the Royal Navy after Trafalgar, Ralph Clarke's fortune was made, but his cowardice in battle remained undisputed.

And so Ross informed his wide-eyed cousin— that tender, trusting soul—as they pulled up to the inn yard in late afternoon.

'I don't want to stop here, then,' she told him. 'It's just brown bread.'

She was probably right. When he'd left home for sea years ago in the last century, his father had admonished him to listen to good advice and take it. Like most young men, he ignored wisdom. Now that he was well-seasoned, he still ignored it.

'Ovenshine and brown bread are on my list,' he reminded her, knowing how childish and stubborn he sounded.

'Very well,' Mary said, sounding a little stubborn and childish herself. Maybe he could tease her about it later.

If his former purser was surprised to see him, he never let it show. After a glance and then a stare, Clarke's smile of welcome seemed genuine enough. Of course, the man played host to Ovenshine in the Bloody Swash and business probably outranked sincerity. Ross felt his misgivings gather like sea birds around a whale's carcase. He wanted to pull Mary close to him, but he didn't.

For some reason, he introduced Mary merely as Mary Rennie, not mentioning their cousinly connection. Mary made no move to edit his introduction, beyond putting her hands on his son's shoulders in a possessive fashion that made Ross smile. When Nathan just seemed to naturally back up closer to her, Mary's hands slipped from his shoulders to his chest, folding him in her gentle embrace. If Ross had suddenly introduced Mary as his cousin and not the mother of his son, Clarke would never have believed him.

Amid the misgivings, something magic was happening; Ross couldn't have explained it. He asked for a private parlour and two chambers connecting, and then for brown bread and quince jelly.

'We can do better than that, Captain,' his former purser assured him. 'I can get you an excellent roast squab.'

In answer, Ross held out the list. 'Remember? The South Atlantic, with no wind for weeks.'

Clarke's smile went from businesslike to genuine, if only briefly. He looked at Ross and his eyes were bright. 'We were a lonely bunch of men.' He inclined his head towards the commons room. 'I can accommodate you, Captain. Do have a seat. This will be my pleasure.'

Perhaps she had been foolish to worry about Ralph Clarke, Mary decided, after raising both hands against another slice of the most amazing brown bread she had ever eaten. Whatever his moral failings, if she could believe the captain, Mr Clarke was right about the quince jelly, too. It was tart and sweet in turn, almost depending upon the whim of where it sat in the mouth.

However stilted their conversation had begun, the captain and his purser relaxed and began a tentative reminiscence. Of course, such camaraderie may have been encouraged by the arrival of hot buttered rum toddies. Mary shook her head over that and drank tea instead. Napkin around his neck, Nathan tucked away a respectable bowl of kidney pie and more brown bread.

Nathan's eyes began to droop and he leaned against Mary. She looked at the two convivial men, frowning to notice that the former purser seemed to be nursing his toddy along, while the captain drank rather more deeply. *I should talk to my cousin about that*, she thought before reminding herself that it was none of her business. They would be in York tomorrow, anyway. Maybe a throbbing head would be a more convincing tutorial than the sharp tongue of a nagging woman.

But here was Nathan, drooping and sagging, as his father drank deeper. 'Ross, I'm going to put Nathan to bed,' she said.

Ross gave her an owlish look, and she itched to slap his head. '*You* are about fifty per cent to let,' she said, which made Mr Clarke giggle.

The captain looked at his cup, as though wondering why there was nothing in it.

When his garrulous host noticed the same thing, the man snapped his fingers for the barmaid's attention.

'No more, Mr Clarke,' Mary said distinctly. 'Not unless you drain your own cup and start filling it with toddy as well, instead of letting the captain drink it all. Do you have malicious plans?'

'Really, Mary,' Ross said. He gestured to his former purser. 'Mr Clarke and I have had our differences, but the war is over, is it not?'

She opened her mouth to object, then closed it. Her face felt suddenly warm, but she could not blame the captain—at least she did not—because Mr Clarke's smug look was embarrassment enough.

On second thought, perhaps the former purser was not so congenial. The look he gave Mary contained equal parts of vitriol and venom, much like the balance of the toddy's rum and sugar. Mary gave him stare for stare until he looked away. She gathered Nathan close to her and walked from the commons room. She would have preferred to flounce off, the way it was done in those overheated novels Dina preferred to read, but she had no practice in flouncing.

She heard a loud laugh and turned around to see Captain Rennie on his feet, his cup raised. 'A toast to Napoleon Bonaparte, my employer these twenty years,' he announced to the room at large, which suddenly became silent.

Her urge was strong to return and drag off the captain, too.

'What's wrong with my da?' Nathan asked, more alert.

He's drunk, he's tired, he's weary of war, he's taking a little memory trip that might not be so good for him. Perhaps it's better than the one I forced on him yesterday. The thoughts chased each other around in Mary's brain until she hardly knew how to reply.

Nathan offered a solution, which touched Mary. 'I get happy like that when school is finished,' he confided.

I only have to do this for another day, she reminded herself as she squeezed his hand. 'I believe he has earned a break, too. But it's bed for you now, lad.'

She couldn't fault the accommodations at the Bloody Swash. After a sleepy face wash, the little boy left a trail of clothes to the bed, stopping only long enough for Mary to help him into his nightshirt, which looked like a cutdown affair from his father. Some put-upon servant had provided a warming pan, so Nathan's sigh of contentment was genuine.

She sat for a moment on the edge of the bed, watching him settle into sleep. She thought of Inez, his long-dead mother, who had never enjoyed such a moment with this child of hers and Captain Rennie. She had no doubt that Mrs Pritchert did the same thing, night after night, the homely task of women. With a pang, she suddenly realised that she did not want life to pass her by for even one more second. She did not know what lay ahead after York, beyond fetching a fruitcake, but she had no urge to return to Edinburgh and pick up where she had left off. It was a daunting thought because she had no idea how to change her fortunes.

There wasn't any reason to return to the commons room. Mary looked in the other bedchamber, smiling to see a lump in that bed which meant another warming pan. She started to unbutton her bodice, then changed her mind, knowing she would not be easy until Captain Rennie was sleeping beside his son.

The commons room was still full of patrons, but they seemed to be talking among themselves now, casting glances towards the other open door. She looked for the captain, but he was either passed out on the bench, or not there.

One of the farmers pointed. 'If you want your soggy man, look in there.'

She did as he said, her cheeks flaming as they laughed at her. No wonder her father used to preach any number of sermons from the pulpit about the evils of strong brew. The sooner they left the Bloody Swash and Ovenshine, the better she would feel.

Mary stood in the doorway to the kitchen and couldn't help smiling. His feet planted wide apart, as though on a pitching deck, Ross Rennie stood at the Rumford, stirring a pot. Mr Clarke perched on the table, his attention on the captain. He glanced at her, then looked away, the smile gone.

'Whatever is going on in here?' Mary asked.

Ross turned around at the sound of her voice. The owlish look was gone, replaced by a satisfied expression. He bowed. 'Madam Mary, I am making the purser a pot of burgoo. He claims he misses it. I know I do.'

'Burgoo?' she asked, coming closer to look into the pot. 'It looks just like porridge.'

He handed her the spoon, and she stirred, while

he added more finely ground oatmeal. 'I suppose it is. I make it sugary.'

She stared as he poured in a generous handful of caster sugar, grated from a large block, then felt her heart settle as he stirred the spoon round. She glanced at his face, which was red from the combined effects of cooking and drinking. She saw something more, something wistful in his expression, which forcefully bore home to her that he truly wasn't comfortable away from the sea, or food that a lubber would scorn. She peered in the pot.

'Burgoo. How many times a day?'

'One or two. Before a battle, cooks on my frigates were always under orders to make a big pot of the stuff before extinguishing their fire. Crew and officers alike, we ate it.'

He dipped in a smaller spoon and held it out to her. 'Try it.'

She did, tasting nothing but over-sugared oatmeal.

'After a battle, sometimes it was a day before anyone had time to relight the cooking fire.' He glanced at the purser and lowered his voice, but not by much. 'Mr Clarke there, he was generally hiding on the orlop deck before burgoo, so I doubt he remembers it.'

Mary put her hand on the captain's arm and shook her head. 'Don't,' she said softly.

He took the spoon from her, turned back to the pot and kept stirring. She felt Mr Clarke's eyes boring into her back as she took three bowls to the Rumford.

'Only a little, then it's time you came to bed, Ross,' she said, suddenly aware how intimate that sounded.

To her relief, he nodded. He poured in another generous handful of sugar, then dealt out three portions. In went a lump of butter large enough to rim the porridge as it melted. They ate in silence. Mary nodded her approval. 'You never put in any milk or cream?' she asked, hopeful of starting a convivial conversation to drain some of the tension in the kitchen.

'Hardly ever. D'ye like it, Mary?'

She did, even after a lifetime of porridge. Maybe it was all the butter. Mr Clarke frowned into his burgoo, his face deadly serious. There was more afoot here than she understood, but she tried conversation again. 'What's next on your list?' she asked, wondering what subject would be safe in a place where the captain must have spoken his mind to his former purser.

He took the much-creased list from his pocket. 'Looks like an encryption,' he joked. 'See here: Walmsey—lobscouse. Pickering—Naples biscuits. And my personal favourite: Shoreham—Pigs Pettitoes. Ah, Mary, I'm tired. Lend me a hand?'

She could have knelt on the floor in relief. She wasn't a big woman, but she hauled her cousin to his feet, balanced him against her hip like a married woman and started him towards the door. He had a slight smile on his face and she wanted to thrash him into the twentieth century. *I am cured of whatever affection I might have felt for this man*, she told herself as she towed him from the commons room and more laughter, and down the hall. *York cannot come soon enough.* She pressed her hands against his back when they reached the stairs and he made a creditable attempt to climb them before he sat down and pulled her onto his lap. Before she could turn her head, he kissed her most thoroughly.

His lips were sugary from all that burgoo and she had never minded oats. 'You are a disgrace to your uniform,' she informed him.

'I'll take it off, then,' he said, and started on his buttons.

She was at a loss to know what would stop him, and for one fleeting moment she didn't want him to stop. The maggoty thought vanished soon enough, when she noticed the purser peeking around the corner, his eyes lively, glee mingled with satisfaction that worried her more than Ross Rennie, who had started on *her* buttons.

Uncomfortable with artifice, Mary glanced at Mr Clarke. She knew it was completely within her power to act quite wifely.

'Later,' she told the captain and flicked her middle finger against his cheek, as her least-favourite governess used to do. The wounded look she received nearly pleased her. 'Get up before I do something drastic.'

Maybe it sounded more threatening in her lowland Scots burr, because he did exactly that, hanging on to the wall and pulling himself up the stairs while she pushed from behind. After a long moment in the hall, where he swayed back and forth, she opened the door and shoved him in. She closed it with monumental relief and turned the key in the lock so hard that a deaf man could have heard it.

'This is the end of your list, Captain Rennie,' she

told him, biting off each word as he stood weaving back and forth in the parlour. 'Tomorrow it is Apollo Street in York!'

He nodded vigorously, which made him stagger. 'There was more in that toddy than rum,' he informed her solemnly, which made Mary roll her eyes.

'You *would* say that,' she accused. 'Mr Clarke is a bad man, but I doubt even *he* is that wicked.'

She poured the captain a large glass of water and stood over him until he drained every drop. She filled it again and repeated the only cure she could think of. It was no cure, but when he finished the second glass, he was sweating and his eyes could focus again.

Mary knew she was not an unkind woman and gradually her anger dissipated, replaced by misery of the acutest sort. She wished she had never stopped at the inn in Carlisle and never accepted his invitation of an escort to York. She was a grown woman and any grown woman could find York. If this was what Mrs Morison called an adventure, Mary wanted no more of it, because it was making her unhappy.

She reconsidered. Not precisely unhappy, but edgy and tense, where life before had been flowing as smoothly as treacle. Here was this man and she didn't know what to do with him.

'I'm sorry, Mary,' he said finally, as she just looked at him. 'We'll leave early in the morning.'

'We could leave right now,' she said as vast disquiet filled her. 'I'll wake Nathan and go find the postilions. You just—just—sit here and behave yourself.' She leaned closer, whispering even in the little parlour that held no one but them. 'Did you make some comment to Mr Clarke about his shipboard behaviour?'

He thought for a long moment, as if opening and closing ledgers in his brain. Mary watched him and resolved never to serve anything stronger in her house than extract of vanilla, if she ever had a place of her own some day.

'Not beyond what you heard me say in the kitchen. At least what I *think* I said.'

'You did,' she assured him. She gave his arm a little shake. 'Think a minute! You told me he cheated your crew. Did you say anything to…oh, I don't know who you report to…'

'The Navy Board.'

'Aye, them!'

He nodded. 'It was at least two years later and my first opportunity on land. Portsmouth. I took his doctored ledgers and my suspicions. Apparently, mine were not the first complaints. I never saw him again.' He shrugged. 'He was a worthless coward and he grew rich off the Royal Navy. But this was several years after he left my ship.'

Mary sat down, deflated. 'Hopefully he has only suspicions and no facts and isn't one to nurse a grudge.' She gave her cousin a squinty-eyed glare. 'And hopefully he has had his fun with you. Ross, go to bed.'

She stood up and managed what she thought was a rather effective flounce from the parlour, considering that she only took a peek now and then at Dina's florid novels. Her lips firm, she propped her chair against the doorknob and went to bed. The captain could figure out his own buttons and remove his leg and why, oh, why was she worried about it anyway?

'I don't even like fruitcake,' she told the ceiling quite distinctly.

Maybe she said it louder than she intended. She thought she heard someone laugh in the next bedroom.

Chapter Fourteen

'Miss Rennie? Miss Rennie? Oh, please!'

Mary opened her eyes, happy enough to wake up from a dream where people were shouting and banging about, and swearing in a most ungentlemanly fashion.

'Miss Rennie?' The voice sounded so young and she heard tears. It was Nathan.

She leaped out of bed and yanked away the chair she had propped against the door. When she opened it, Nathan stood there, his hands out, pleading.

He was in her arms in a moment. She held him close as she looked around the parlour, where chairs had been turned over, a tablecloth ripped away and pictures tilted. A vase lay on its side as water dripped to the floor.

'What in the world...? Where is the captain?'

Nathan sobbed into her shoulder. 'A man in uniform hauled him away! Miss Rennie, he's in his nightshirt and it's cold out. And look there.'

She looked where he pointed and saw the captain's peg-leg, looking small and discarded without the man attached. 'They just dragged him away without giving him a chance to put on his leg?' she asked, aghast. 'He's a frigate captain! A hero, most likely.'

'Not for long, I fear.'

Mary looked at the open door, where Mr Clarke stood, impeccable and smug. She stared at him open-mouthed, then understood precisely what he had done. Her hand went to Nathan's head and then her lips as she kissed the shivering boy. 'It will be all right, Son,' she told him, deciding immediately on the best tactic. 'Get your clothes on and gather together your father's effects. I'll take his leg.' She gave him a gentle swat. 'Go on now. Get dressed.'

To her relief, he did not question their sudden change of relationship. She turned her attention to the owner of the Bloody Swash, where the brown bread was magic, even if the proprietor was spiteful. She had spent her life in calm and quiet and it came to an end at midnight. Clad in just her nightgown and her hair in a tangle, she stalked right up to the man and had the infinite satisfaction of making him back up into the hallway.

'You have done a mean thing, sir!' she raged, as doors opened all along the narrow hall, then closed again just as quickly. 'You *knew* what he would say, when in his cups! You've…you've contacted someone—'

'Our Justice of the Peace, Sir Henry Pontifract.'

'—and told him there is a spy at the Bloody Swash.'

He smiled at her, but did not try to re-enter the parlour.

'Someone should have shot you with a firing squad!' she sputtered.

The supercilious grin left his face. 'He fair ruined me!'

'Him and others, I suspect,' she shot back. 'How were you ruined, sir, how? Ross told me you served no gaol time in the fleet, even though you should have. You spirited away your embezzlement from Navy funds and bought an inn with the money that should have purchased clothing and better food for the men of the fleet. Shame on you!'

She stopped for breath, amazed at herself, as he began to laugh. Shocked, she wondered if anyone had a conscience after all these years of war.

'Shame on me? Oh, Mrs Rennie, I am all a-tremble.'

Without a word, she turned on her heel and slammed the door behind her. It was a matter of a few minutes to pull on her clothes and gather up Ross's leg. His face pale, Nathan watched her.

Mary took a deep breath and went into the Rennies' room. Nathan had gathered his father's uniform and smallclothes, which she carefully folded and replaced in the shabby duffel he used. She looked around. 'Does he have any money? A purse?'

Nathan felt underneath his father's pillow and pulled out a wallet. 'He told me he always keeps it under his head, ever since he was a midshipman. "Don't trust too many people," he tells me.' He started to cry again.

'You can trust me,' she said in complete earnest. She put the wallet in her reticule, rethought the matter and tucked it down her dress front instead. Mr Clarke was probably still standing in the hall and she wasn't about to give him anything. 'I am going to have to pretend to be your mother, and—'

'I don't mind,' he said quickly.

She smiled at him, touched. 'I don't mind, either.'

The little boy wavered so close to tears. His need

gave her strength, even more than the captain's dilemma. When things settled out from this evening's work, she intended to remind Ross Rennie that he had brought this entirely upon himself. Nathan needed a parent. Maybe she was a cousin so distant that their ties were nearly non-existent, but she was the only parent he had right now. She thought the responsibility might feel onerous, she who was used to letting her aunt and uncle control her life, but it descended on her like a little blessing, to her gratification.

'I'll find him, my dear,' she said. 'Pack your clothes. We're leaving this place.'

Mary took her own advice, cramming everything into her travelling case. When she came into the parlour again, Nathan was ready, too, his duffel slung on his shoulder, the son of a seaman, and his father's tall hat tucked close to his side.

He looked at her with that patient expression she had directed at her aunt and uncle through the years as she let them guide her. Now it was her turn to do some good.

'Suppose we can't find him?' Nathan asked, his eyes bleak.

Mary knelt and rested her cheek against his.

'Never fear. I'm not about to leave Ovenshine without your father. And let me tell you, he will get a generous piece of my mind once we're on the road again. Do overlook that, if you will.'

Her words had the desired effect. Nathan grinned.

She put her hands on both his cheeks now. 'All I ask is that you do exactly what I tell you to do. Only trust me.'

He nodded, his face so serious, then surprised her by kissing her cheek. Her heart beat a little faster as she realised that for the first time in her life, two people needed her.

Mr Clarke stood outside the door, a self-satisfied smile on his face that she longed to peel off with her fingernails. Instead, she raised her head a little higher and addressed the curious bunch of onlookers that stood behind him in the hall.

'I cannot imagine people who would trundle away an officer of the Royal Navy without not only his clothing, but his leg. I ask you, how much must a man give in defence of his king and country?'

She looked around in all her serenity, satisfied to notice that hardly anyone in that gathering could meet her eyes, even Mr Clarke, who cleared his throat.

'Where is he?' she asked.

'In the cellar of the guildhall,' the former purser said and offered not one more direction.

'Very well, then,' Mary replied. 'Come, Nathan. Let's…uh…fetch your father.'

Nathan took her travelling case and she shouldered the captain's duffel, tucking his leg under her arm. Head high, she walked quickly to the stables and routed out the postilions, who did as she said and prepared the post chaise for travel.

'Captain Rennie is in the guildhall, but I don't know where that is,' she told the Prestons, both so serious.

'Not a problem,' the father said. He went in search of the ostler, returning with him. The application of a little pressure on the ostler soon resulted in a satisfactory answer. In another moment the luggage was stowed, the door opened and Mary and Nathan ushered inside. For good measure, the postilion tossed the ostler in with them. 'In case we need more directions', was the man's practical reasoning.

Mary took a deep breath when they pulled up in front of a stone building. There were a few winking lights on the bottom floor and a grand but antiquated carriage out front.

The ostler rubbed his hands together, as though anticipating more action than Mary guessed Ovenshine ever saw. 'Sir Henry Pontifract, he what is justice of the peace,' he announced. 'He's not one to enjoy being dragged from bed at midnight.'

'None of us is,' Mary snapped, fixing the ostler with a glare that made him open the door and make a quick exit.

'I think you frightened him, Mary,' Nathan whispered, his eyes big.

'I should hope I did,' she told him. 'Now, my dear, if you must address me, call me Mama. We have some work to do here. I am now Mrs Rennie, a woman who does not suffer fools gladly, especially the one she married!'

'My Da?' Nathan asked, his eyes wide.

'Your da.'

Nathan laughed out loud, a little boy again and not a frightened child. 'He told me this was going to be such an ordinary visit to my aunt in Scotland,' he confided.

'Maybe it started out that way,' Mary said, happy for his company. 'I was just looking for fruitcakes.'

* * *

It seemed like a huge chance to take, she who had never dissembled or prevaricated, or even engaged in half-truths that Dina insisted the Lord God Almighty didn't give a fig about—although where Dina acquired her theology, Mary could never have said.

Brazen it out, she told herself, as Nathan helped her so nicely from the chaise. Going far above and beyond their duties, the postilions accompanied her up the steps to the guildhall. Neither father nor son were tall—what post riders are?—but their presence stiffened her spine. The ostler gave them a wide berth, perhaps not wishing to be thrown somewhere else.

The door was opened by an elderly gent with a long and lugubrious face, rather like a basset hound after a trying week.

'Mrs Rennie needs to find her husband.'

She turned around, surprised to see the Bloody Swash's ostler. The man had obviously decided there was more excitement to be had in this place than back at the inn. He still kept himself a respectful distance from the postilions.

'Aye, sir,' she said, taking Nathan's hand and addressing the older fellow, perhaps a servant.

'A constable has hauled him here in a half-naked state.' She drew herself up. 'I will remind you it is December and cold out.'

The elderly gent looked at her over his spectacles, his expression mournful. 'My master, Sir Henry Pontifract, has been informed that the felon in the dungeon is a spy.'

'A dungeon? My father?' Nathan said. His lips quivered and Mary rested her hand firmly on his head.

'Sir Henry was woefully *misinformed* by that scoundrel who runs the Bloody Swash,' Mary said. 'Captain Rennie is nothing of the sort. Please let me see him.' She held up the peg-leg, which made the servant blink and step back. 'A man ought to at least have his leg on if he is to answer charges!'

There was no logic to her statement and she knew it. The servant eyed the leg with real discomfort, then his expression mellowed. 'It *is* cold out, and a man ought to have a leg,' he muttered. 'Follow me.'

Mary heaved a quiet sigh and tightened her grip on Nathan. Preston took Captain Rennie's duffel from her and shouldered it, following her down the hall. He stopped and whispered to her, 'Mum, my name is Thomas.'

'I can't begin to tell you how grateful I am for you and your son, Thomas,' she whispered back. 'Just continue my charade, please.'

He touched his cap with a smile.

They descended a long flight of stairs, where the air was damp and foul-smelling.

'Dear me,' Mary said, as a trio of nasty customers that looked like rats ran across the stone flagway in front of them. Sir Henry's servant shrieked like a girl and Nathan gave him a disgusted look, even as he tightened his grip on Mary.

Mary shivered in the damp, squinting into the gloom to see a uniformed man sitting in a chair tipped back against a wooden door with bars.

'You, sir,' she said as she came closer. 'Please let me in to see Captain Rennie.'

The chair came down with a bang. 'God help us!' the constable exclaimed. 'I suppose you will tell me you are his wife.'

'I suppose I will,' Mary snapped, hoping to sound like the world's most put-upon wife. She touched Nathan's head. 'This is his son and I am Mary Rennie. You're holding an innocent man who gets intemperate with drink—oh, how I have railed at him about this!—and claims he is in the employ of Napoleon.'

'Exactly! We know spies in Ovenshine when we see them,' the constable declared, managing to sound prim and virtuous when he obviously was neither.

'How many spies do you see skulking about on a daily basis?' Mary challenged, walking right up to him to practically stand on his toes.

'Bravo, wife,' she heard from the other side of the door.

Mary looked at the constable. In a fit of rare creativity, her long-ago fiancé Lieutenant MacDowell used to tell her she had eyes that spoke their own language. She tried them on the constable, managing to add tears that just threatened to fall. Coupled with a sobbing breath or two, and the man was blancmange.

'Oh, for the Lord's sake, go inside!' he said, turning the key in the lock. 'You, too, sonny.' He stared at the peg-leg in Mary's hands. 'If a man can't have his leg, what's an England for?'

The sound on the other side of the door this time was a strangled yelp between a laugh and a cough.

I swear I will hurt you, Ross, Mary thought. *You're making this difficult.* She tried another tack and sobbed out loud, 'I pray he is not at his last gasp. Let me in.'

Chapter Fifteen

Captain Rennie had been in a worse prison in Spain, but at least he hadn't been cold in Cadiz. He couldn't stop shivering as Mary and Nathan came into his cell. She jumped when the door clanged behind them, which he found endearing. Whatever Miss Rennie's quietly lived existence in Edinburgh, he could have successfully wagered that it had never included a turn in a dungeon, not even for a visit.

Good Lord, but the woman had beautiful eyes. There was a certain snap and fire in them right now, which hardly surprised him. She looked like a woman with a huge grievance, a wife, perhaps. As he admired the view, she opened and closed one eye in an elaborate wink. She turned around to address the constable.

'Sir, I would greatly appreciate it if you would get a blanket for my wretched husband.'

So that was the game. He liked it. Mary Rennie might know nothing about prisons, but she seemed to understand that only close relatives would be allowed in dungeons after midnight, if at all.

The constable attempted an argument, but he got nowhere. Quite possibly the look that Mary was directing at *him* contrasted with the captain's view. As he watched, appreciative, she ushered his son towards the constable.

'If you don't feel secure about leaving the captain with me, send Nathan upstairs with a note. Captain Rennie needs a blanket and he needs one *now*.'

She said it calmly and with vast authority, reminding Ross of Admiralty lords. The constable gestured to his son and they left the hall without a word. Nathan looked back, anxious, and Mary blew him a kiss, which seemed to reassure his boy. Like father, like son; he could remember a kiss or two like that from Inez.

'Well, now,' Mary began, when they were alone. 'Let's put on your leg and get you dressed and you can tell me why on earth you ever trusted that purser for a single moment. Honestly, Ross, you are trying my very last nerve and I have a limited supply.'

Her calm acceptance of the situation amazed him. She handed him the wadding to pad his stump, then eased his wooden leg in place. Unperturbed by his naked body under that nightshirt he should have discarded years ago, she strapped the belt around his waist, then started to help him into his smallclothes while he stood and leaned against her.

He did try her once. When he told her he preferred his drawers on *before* his leg, because then the belt wouldn't chafe his waist, she started over, after muttering something under her breath that he never intended to question. When her hand brushed his genitals, he found her touch entirely pleasing. Her hand didn't linger there, but she wasn't missish about the matter.

He probably didn't need to lean against her—he had been dressing himself for years, after all—but her touch comforted him.

'Do you have a plan?' he asked after she helped him into his trousers and shook the wrinkles from his shirt. 'I'm fresh out.'

'I favour the truth. I assure you I can lard the whole thing with an ocean of tears that would likely upset our good king himself, be he ever so addled.'

He laughed and considered himself in capable hands. Then she spoke so seriously, and he knew she was right, as much as he disliked the matter.

'Captain Rennie, when I get you out of this dungeon, and I will, we simply must part company tomorrow in York. I can find Apollo Street, retrieve that final fruitcake and you can be on your way.'

'Am I disappointing you, Mary?'

To his chagrin, he who fought foreign navies and dealt in blood, her eyes filled with tears, and he knew these were genuine. He could have done a lot of things just then, most specifically agreeing with her and assuring her he would resume his previous plans. Instead, he held out his arms and she went into them, not crying, just resting her head against his chest because she seemed even more weary than he was. They sat together on the noisome straw until he heard his gaoler returning.

Mary heard them, too. She sat up, getting nimbly to her feet in that way he still envied of people with two sound limbs. She held out her hand to him and helped him to stand.

'I think I am just not good at adventures,' she told him, and it sounded like an apology. 'You frightened me when you spoke so intemperately about Napoleon and now you are in a prison and there is much at stake.'

'There are worse prisons than this one,' he began, and she put her finger to his lips. 'And it's not your fault,' he said around her finger.

'And you have probably been in one or two, I shouldn't doubt. *I* have not. I'm just a quiet lady and I'd rather be anywhere but here.' She squared her shoulders, which touched his heart. That alone would have startled a generation of midshipmen, who were probably certain he had no heart. 'But now I have to get you out of here, so don't give me grief, Ross.'

The constable unlocked the cell and gestured to them.

'Where is the captain's blanket?' Mary said, the spark back in her voice and the stiffening in her spine.

'Damn the blanket. You're coming with me,' the constable said. 'Sir Henry Pontifract will see you now.'

They were joined on the stairs by two healthy-looking rural types who had probably been routed from warm beds because the constable felt *he* needed some stiffening. The postilions still waited at the top of the stairs, neither of them as hulking as the constable's stooges, but lean, in that way of city men. Ross took heart to see them, mainly because he was beginning to suspect he was not the only man around who wanted to protect Mary Rennie. It was not a pleasant reflection to realise that he was in no position to help her or his own son. He was honest enough to know he had not a soul to blame but himself.

He had been in uncomfortable circumstances like this before, most notably in Cadiz, and again in Mersin, a plaguey Turkish backwater, where he and his crew had languished for nearly a year, waiting for the tide of their fortunes to turn. By the time the unpredictable Lord Thomas Cochrane had liberated the prison, Ross was thirty pounds lighter and could speak fair Arabic. At least Sir Henry Pontifract, whoever he was, wouldn't require a translator. It was some consolation.

Still, he hesitated at the door, suddenly weary down to his toenails and convinced he was the most naive man ever let loose on an unsuspecting population. His hesitation earned him a mighty prod from one of the constable's goons, which put him off balance and sent him sprawling in a massively undignified way.

No fears, though, because Mary was at his side immediately, gathering him tight in her arms, as if daring anyone to touch him again. He wasn't so certain he needed to be protected, but he also wasn't so certain he wanted her to ever let him go. And there was Nathan on his knees, too. With a sudden lift to his heart, he knew he had two champions.

'How can you be so unkind?'

Mary was on her feet again, backing his assailant into a corner, reminding him of wrens he used to watch from his bedroom window when he was a boy Nathan's age. The wrens regularly did battle with much larger birds, but they never lost an engagement.

'I'm well enough, Mary,' he told her. 'Just give me a hand up.'

She did, tears sparkling in her eyes, but somehow not falling yet. He began to think she had a mighty arsenal of feminine weapons. He glanced at the massively rotund man seated behind a desk who must be Sir Henry Pontifract, Ovenshine's magistrate and Justice of the Peace. Sir Henry's eyes were on Mary, too, and he appeared none too confident.

When Ross was on his feet again, Mary asked

for a chair. Sir Henry shook his head and she did not argue, but stood close to Ross, one arm around his waist, and the other around Nathan. Sir Henry opened his mouth to speak, but he was overruled by other voices in the hall, then the entry of his former purser, looking smug as only Ralph Clarke could, and several other men, one or two who seemed familiar. He recognised them from the commons room of the Bloody Swash.

His expression sour—Ross thought Sir Henry did not often see the shady side of midnight—the magistrate turned his attention to Mr Clarke.

'Well, sir, well, sir, you have insisted this matter could not wait until morning,' Sir Henry began, with no preamble. 'You tell me about spies and I see before me one post captain, a wife and son.'

'Appearances are deceiving, Sir Henry,' Mr Clarke said with a smirk. 'That's what they want you to think.'

He paused and struck a funny little pose, one that Ross was familiar with. He had seen it often enough at sea, when his former purser had some minuscule complaint to trouble him with, usually something that a better-regulated officer could have dealt with by himself and solved with no fanfare.

Sir Henry appeared to be of the same mind. 'Well, sir, *what*? My bed is getting cold.'

Elaborately, Mr Clarke drew out the much-folded list of towns and food. Ross almost expected to hear a fanfare from somewhere, but the only sound was the breaking of wind from a geriatric hound of questionable lineage who must have come inside seeking warmth. Nathan turned his face into Mary's sleeve so he would not giggle.

His face red, the former purser took the list the Sir Henry, who picked it up.

The magistrate frowned as he read down the list. 'All I see is a list of towns, some of which I know, and food.'

'I am convinced it is code, Sir Henry. Perhaps the food stands for something else.'

Sir Henry nodded and looked at the list again. 'Or it could just stand for food.' He jabbed a pudgy finger somewhere in the middle of the list. 'The Orion, shepherd's pie, Everly.' His expression became contemplative. 'I had a shepherd's pie at the Orion once. It was a mouthful of heaven.' He looked at Ross. 'A little inn located in the wilds of Northumbria? Somewhere near Leel?'

Ross felt himself relax. 'The very place, Sir Henry. I ate there last week, on my way to Carlisle.'

Sir Henry absorbed that news and proved he was no fool. 'Northumbria. Carlisle. Ovenshine. Captain, *where* are you going? Hopefully your sense of direction is better at sea than on land, or this nation is in deep trouble.'

Everyone laughed, including Mary, who seemed to think this was the funniest witticism she had ever heard. Her laugh was so charming and infectious that Ross had to smile, too, even though he knew not even Ben Pritchert had been better at finding latitude and longitude than he was. A man had his pride.

Mary cleared her throat and picked up the tale. 'Sir Henry, if you please, my dear husband was on his way to retrieve us. We're usually in Dumfries, but we had started out to find *him* and we have been backtracking here and there.'

It was a lovely lie and Ross believed her completely; more usefully, Sir Henry appeared to believe her, too. Ross sighed. 'I haven't seen them in nearly two years and, wouldn't you know it, we miscommunicated.' He rested his arm on Mary's shoulder and caressed her neck. 'Two years. That's a long time to be without a wife.'

Sir Henry nodded, a small spot of colour blooming in each jowl. 'And I suppose you have a limited time on short leave.' He peered closer at Mary. 'My, but she's a pretty one.'

Mary blushed and turned her face into Ross's sleeve.

'Aye, she is a bonny lass, Sir Henry. I must report back to Plymouth in two weeks.' He shook his head. 'We found each other in Carlisle. Now we're on our way to relatives in York.' *There, Mary, I can lie, too*, he told himself with some satisfaction.

Mary gave him a shy glance, which made the larger of the constable's goons sigh. The hound passed more gas and Nathan giggled. The corner of Sir Henry's mouth twitched.

Apparently, Mr Clarke began to suspect his quickly constructed plan was unravelling. After a hissed comment, he pushed the two men forwards that he must have brought from the Bloody Swash. Both of them swayed, suggesting too much libation. Sir Henry frowned.

'Speak, sirs,' he said, adding, 'if you can.'

'Your Excellency, we heard this man propose a toast to Napoleon himself, and call the Corsican Devil an employer!' The man from the Bloody Swash looked around, satisfied with himself and righteously prim. 'I know what I heard.'

The room was silent. Even the hound seemed to

sense something else in the wind besides his own contribution.

'Ah, yes. There is that matter, Captain. How do you explain this?' the magistrate asked.

'Allow me, Sir Henry,' Mary said, the blush gone now and replaced by a look so wifely—and not in a kind way—that Ross felt his insides rearrange themselves. How did she *do* that?

'I have been trying to break my husband of that regrettable habit.' She looked at Ross, her glance softer. 'I believe I understand it now.' She tucked her arm through his. 'For twenty years, we have all danced to the Corsican Devil's tune.'

Mr Clarke started to say something. A glance from Sir Henry stopped him.

Mary was in tears now, the beautiful kind that slid down her cheeks and not the kind that would have made another woman's eyes redden and her nose run. Ross wondered if she had practised such artifice and decided that Mary would never do that. Maybe she was just gifted. He wondered if her Edinburgh relatives had any idea what kind of woman lurked beneath her calm demeanour. More to the point, he wondered if Mary even realised it.

'I have walked the floor many nights, wondering where my darling was,' she said. 'When he was in prison, I was in prison, too. When he lost a leg in the service of his country at Trafalgar...'

She paused, giving the constable's goons a moment to collect themselves.

'...it was as though I felt his terrible pain, too. Sir Henry, we have all danced to Napoleon's tune. Surely you cannot deny it.'

'I suppose I cannot,' the magistrate agreed.

She went forwards and took the list from Sir Henry, then returned to Ross's grasp. 'Last night we stayed in Skowcroft with the vicar and his wife. Their youngest son served with my husband and died at sea of a fever.' She swallowed, and Ross knew her plea was genuine. 'The Everetts of Skowcroft have been in Napoleon's employ, too. That's all he meant. Through no one's fault but Napoleon's, we have suffered grievously. Think of the worst employer you can imagine, Sir Henry. Granted, it is an unorthodox way to put it, but surely you understand.' She shook her head. 'I know I have danced in the employ of the monster, my son and I.'

Mary smiled at him, and Ross felt the power of her words so softly spoken. He suspected that she, who had probably never put herself forwards in her life, was giving him a defence worthy of England's finest barrister, whoever he was. He had never been so moved.

'That's all it was, Sir Henry. I will do my best to see that Ross never gives such a toast again, but I can make no guarantee. We are as you see us: a family so long separated by war that it's hard for us to imagine anything else. Please let us go our way.'

She stopped then, looking around at her captivated audience and suddenly shy. The look she gave Sir Henry—reaching for his handkerchief—would have turned any man to mush. 'All we want is to have a happy Christmas together. We have never had such a thing before. I hope I didn't speak out of turn, Sir Henry.'

The magistrate blew his nose. Even the postilions in the doorway dabbed at their eyes and *they* knew the deception. Ross looked around. Mr Clarke and his witnesses had left the room. Ross knew he could probably take a moment to acquaint Sir Henry with the exact nature and faulty character of the man who was part-owner of the Bloody Swash, but he said nothing. He knew Ralph Clarke well. In a year or so, maybe sooner, he would muddy his nest and Ovenshine would understand what a viper he was.

'Please, Sir Henry,' Mary said.

Her quiet words must have reminded the magistrate that the hour was late, he was tired and there was no need to continue the matter before him.

Sir Henry leaned across the desk and gestured Mary closer. She released her death grip on Ross and came forwards.

'Take good care of him, Mrs Rennie,' Sir Henry said. 'And perhaps it would be better if he not show himself in Ovenshine any time soon.' His tone became conspiratorial. 'You never know who might take offence over something trite and trivial. *I* would never, but there are some...' He looked around and caught the constable's eye.

'Aye, Sir Henry. Once we visit those relatives in York, Nathan and I will see him safely to Dumfries for Christmas.' She sighed again. 'And then it's back to Plymouth and the Channel Fleet.' She put her hand in Sir Henry's. 'And do, sir, pray for peace. I want my darling with me evermore.'

Sir Henry adroitly turned a gasping sob into a sneeze and buried his face in his handkerchief. Mary gave him a lovely curtsy, then led her men from the chamber.

The night air braced him as they waited at the bottom of the steps for the postilions to remove the blankets from their horses. He wasn't brave enough to look at Mary Rennie, who stood so quietly beside him, her arm still in the crook of his arm as though it belonged there.

When they were seated inside, the postilion stood by the open door. 'Are we going back to the Bloody Swash?'

'No need,' Ross said. He looked at Mary, so composed, but with a level of sadness in her eyes, even though the charade was done and he was free—if one could overlook the admonition never to return to Ovenshine. 'Where, my dear?'

'York. You know it must be so.'

Chapter Sixteen

They travelled through the night in silence. *I meant every word I said*, Mary thought, dazed. *Ross probably thinks it was all for show, but not a word of it was false. I doubt Mrs Morison intended this much adventure.* She took a deep breath, wondering just when an admittedly odd journey turned into that moment in her life that Mama had predicted, but which Mary had thought would never happen, events being what they were. *Mary, you cannot possibly be in love*, she scolded herself. *It doesn't happen like this.*

'How would you know how it happens?' she murmured under her breath, her face turned towards the window.

'Beg pardon?' Ross asked, and Mary thought he sounded a little breathless.

'It's nothing,' she whispered back, mortified that she had spoken out loud.

She glanced at Ross, who stared out the window, Nathan's head resting on his lap. She watched how his hand caressed his child, this boy he saw only now and then. Whatever peculiar emotion had gripped her was destined to pass. She could hurry it along by putting Ovenshine completely out of her mind. She thought it might be a little harder to dismiss Captain Rennie in a skimpy nightshirt, but anything was possible, she reasoned. As embarrassment washed over Mary, it was followed by remorse of the acutest kind. She regretted taking up one more minute of the father and son's time together because of her silly quest. Whatever she was feeling was her problem and not theirs.

When Nathan was asleep, Mary cleared her throat and Ross turned towards her. She opened her mouth to speak and he put his hand up to stop her.

'Allow me to be ungentlemanly and go first, Cousin,' he said. 'Please accept my apology for this whole wretched turn of events.' He looked out the window again as if collecting himself. She waited. 'There are times when I wonder if I will ever be fit for land.'

'Ross, you know you will,' she assured him, puzzled at his train of thought. 'Napoleon—your employer—' he chuckled at that '—will remain on Elba. You can buy an estate in…in…'

'Dumfries. Or was it Kirkbean?'

'Whichever, and turn into a country gentleman.' She stopped, because the whole idea seemed suddenly unpalatable to her, never mind how *he* felt. 'Or not,' she concluded, chastising herself with how lame she sounded. 'You will be on half-pay, won't you? Perhaps I shouldn't wish unemployment on you.'

'Doesn't matter. I have prize money being put to good use by Brustein and Carter in Plymouth. The damned thing is this: I want to go back to sea right now and it isn't even Christmas. I have two more weeks of shore leave. Two whole weeks.' He shook his head, as though the idea of that much leisure was a plot hatched by Talleyrand himself.

'Only think how disappointed your sister would be,' Mary said, dismayed how eager he was to put real distance between him and her.

He shrugged again. 'My sister's disappointment will pass. She told me once that I only come to go away. Do you have the list?' He held out his hand.

She took it from her reticule and handed it to

him. He stared at it for a long time, then he smiled. 'The Orion, shepherd's pie in Everly; Quarie, steak-and-kidney pie at the Bugle; The Last Judgement and Ragoo'd Mutton in Frampton. It *does* sound suspicious. I spy and what do I spy? Did you ever play that child's game?'

'We all did.' She looked at his face. It was bland now, with no show of emotion, a contrast to his bare pleading when he sat so vulnerable without his leg. Or perhaps she had imagined any concern or fear. He was a man in perfect control. 'How close did Mr Clarke come to the truth? *Did* you ever spy?'

He folded the list and tucked it in his inside uniform pocket. 'Not how you are thinking. Or him. For a man at sea, Mr Clarke was amazingly oblivious. Maybe that came from too much drinking or too much hiding when we engaged the enemy. Did you know it's a hanging offence to hide during a battle?'

'I would have hid myself at the first sign of a French ship,' Mary declared.

'I doubt that supremely, Mary, my handy wife,' he teased. 'You're at least as brave as Mr Clarke.' He ducked when she threw her tatting spool at him. 'Mind your manners.' He tossed it back. 'Actually, we dropped off many a British agent on the Spanish and French coasts and retrieved others. It was a dangerous game.'

His eyes seemed to light up with the animation that had been missing since they arrived in Skowcroft for the lemon-curd pudding, reminding her again how taxing it was for him to visit the relatives of a dead man. *I shouldn't have forced him to do that* warred with *But the Everetts needed to talk about their boy,* but she did not make herself happy with her interference. The light in his eyes brought home to her his need for the excitement of his life, which was bound up with war. With a pang, Mary realised she had nothing to offer such a man. He was nothing more than a supremely distant relative who thought to help her.

The notion shook her, because, just for a moment in the guildhall, Mary was certain she had been essential to his salvation from the charges levelled against him. Under the cover of darkness, she looked at his face, contrasting it with the more vulnerable man in the dungeon of the guildhall, the man who needed her briefly. She could tell he didn't need her now, which was going to make York simpler. So what if she had meant every word she said to the magistrate? Captain Rennie preferred the thrill and terror of war; better she understand that now. They truly had nothing in common and matters were not likely to change that understanding.

'You were going to tell me something?' he asked.

'Nothing important,' she replied and closed her eyes to stop any further enquiry. She had never felt such pain in her heart before, which caused her even more anxiety. She took a deep breath and faced an unpleasant truth: She, Mary Elizabeth Rennie, had been dwindling into more than old maidenhood. She was becoming bland and colourless. Soon she would blend into the very walls at Wapping Street and no one would know she had ever lived. In a few years, maybe only a few months, she might tell a friend about the time she fell in love and the friend would have to turn away to keep from laughing at her.

Too bad that her only guide to love and nuptials was her cousin Dina. All Dina could do was complain about her fiancé, then go into spasms when she realised that the ring she had so wilfully thrown away was valuable.

'Come now, Mary, what is it?' Ross asked.

Mary didn't know what his ocean-going voice sounded like, but there was a firmly persuasive tone she had not heard before. Perhaps she owed him some sort of comment. 'It's this,' she began. 'You are eager to return to sea, because it has become your natural habitat.'

'Aye, lass. You have more insight than most.'

'I, on the other hand, have no wish to return to my chair by the fireplace in Wapping Street. Edinburgh is starting to seem tame. Is that what happens with adventure? Once I find that dratted ring in York, I'm not certain what to do.'

Ross thought a moment. 'You could emigrate to Canada.'

That seals it, Mary thought, as wry amusement rendered moot whatever she thought she had felt for Captain Rennie. *My affection for this man might be growing, but he is not interested, if he would send me to Canada.* 'And do what in Canada, once I have emigrated?'

He considered the question for so long she thought he had dropped off to sleep. The rhythm of the post chaise was making her eyelids droop, too. He startled her when he spoke, partly because he had covered Nathan with his boat cloak and moved to her side of the chaise.

'Not many avenues open to single ladies who emigrate, I suppose.'

'None, I should think,' she said. 'I suppose I could be a governess, except that my aunt and uncle would likely object and consider it beneath me.'

'Why does it matter what they think?'

'Why, indeed?' she said. 'I have it. I will take ship to Canada and hang a placard around my neck.' She spelled it out with her hand. "Governess for hire. Is not afraid of Indians or polar bears." At any rate, I've never met either, so how would I know?'

He smiled, which only reminded her how much she was going to miss his company after he dropped her off at Apollo Street. 'I suppose we all have our worries,' she told him. 'Mine are lighter than yours, sir.'

'I doubt that. I'm used to dealing in death.' His tone was matter of fact. She wished he had not taken her hand just then. 'You're just not used to adventures.'

'I suppose I am not.'

'But what, above all things, would you like to do, Mary Rennie?'

No one had ever asked her that, not even her own parents, because there was only so much a female could do. 'I've never thought of that,' she told him.

'Come now. Everyone does.'

'Men do,' she said quietly.

He took her hand and kissed it, then put it back in her lap. 'I'm an ass.'

'No, you're not. If it were within my scope, and I doubt that it is now, I would love to have children.' She felt her face grow warm. This was no subject to ever discuss with a man and hardly even a husband, probably. 'I would love them and take care of them. I wish I could tell you something more dramatic, Captain, but I cannot.'

'It's a noble occupation; only ask poets and painters. But if that does not happen, what then?'

She felt a flash of irritation, wondering at his probing. What would she do? Remain quietly in Wapping Street until she died? She stirred restlessly, wishing he would return to his side of the chaise. The space was crowded and he sat too close. What would she do?

She thought to lighten the whole subject. 'It hardly matters. Better you should be asking yourself what that charming, tall, blonde lady with the French-Caribbean accent is doing now.'

He gave her a blank stare, then started to chuckle. 'Our Lady of the List?' he teased. 'P'raps if the war ever ends, I shall return to Martinique. Come, come, Mary Rennie—what will *you* do?'

'I know,' she said suddenly. 'I would be a clerk in my uncle's counting house. I'm clever with figures and columns. I would get my own house and library subscription, and…and eat luncheon in a public house now and then, because I like…Cumberland sausage.'

He laughed along with her. 'Could it happen?'

'Never in Edinburgh, I suppose. I wonder…do you think there is room for someone like me in Canada or the United States? I would probably get a kitten or two, because I like them, and cats make my uncle sneeze so we have none. Oh, bother it! I am running on. Maybe you're giving me ideas.' She turned her head away. Maybe he would think she slept now. After all, it was long past midnight. She decided it was not wise to think about independence too much—not for a woman, anyway.

Ross didn't think she slept, but he respected her silence. He thought for a long moment about returning to the other side of the chaise, but stayed where he was, not wanting to embarrass her by moving away. But was that it? He took a deep breath, enjoying the fragrance of what smelled like cloves.

He knew she wasn't asleep. 'Mary, do I smell cloves in your hair?' It sounded stupid, but he was curious.

She opened her eyes. He saw inexplicable sadness first, which quickly changed, as though she did not want him to question her mood. 'Aye, it is. Mrs Morison brews a hair tonic with cloves.'

'I like it.'

To his chagrin, that covered the subject and she turned away again, her eyes slowly closing until he knew she slept this time. When her head started to bump against the side of the chaise, Ross reached for her, pulling her to his chest. She opened her eyes for a groggy moment, then settled against him. The fragrance was more pronounced; he decided he would always think of Mary whenever he smelled cloves. Maybe—if he ever found that blonde lady—he would suggest a hair tonic with cloves.

Ross thought he would sleep, too, but his leg pained him where the constable's guard had shoved him down. He remembered the humiliation of the moment, grateful at least that he hadn't been upended, to thrash about like a turtle. In an amazing flight of fancy, probably brought about by the late hour and stomach sour with ale from the Bloody Swash, Ross wondered if Mary would be repulsed by his naked body if they made love. He decided she wouldn't. After all, she had expressed no qualms helping him into his peg-leg in the cell, with all his assets on display.

Mind your manners, Ross told himself. Once his visit to Dumfries ended and Natham was back in Plymouth with Mrs Pritchert, he knew a discreet establishment where men gamed on the first floor and sported on the second. He could relieve his tension there and return to sea with a spring in his step; he had done it before. Those women never complained about a leg and three-quarters. He frowned; they were paid not to complain.

Looking at Mary, admiring the length of her eyelashes and the softness of her bosom as she leaned against him, he wondered if such sport would satisfy him now. Maybe peace wasn't such a bad thought—he could lie down at night with a wife, remain with her through all the hours and wake up in the morning with her beside him. He had never felt inclined to do that with second-floor women.

Yes, definitely someone like Mary, even if his

cousin did not meet a single of the criteria he had established years ago. As the post chaise travelled closer to York, the idea beguiled him. Imagine waking up, warm and comfortable, with perhaps a child or two bounding into their room to jump on the bed. In a distant life he barely remembered, he recalled the pleasure of snuggling between his parents as they laughed and teased him.

He wondered what would happen to Mary if she never found a husband. Such a prospect seemed more likely than the alternative, he decided, re-calling countless wardroom discussions. Depend-ing on the length of the voyage, his fellow officers might be more inclined to speak of women than compose food lists. First, Mary's hypothetical hus-band would have to be indifferent to the idea of money, because she had already said she had lit-tle. He appraised her travelling outfit, which was well cut and of good fabric. Obviously, her aunt and uncle didn't skimp on her. He had no idea of their circumstances, but it wasn't likely they were inclined to lay out a respectable dowry. They had taken her in and would do their duty, but he doubted that their duty extended to the financial arrangements of a marriage.

Ross studied Mary more carefully, admiring

how relaxed she looked when she slept and the length of her eyelashes. Nothing wrong there, he decided. Discounting a cinnamon sprinkle of freckles across her nose, which he found personally beguiling, she had the kind of skin that most females less endowed probably envied. Her lips were not like his, tight and Scottish, and she had a way of pursing them that made him imitate her unconsciously, until he stopped himself. Viewed a bit at a time or altogether, there was nothing unpleasant about Mary Rennie. Surely there was a man somewhere who wasn't immune to her.

He had to own to feeling a little personal tightness as he surveyed her shape. Since he had put his arm around her to keep her from banging her head against the side of the chaise, the gentle pressure of her bosom against his ribs made Ross edgy. He began to wish he had visited that discreet establishment before he'd started north with Nathan. He knew Mary hadn't meant to touch his genitals when she helped him into his leg, but she had, and he remembered the feeling.

A man of certain years and experience in a middling-to-dark post chaise could be pardoned for woolgathering. Mary wasn't one to chatter, and he liked how restful she made him feel, almost as though he could relax or say something, or say nothing, and she would not insist on more than he could provide at once. Certainly a husband would enjoy some conjugal fanfare upon his return from the Channel, but there wasn't anything about Mary to suggest she could not provide that, too. She had a hearty laugh, which suggested she could be as animated as any woman, given the opportunity that a healthy man could furnish. Perhaps a low laugh wasn't as necessary as he had imagined.

Great God above, this was sweet Mary Rennie and he was havering on like a randy mariner who hadn't left his quarterdeck in five years. Thank the Lord she could not read his mind, he decided, closing his eyes with what he felt was an audible snap, causing him to chuckle, which caused Mary to open her eyes—they were so green—then shut them again with a little sigh that went right to his heart as she snuggled closer.

With any luck at all, he'd find the woman he was looking for—maybe with a few of Mary's qualities. Ross knew in his bones, those present and those missing, that Elba wasn't far enough for Napoleon. And because there might be years more of battle, he knew better than to claim any woman's ultimate affection before the whole turmoil finally ended. That would be unfair.

He had decided on such a rational plan years ago, when he hadn't thought the war would drag on much longer than a year or two. As he stared out the window and watched night turn to dawn, he rubbed his stump and admitted finally that such nobility had lost its appeal.

Chapter Seventeen

Drat the captain. There was no call for him to be so grumpy and out of sorts as they turned on to Apollo Street, Mary decided. She had no idea what had set him off, except that he had been rubbing his stump for more than an hour.

Earlier, when she had opened her mouth to commiserate, he growled, 'Snow's coming', in such an unpleasant tone that Mary turned her attention to a skinny dog lifting his leg against a lamp post.

When she looked away from that spectacle, Nathan gave her a glance of real sympathy. 'Da gets that way when his leg hurts,' the boy whispered, which made Da grimace and apologise.

And you're probably starving, Mary thought, wondering why he had insisted on staying in the post chaise during a luncheon stop. She knew he was too experienced and adult to be pouting. The sooner he was on his way to Scotland, the better, she decided. Heaven knows, *she* didn't know what to do with him.

Since Captain Rennie had made no attempt to talk beyond a few monosyllables, Mary had turned her attention to his son, who still found the journey to his liking. While his father glowered in his corner of the chaise and the day wore on, Nathan had entertained her with stories of Plymouth and school. Mary had nothing of interest to tell him about her own modest life, so she described Edinburgh, from the Castle to Holyrood House and the Royal Mile between. In the telling, she found herself a little homesick.

She had tried to involve the captain in their discussion, timidly asking him if he had a particular favourite place. He didn't say anything for a while, but he stopped rubbing his leg. He leaned back and regarded his son. 'Probably Oporto,' was all he said. 'Aye, Oporto. Good port. Lovely women.' He rubbed his knee again and returned his attention to the village they passed through, with smoke rising from chimneys and men walking home from work now.

Poor man, Mary told herself. *He is thinking of*

the wife he spent so little time with. I can be kind and overlook his megrims.

'Is Edinburgh your true home?' Nathan asked her. 'I think mine is Plymouth.'

I don't know, Mary thought. She gave the matter some attention, because Nathan seemed to be genuinely interested. She reminded herself that children had no skill in idle chatter; he probably did want to know.

To answer, she told him about Mrs Morison, the cook and her confidante. In the telling, she became aware that her life was most comfortable below-stairs at Wapping Street, rather than above. She glanced at Captain Rennie, hoping that he wasn't paying attention. Her life was ludicrously small. She doubted Nathan would notice, but all of a sudden she didn't want her distant cousin to feel sorry for her. All in all, it wasn't a bad life.

To her dismay, the captain had stopped rubbing his knee. His expression had turned thoughtful.

'As slow as it would probably seem to your father, I like my life well enough, Nathan,' she said, deeply aware of the stinginess of it. As much as Dina complained about Mr Page, they would likely marry and she would have children. Silly Dina would have more experiences than Mary could ever even dream of and it suddenly seemed so unfair. With great effort, Mary swallowed her tears and turned her attention to her tatting. *My life isn't that bad*, she thought.

She knew she would find the ring in York and return to Edinburgh. Years from now, no one would ever know anything about her. She would live her quiet life and pass from the scene.

As they finally turned onto Apollo Street, Mary had to admit that perhaps she was the traveller who was feeling cross and out of sorts, grumpy even. She just didn't show it; perhaps that made her a hypocrite.

'Number Fifteen Apollo Street,' Mary said, reminding herself painfully of her aunt, who was famous in family circles for stating the obvious. She glanced at her fellow travellers. Nathan's expression was all interest. His father's was less so. In fact, he had leaned back and folded his arms across his chest. When the chaise stopped and the footman opened the door, she knew this was the right time to end their decidedly odd journey.

Mary held out her hand to Nathan. 'Dear boy, it's been a pleasure,' she told him, overlooking the puzzlement in his eyes. She shook the captain's hand next. 'You, too, Cousin,' she said, hoping she sounded more resolute and decisive than she felt. 'I can handle the matter from here. Tom Preston can take down my travelling case and you can ride on. Thank you for your assistance. It was a decided pleasure to meet you both.' She couldn't help but laugh. 'If our fractious and odd ancestors had ever got along, we would likely have met at a family reunion!'

The captain's expression grew thoughtful. 'Are you abandoning us?'

'We're in York,' she reminded him. 'I have taken far too much advantage of you, and this is my destination.'

She stepped from the post chaise, helped by Preston's son, and asked for her luggage. When she tried to close the door, she discovered that Captain Rennie held it open.

'Not so fast, Cousin. I haven't come all this way not to see the ring in the cake.'

He had a clipped way of speech, as though he walked his quarterdeck just then. His own Scottish accent sounded more precise, which caused Nathan to look from her to his father, a question in his eyes.

Mary decided not to back down. She smiled at the postilion when he handed her the travelling case. 'It's just a small ring and you should be on your way. Your sister must be wondering where you are.'

'Let her wonder,' Captain Rennie said with a shrug. 'I suppose once you acquire the ring, you will just walk until you find lodging for tonight?'

'Aye,' she assured him. 'It served me well enough for the other three cakes.' She started for the front door, but the captain took her arm. His touch was gentle. She could easily have ignored him and extricated herself, except that Nathan watched them both.

'I want to see this ring,' he repeated. He released her, stepped back and offered no restraint.

He thinks I will fold like a hand of cards, she thought, and continued to the door, where she knocked.

Something in the way he had spoken told Mary there wasn't any need to look behind her. In another moment, Nathan stood next to her on the step. Captain Rennie was just a step below, his expression daring her to do anything about it.

'For goodness' sake,' she murmured under her breath and raised her hand to knock again.

The door opened before she could knock and she nearly hit the butler, an old ancient of days who probably would have toppled, if she had touched him.

His eyes filmy, he looked at her, then his smiled brightened. 'Oh, it cannot be.' He peered closer. 'Are you Miss Ella Bruce from Carlisle, her what my master still yearns for after all these years?'

The poor old dear was mistaking her for Mr Maxfield's long-gone lady love, if she could believe her ears. 'I'm Mary Rennie,' she said, 'and I have come to see your employer about a fruitcake.'

Before she could stop him, the butler took Mary by the wrist and tugged her inside the house. He looked at the others on the doorstep. 'Do you *know* these people?'

As much as she wanted to assure him she did not, which would probably force Captain Rennie to see the wisdom in her action and return to his own plans, she never had a chance. Ross ushered his son inside and shut the door behind the two of them.

'We're all Rennies,' he said, after a glance in her direction that dared her to make any amendment to his bland statement.

'What commotion is this, Reading?'

The man she assumed must be Tavish Maxfield came into the hall. His voice could not be called anything less than commanding, but it seemed to bear no relation to the little fellow with wispy white hair who stood fully a half head shorter than Mary. She tried not to gape.

The butler took all attention from her. Reading turned to his master, his hands fluttering about. 'I do believe this is Miss Ella Bruce, sir! She has come from Carlisle, as I know you have been wishing and dreaming for decades.' He gave her a fond look. 'Now you can put that kissing ball to good use that you have been hanging for these past thirty Yuletides.'

'Oh, no, I…' Mary stopped when Mr Maxfield gave her the slightest shake of his head, his eyes lively.

'Reading, take their cloaks and bring us some tea.' He spoke firmly, and the butler nodded, doing as he was asked, then hurrying down the hall, rubbing his hands together and murmuring to himself. Mary watched, mystified.

Mr Maxfield cleared his throat. 'My dear Rennies, won't you come into my sitting room? Let me explain Reading to you and you can tell me more about the fruitcake.' He gestured. 'Mrs Rennie, allow me.'

They went into a cheery room that could only

have belonged to a bachelor of long standing. Books perched on every chair, the mantelpiece and window ledges.

His eyes bright with amusement, Captain Rennie nodded to Nathan, who quickly picked up books and manuscripts from the sofas and wing-back chairs. Mr Maxfield nodded his approval.

'Helpful lad,' he said. 'Do be seated, my dears.' He looked at them for only a short moment; perhaps he was making sure his butler was out of earshot. 'Dear Reading has been with me since I was a pup. He woolgathers now and is well-nigh convinced we're both thirty years younger.'

'It happens,' Captain Rennie said.

'Not in your line of work, I should think,' Mr Maxfield replied.

'No, indeed. Thanks to my—' he glanced at Mary '—to Napoleon, there's hardly a captain alive who rejoices in a thirty-year career.' He looked down at his own deficiency and gave his wooden leg an experimental tap that made Mary smile. 'Or at least survives with all the parts he started with. If your butler thinks Mrs Rennie is Miss Ella Bruce, I assure you my...Mrs Rennie is game enough to play along. Aren't you, honey?'

I will thrash you some day, Mary thought. 'Certainly I am game, my love,' she replied just as sweetly and had the pleasure of watching the captain blush.

'Good,' Mr Maxfield said. He laughed, but it was a wistful sound. 'Age has a way of catching us up. I must confess that since the fruitcake arrived, with its startling message, Miss Bruce has been the subject of some commentary in this little household.' He sat back and steepled his hands, looking like the solicitor he was, albeit a short one. 'Now tell me what little plot Ella's silly nephew Malcolm Barraclough has hatched. I fear he is a frustrated romantic.'

Captain Rennie waited for Mary to speak. When she continued to regard the old fellow in silence, perhaps amazed at his frank understanding of his nephew, Ross decided he should atone for 'honey'. After all, Mary *had* sprung him from the clutches of the law in Ovenshine. She had also forced him to spend time with the Everetts, perhaps the furthest thing from his mind when they went to Skowcroft, but probably the most correct. To be honest, he had enjoyed his visit with the vicar and his wife.

'We're after a Christmas cake, sir, a fruitcake, if you will. Apparently, your nephew sent it to you under the pen of Miss Ella Bruce, in the hopes that you would—'

'He meant it most sincerely,' Mary said, interrupting him. 'Mr Barraclough told us that you were in love with Miss Bruce a few years ago…well, maybe more than a few years ago, but you were too shy.'

She stopped. From the charming way her face became so rosy, Ross knew she was shy, too. He put all his eggs in one fragile basket and covered her hand with his, surprising himself how gratified he was when she tightened her grip on his fingers.

'That young scamp thought if he could send you a letter from Miss Bruce herself, you might work up your own courage,' Ross explained.

'Even after all these years,' Mary added. 'It's probably not ever too late for love, Mr Maxfield.'

She stopped again, her face even more red. Ross could not think of a time in their admittedly brief relationship where he had seen her more lovely. *I hope some man takes a good look at her*, he thought in admiration. *What's wrong with the boyos of Scotland nowadays?*

To his amusement, she gave his palm a little pinch, as if expecting him to do more of the heavy lifting in this conversation. He discovered that the last thing he wanted was to fail Mary Rennie. He shouldered right in.

'That's the short and tall of it, sir. Your nephew is a shameless matchmaker and he has been watching his dear aunt brood for too many years. What do you plan to do about this?'

Ross hadn't meant to sound like a captain addressing a particularly dense midshipman, but that was his life and he expected results. He amended it with a more kindly gaze than he had ever given a midshipman and leaned back, keeping hold of Mary's hand and putting it to rest on his thigh. Inez used to like that. Mary gave a little start, but she didn't withdraw her hand from his leg. He wondered what Mary would do if he inched her hand a bit higher on his leg, but decided his credit wasn't that good.

Mr Maxfield looked around, as though seeing his own sitting room for the first time. A ruddy colour had arrived in his own cheeks, which Ross thought quite charming. He didn't know that elderly fellows blushed. The old fellow didn't speak, though; Mr Maxfield was either filled with stronger stuffing than most midshipmen, or Ross was losing his touch this far from the ocean.

Mary took the initiative. She leaned forwards

and touched Mr Maxfield's sleeve with her free hand. Ross knew she could have just as easily pulled away her hand from his leg, but she did not.

'Please, sir, I hope you will consider the matter. Your nephew was most in earnest. There is a woman who loves you and here you sit.'

Look at her. Amazing woman! He recognised the lip tremble from last night with Sir Henry Pontifract in Ovenshine. He stared at Mary in admiration, convinced that Siddons herself could take lessons from his sweet cousin. He looked closer, wondering if she was in earnest herself. Touched, he dredged a handkerchief from his uniform jacket and handed it to her. He sat back to watch Mary Rennie work her magic.

'Mr Barraclough told us that each Christmas season, Miss Ella Bruce droops a little. She puts up a kissing ball, then mopes about the place until she leaves for Stirling. I suspect it has something to do with you.'

Mr Maxfield was not any more immune to bare pleading than Sir Henry Pontifract. Although he had not known Mary beyond twenty minutes, the solicitor opened his heart. 'Let me explain,' he began, then stopped when the butler returned, staggering under a tray too heavy for him.

A nod in Nathan's direction sent Ross's son leaping to his feet to help. When the tray was safely lodged on a table and Reading dismissed—not without a pout and a forlorn backward glance—Mr Maxfield asked Mary to pour. She did, taking her time, while Ross wanted to climb the rose trellis in the wallpaper pattern in his urge to hear the old man's story.

'Now then, sir,' Mary said, when everyone had tea in hand and bread and butter within reach.

That was all the invitation Mr Maxfield needed. 'I'm so short,' he began, and described his humiliations as a youth growing up in Carlisle next door to Ella Bruce. To hear him tell it, Miss Bruce was the envy of nations with her fine looks, even temper and wisdom, which made Ross wonder why, with all these qualities, she had arrived at an antique virgin state. 'How could I impress someone like her?' the solicitor concluded with a violent shake of his head that sent his wispy hair into curious patterns. 'So many times I tried to work up my nerve to travel beyond neighbourly small talk.' He shook his head in sorrow. 'I was never brave enough.'

'Why the kissing ball?' Mary asked.

The little man heaved a sigh worthy of one far

more substantial. 'I last saw her thirty years ago at this time of year. There she stood, in close proximity to a kissing ball.' He shook his head. 'I just wasn't brave enough to kiss her.' He thumped his leg with his hand. 'That was all that stood between me and possible success!'

'She never married,' Mary said. 'As you know, sir, ladies cannot move the matter forward.' It was gently put, but Ross could have sworn he heard some real longing.

A little pressure on his thigh told Ross it was his turn. 'Her nephew told us how many letters she wrote through the years and then tore into scraps,' he said promptly.

He hadn't told a lie that big since he was eight, but it had the desired effect. Mr Maxfield absent-mindedly took the handkerchief from Mary's hand and pressed it to his own eyes. 'In the note her nephew manufactured, she is at Stirling?' he asked from the depths of the handkerchief.

'Her sister's,' Mary replied. 'I don't know the address.'

'I do,' Mr Maxfield said. He gave his nose a fierce blow.

'Well, then?' Mary asked, her voice so soft.

'I will leave for Stirling tomorrow morning!' Mr

Maxfield declared. 'I have been teetering on the brink ever since the fruitcake arrived with that little note tucked inside. You have swayed me,' he said to Mary, then turned his solicitor's gaze upon Captain Rennie, which Ross reckoned was only slightly more kind than the look he fixed upon midshipmen,'You probably have no idea what a gem you have in Mrs Rennie.'

'Guilty as charged, like any husband,' Ross replied promptly. 'She tolerates me because I am so often at sea.'

He couldn't help a sidelong glance at Mary, who looked away. Even the back of her neck was red.

Trust Nathan to reel in the conversation. Ross had thought he was packing away bread-and-butter sandwiches and paying no attention. Obviously he misjudged his son.

'Please, Mr Maxfield, where is the fruitcake?'

Mary seemed to pounce on Nathan's question with great relief. 'Yes! Where, indeed? You see, sir, I was sent on a commission to retrieve four fruitcakes for my aunt in Edinburgh, who fears the ingredients are slightly off.' She smoothed down her dress. 'That is really why we are here. After fruitcake.'

'I would have thought you would hurry to be with your husband, Mrs Rennie,' the solicitor said.

Your turn to prevaricate, Ross thought gleefully.

'This was an errand I…we…Nathan and I… could handle as we made our way south,' she lied, every bit as facile as he. Chalk up another tally for Mary Rennie. 'And as you can see, we found him.'

She astounded Ross then by voluntarily running her hand up his thigh a little higher. He broke out in a sweat. 'It's somewhere in the city, then? Further afield?' Ross asked, not adverse to another day or more in Mary's company.

They all looked at the old man, who threw up his hands. 'Only yesterday, I mailed it to a friend in Knaresborough.' He touched Nathan's knee. 'Dear boy, no one actually *eats* fruitcake.'

Chapter Eighteen

That cinches the matter, Mary thought, embarrassed, as the captain groaned and swore an oath probably only heard on his quarterdeck during times of stress. *Our journey ends right here. I have finally disgusted this man with my silly errand.* She took her hand from his thigh, something she should have done several minutes ago. She had only inched it higher to get him back for the 'honey'. Trouble was, she was starting to perspire and she knew the room wasn't hot.

'Pardon me,' Captain Rennie said quickly, and there was no mistaking his own embarrassment. 'It's just that…Knaresborough, you say? Out of curiosity, why didn't you just throw it away?'

It was Mr Maxfield's turn to look askance. Mary held her breath, wondering what the solicitor must think of them. Not that Captain Rennie's language reflected on her, precisely.

'Sir! I think that from our combined accents—Nathan is our exception—we are three Scots. Have ye no national pride?' the solicitor scolded. 'I wouldn't dream of throwing away food. One merely sends fruitcake on.'

Mary glanced at Captain Rennie. His lips began to twitch. In another moment, he seemed to cast all burdens to the wind as he laughed. 'Mercy!' he said finally, dabbing his eyes. 'My dear Mary—all kindness to your aunt aside—there is a reason why no one put fruitcake on my wardroom list.'

A puzzled look on Mr Maxfield's face led to more explanation of the list and the vicar in Skowcroft, followed by evil tidings in Ovenshine. By then, the solicitor was eating his way steadily through the bread and butter that Nathan had left, amazed at their journey. Shadows began to slant across the sitting room and the old butler had been peeking inside the room for the past half-hour, at least

It was Mary's turn to steer the conversation back to the fourth fruitcake. 'Who did you send it to, sir?' she asked.

'Bartemus Whitney, Number Twenty-five Corydon Circle,' Mr Maxfield replied. 'He is in the export business.' The solicitor giggled. 'Perhaps he will send your Christmas cake to Napoleon on Elba!'

'I sincerely hope not,' Mary said, suddenly tired of her adventure. 'I don't fancy an ocean voyage. I don't know your country, sir. How far is Knaresborough from here?'

Mr Maxfield fixed her with a kindly eye. 'I am teasing you, Mrs Rennie. It's a mere fifteen miles. I could send him a note to dispose of it and—'

'Oh, no!' Mary exclaimed, chagrined at the puzzled look Mr Maxfield gave her. 'I mean...Knaresborough is on our way to Scotland, is it not?'

'Aye, lass.'

'We can pick it up on our way through the town, sir,' she assured him. 'Nothing simpler. No need to write to Mr Whitney.'

'I suppose it is on your way,' their host agreed. 'But I do insist that you stay the night with me. It's nearly dark now.'

'We could never do that,' she replied, looking to Captain Rennie to back her up. To her dismay, he seemed to be enjoying the whole exchange. 'Could we, my dear?' she asked him point blank.

* * *

'Certainly not,' he agreed. 'You barely know us, sir.' He took out his much-folded list. 'Besides, there is a duck à l'orange I most specifically want to try at the Maiden's Prayers on Hinckley Street in your very own York. We will leave for Knaresborough in the morning.' He bowed to Mr Maxfield, then gathered Mary close with his arm around her waist. 'Good luck with Miss Bruce, sir. I trust you will be as pleased with her as I am with Mary Rennie.'

His fingers were warm on her waist, even edging a little lower than Mary thought proper. There wasn't a thing she could do except smile at their host, wish him Happy Christmas while she wished Ross Rennie to the devil and let Reading retrieve their coats.

'Let's find the Maiden's Prayers,' Captain Rennie told the postilion as he helped them into the chaise again. Light snow was falling now.

She still couldn't say anything, not with Nathan so lively and wide awake. She tried, though. 'Captain Rennie, you really don't owe me any more attention,' she said as they started off. 'Knaresborough was never in the bargain!'

Trust such an unscrupulous man to bend her will

to his so adroitly. The captain turned to his son. 'Nathan, she doesn't want us around.'

The little boy's face fell. 'It's hard to imagine anyone not wanting us around,' he said.

'Certainly I want you around,' Mary declared after a speaking glance at Nathan's father, grinning in the shadows from his corner of the chaise. 'Nathan, you are a delight. It's just that you have a journey and I have a journey and they are not one and the same.'

The boy nodded. '*I* couldn't have sprung Da from the magistrate last night,' he told her simply. He leaned close to her and whispered, 'I don't think he would have visited the Everetts, either.'

'I was glad to help,' she whispered back, 'but you are overdue in Dumfries.'

'Are we, Da?'

The captain shook his head. He took out the list again, tracing his finger down the page. 'Aha! Apple turnovers at the King's Arms in Knaresborough. That settles it. Besides, Mary Rennie, Knaresborough is on our way.'

All misgivings aside, Mary had to agree that the duck à l'orange at the Maiden's Prayers was far superior to any of the plain fare she was used to in Edinburgh. How the cook kept the duck both moist and crackling was probably a state secret. She needed no particular coaxing to try some of the ale that was the public house's other speciality. She drank enough of it to make her laugh at the pub's swinging sign, an old woman kneeling by her bed with a man peeking out from underneath it.

After an hour, Mary took Nathan upstairs to his room while Captain Rennie, encouraged by the ale, described Trafalgar to an interested audience. The Maiden's Prayers's excellence didn't extend above the ground floor. The rooms were small and spartan, with no chambers off private parlours. As usual, Captain Rennie was sufficiently intimidating to get a chamber with a larger bed, and a smaller room on the next floor up, even though the publican assured him that they could easily fit a truckle bed in the larger room for their son. No need for the man to know that Mary's room was the one up another flight.

Although they had been travelling in close quarters for four days, she felt a little embarrassment at even entering the chamber Nathan shared with his father. There wasn't any warming pan, so Nathan had no trouble convincing Mary to get into bed with him for as long as it took to read another page in the *Naval Chronicle*, which formed the boy's curious bedtime routine. When Mary had questioned it earlier, Ross had told her, 'It puts us both to sleep.'

Mary struggled to keep her eyes open as she read a column on the hails and farewells from Portsmouth and Plymouth, then a stifling article on the proper way to store victuals in the hold in tropical climes. When she finished the last dreary paragraph, Nathan slumbered beside her, his head resting against her bosom.

She kissed his forehead and got out of bed, pulling the coverlet high around his neck, because the room was so cold.

She stayed in the room a little longer, bracing herself for her solitary bed upstairs, which she knew would never warm up. The captain had already arranged his shaving gear on the bureau and there was a bottle of lemon cologne. She took a whiff, a little sad because she knew she was going to miss the Rennies after Knaresborough.

He had left his food list on the bureau. She opened it and looked for apple turnover at the King's Arms in Knaresborough. She found no turnovers of any sort, and no King's Arms, and her over-active conscience smote her soundly. Ross Rennie was just wasting his shore leave when he could be in Dumfries with his sister's family. It was time to pull the plug on such good intentions, however kindly meant. She had tried before, tried several times, in fact, but she meant it now.

Mary sat for a long time on the narrow bed upstairs, wondering why on earth she had let herself be talked into chasing after fruitcake in the first place, and then succumbing to Captain Rennie's insistence on accompanying her on such a silly errand. True, she was pretty certain she loved him, but once she had given herself that stern talking-to a few nights back, she had stifled the matter.

The bed was as chilly as she had feared. Mary removed only her dress and shoes and put her cloak on the coverlet, wishing for a warming pan. She couldn't help but think of the hour she had shared her bed in Skowcroft with the captain. She certainly hadn't been bold enough to put her bare feet on his legs, but she had slid her feet as close as she dared, enjoying the little warmth. *Heavens, Mary, stop it*, she scolded herself. *Think of something else!*

Mary thought about the United States, wondering if a brand-spanking-new country would employ a female banking clerk somewhere. She had a little money from her father's estate and Uncle Samuel had kindly put it to work in his banking firm. In another year or so, there might be sufficient to provide passage to North America. She knew a little about bookkeeping and was willing to learn.

She held her eyes closed long enough to actually fall asleep.

When Mary woke up, the sky wasn't beginning to lighten yet. A few minutes sufficed to render her tidy and write a short note to push under the door on the floor below. She thanked them both for their escort, assured them she could manage Knaresborough and wished them Happy Christmas.

The taproom was dark, so she did not have to explain herself to the publican. Last night, she had overheard him tell another patron that the Royal Mail left from a public house on Edgecombe Street, but two streets away. Snow still fell, but her travelling case was light. She travelled the short distance in time to secure herself a seat on the Royal Mail, leaving at sunrise, and a cup of tea and a roll.

Knaresborough wasn't so far. With any luck, she would be on her way to Edinburgh by tomorrow, mission accomplished. She hated to think how disappointed Nathan might be, but she knew he would be more upset than his father. Captain Rennie would probably chalk the whole thing up to a little detour on his well-deserved shore leave. By spring, he wouldn't give the matter a thought.

They left town as the sun rose behind the bulk of York Minster. With an ache in her heart, Mary knew down to the last memory just how much she was going to miss both Rennies. Apple turnovers at the King's Arms? There was no such place. Drat the man and his wardroom list.

Chapter Nineteen

'Da, she's pulled a runner on us.'

Ross's head felt too large for his body. Nathan's words seem to pummel him from a great distance. He touched his eyes with tentative fingers, certain they were bulging from their sockets. He resolved right then to never touch spirits again, especially since he thought his son had shouted that Mary had given them the slip.

No, no, Nathan couldn't have shouted, not if the look on his face was any indication. Tears slid down his face as his son mourned silently. In one of her rare bursts of candour, Mrs Pritchert had written to him once that for days after his frigate sailed back to the Channel Fleet, Nathan would just sit by his window, weeping in silence. 'I give him time to grieve,' she had written, 'and then it's back to our lives.'

But watching his father come and go was Nathan's life, Ross realised, as he looked at his son, still dressed in his nightshirt, standing by the bed they had shared, when Captain Rennie had finally dragged himself into it. With a wince—all his parts ached—Ross pulled back the coverlets, holding them high as an invitation. With a sigh, Nathan joined him again.

'How do you know she's gone?' Ross asked. He wiped Nathan's eyes with the pillow slip. 'Surely you didn't go above deck—upstairs—in just your nightshirt?'

'It was still dark,' his son said. 'No one saw me, Da. I just didn't think she was in there. I peeked inside.'

He paused, as though unwilling to unburden himself. Ross wondered how much of his young life he kept bottled inside. He knew Mrs Pritchett was an estimable woman, but Nathan was not her boy. He also knew how little acquainted he was with his own child. By the same token, he knew in his bones that Cousin Mary understood Nathan. Call it a knack. Nathan might be his son, but Mary Rennie had the surer touch.

'What should we do, Son?' he asked.

'Follow her to Knaresborough.'

Ross tried once more. 'She made it pretty plain we weren't to follow.'

'Da!' Nathan made no effort to disguise his bare pleading. 'Don't you want to go, too?'

The fact was, he did. 'Very well. Still…she'll think we're managing her.'

'She won't,' his son replied. 'She likes me a lot.'

'I believe she does.' Ross's reward was a relieved smile.

They set out in the distant backwash of the Royal Mail, easy enough to follow at first. As the weather worsened, his own vehicle moved slower. Amused, and a little exasperated that he had listened to his son, Ross looked out the window at the white world around them. Knaresborough couldn't be more than eight miles away now.

He couldn't help but think of patrolling Arctic waters to keep the Danes in check, during their enforced alliance with Napoleon. He remembered snow on the deck and powder monkeys scampering about and throwing snowballs, when the work was done—if it ever was on a frigate.

'Does Mrs Pritchett allow snowballs?'

Nathan shook his head. 'She says I'll catch my death and won't you be disappointed.' He gave his father a kind look. 'Besides, Da, it doesn't snow much in Plymouth.'

'You've never built a snowman?'

Nathan gave his father a cheery smile. 'Not yet.'

'Then you're an optimist.'

'I could be,' Nathan said after a moment's thought. 'That depends on what an optimist is.'

'Someone who thinks the best of all situations.'

His son considered the matter some more, then brightened. 'I believe I am. After all, I just know Mary will be glad to see us.'

They travelled even slower, then finally stopped. Ross watched out the nearly frost-covered window as the postilion dismounted stiffly. He shook the snow off and trudged in front of the horses, grabbing them by their bridles. The other postboy hopped off to help him. After less than a mile they stopped again.

'Where away?' Ross asked.

Tom Preston pointed. Ross left the chaise and peered into the swirling flakes. The familiar colour and shape of the Royal Mail materialised, barely visible and motionless.

Ross returned to the chaise. 'Nathan, I believe you have your wish. Take a look.'

His son surprised him. He peered out, then leaped from the chaise, running towards the mail coach, calling Mary's name.

His son might have surprised him, but strangely, Mary didn't. The coach door opened and there was Mary, barely waiting for the coachman standing by the road to pull down the step. Ross saw that fine pair of ankles he had admired a day or two ago, then his son grabbed her around the waist.

He wasn't sure what she would do. To his relief, she laughed out loud, returned his hug, then stooped a little and put her forehead against Nathan's. His scamp of a son kissed her cheek, then towed her back to the post chaise through the deepening snow.

Ross had an inkling what she would say, and she didn't disappoint.

'Captain Rennie, there is no Knaresborough and apple turnovers on your infamous list. You continue to waste valuable shore leave with me.'

'My son insisted.'

'*You* did not,' she pointed out in her matter-of-fact way, reinforcing his belief that Mary Rennie was an honest soul not easily bamboozled. 'I have the situation in hand,' she added. When he just smiled, she was frank enough to add, 'But you don't believe me, Cousin.'

'When I tell you I would like to see this ring, I mean it,' he told her.

'Very well, then,' she grumbled, which he took as a good sign to send the footman for her travelling case on the mail coach and stow it where Ross felt it belonged in the post chaise.

'Well, here we are,' he said, sounding more inane than someone's geriatric maiden aunt.

He could have saved his breath. Nathan and Mary were already rolling what was probably going to become the bottom half of a snowman. He watched as a child standing by her mother near the mail coach sidled closer and closer. Mary noticed the little girl and motioned to her. With an affirmative nod from her mother, she came through the snow in that lightfooted way of children and was soon involved in the second portion of snowman anatomy.

Ross smiled to see a child and then another standing in the open doorway of a nearby crofter's cottage. A wave and a beckon from Mary added them to the building crew.

He couldn't resist. A few deft pats and he had a snowball in hand, which he threw at Mary Rennie. It connected with her rump, which made her gasp and whirl around, then pelt him with a snow-ball of her own.

He should have known better; Mary had allies and he had none. Soon Ross was as snow-covered as his postilion, laughing at them.

After another salvo, Mary declared a truce and her crew went back to work. Ross brushed off his boat cloak and put his hat back in the chaise for safe keeping.

'Beg pardon, Captain?'

Ross turned to his postilion, who stood with his hand on his son's shoulder. The young man looked pinched and cold. 'We're not going anywhere, are we?' Ross asked.

'No matter how close Knaresborough is, not to-night, sir.' He indicated the crofter's cottage. 'You might want to see if you three can bed down there for the night.'

'What about you?'

The post rider squeezed his son's shoulders. 'We'll manage.'

'Let's go together, Preston.'

Ross put on his fore-and-aft hat again, smil-ing to himself. He had never tried to intimidate a crofter with maritime power before. This shore leave had turned into something more than he had bargained for.

The crofter proved amenable to Captain Rennie's petition for lodging, even before Ross offered a tidy sum of money that the man likely never saw. With a frown of concentration, he looked at the coins in Ross's outstretched hand and picked up a few.

'That'll do, Captain. Any more and my wife will scold me for being a thief.'

'One more,' Ross insisted, impressed with the man's honesty. 'My postilion and his boy need a place, too.'

'They'll have one here, if they don't mind sleeping with my own pack upstairs in the loft.' The crofter looked at the setting sun. 'Cold tonight. We'll all stay warm close together.' He dared a little familiarity. 'You and your lady can cuddle right good tonight, sir.'

As he walked back to the chaise, Ross asked himself why he never bothered to correct anyone's misconceptions.

Mary took the news of the change of travelling plans with that equanimity he was coming to appreciate with each day passing. 'Do you think the mail coach will travel on?' she asked the postilion.

'He might try, mum, but I doubt he'll get far, even were Knaresborough just over the hill. If I may presume, you're better off here.'

''Pears he's going to try,' the postilion said as the coachman whistled up his tired team. 'I give him ten minutes before he's bogged down.' He turned to Ross, deferential appreciation in his voice. 'Thank'ee, sir, for not making us go on.'

'It was too much,' Ross replied. 'Knaresborough can wait.' And it could. He liked the idea of another evening with Mary Rennie. He watched her as she walked back to the snowman, which was getting stunted twig arms now. Her hand rested on Nathan's shoulder and his arm circled her waist. He held his breath with the loveliness of it all when she leaned down and kissed the top of his head. Nathan put both arms around her then and they just stood together in the falling snow.

He knew that Mrs Pritchert was kind and loving to his son, but as he watched Nathan and Mary, he knew there was something more. It pained him that he had become so inured to the harshness of his own life that he had trouble thinking in terms of peace or just the simple things that constituted everyday living. And here was Mary, showing father and son alike the homely little blessings that were either a by-product of peace, or what happens when ordinary folk are allowed to pursue their lives on a much smaller stage than his own.

He envied them.

Hoping he wasn't obvious, Ross watched Mary during the simple meal the crofter's wife prepared. The kitchen was tiny, but somehow there was room for Callie Blankenship and Mary to work together. Callie started shy, but the two of them were laughing together before the onion-and-potato soup made it to the table. There weren't enough bowls for them all and they had to take turns with spoons. Somehow, no one was embarrassed. He had the strongest suspicion that the loaf of bread passed around as everyone took a chunk would have lasted the family an entire week. When it came to him, Ross made a mental note to leave a few more coins in some out-of-the-way place that the honest crofter wouldn't find until they were gone.

He began to think his cousin had blossomed in the past few days, even though he hadn't known her long. As he admired the efficient way the women worked in the kitchen, he tried to remember her in Carlisle—pale, quiet, too self-conscious to look him in the eyes more than once or twice. This Mary was rosy from the heat of the kitchen. Her hair must have come undone during the exertion of building a snowman. During supper preparations, Callie had tied it back for her with some twine. The effect was homely and workaday, but he began to feel that tightening below his belly again, reminding him he was a post captain, to be sure, but a man, as well.

Absurd. Tomorrow would see them in Knaresborough, the fruitcake in hand. Once his curiosity was satisfied, they would head north-west to Dumfries and Mary north to Edinburgh. Once he was assured of peace, there would be leisure to look around for a stepmother for Nathan. Someone just like Mary Rennie would be nice, but for the life of him, he could not relinquish that blonde, tall lady of his younger dreams.

Is that really it? he asked himself. *Other men have found wives in wartime. What was the matter with him?* Maybe when peace came, he could think about the matter.

Chapter Twenty

Davy and Callie Blankenship evicted their daughters from the tiny room beside their own and sent the girls up the ladder to the loft after supper, full of admonition about not teasing their little brothers and keeping the postilion and his son awake. The cold settled in almost as soon as the darkness.

The Prestons returned from the barn after seeing to their four horses. Mary could tell they were ready to insist all over again that the barn would be good enough for them, but Ross wasn't listening. His firmly stated 'I'm not accustomed to argument' ended the matter. Father and son went up the ladder, too. Ross had turned away by then, but Mary noticed the grateful look the postilion bestowed on the post captain.

She prepared the bed for herself, ready to share with Nathan, but was not surprised when he chose the loft, where general merrymaking seemed the order of the evening. Callie Blankenship had kindly provided Mary with a cloth-covered stone. As she started towards the equally tiny room she shared with her husband, Callie turned her attention to the captain still sitting in the front room. Mary could tell she wanted to say something to him, but there was a gulf of shyness and social order that must have felt too wide to span, even though the Blankenships had opened their home to strangers.

Mary put out her hand to Callie. 'Do you want to ask him something?' she whispered, determined not to tread on the woman's dignity. 'Here, let's ask him together.'

Callie flashed her a grateful smile. 'Will he mind?'

'Oh, no,' Mary assured her. 'He's quite human.'

'Mercy, I didn't mean…'

'I know.'

Ross seemed involved in that inward conversation she had noticed about him. Gently, she put her hand on his shoulder, feeling almost as shy as Callie Blankenship. She felt him tense, then relax when she did nothing more than pat his shoulder. Maybe it was brazen of her. To be sure, it was, but in the past few days of their acquaintance, she found him less and less majestic and fearsome with each day and more a man to be cared for, because he received so little care from any source. How hard it must be to be a post captain in the Royal Navy.

'Ross, if you have a moment for Callie Blankenship...' she began, nearly speaking in his ear.

'Certainly I have.' He stood and, while he did not bow to someone so common, he inclined his head. 'My dear, you are an excellent, impromptu hostess. What may I do for you?'

So much praise seemed to fluster the crofter's wife. For one small moment, Mary feared the woman would burst into tears, or, at the least, cover her face with her apron, as Mary had seen other simple women do when tasked.

Callie was made of sterner stuff. After several deep breaths, she cleared her throat. 'Captain, sir, I have a brother who went to sea.'

She couldn't say anything else for a while. Mary turned her head to allow the woman a measure of privacy, which only brought the captain into her view. She turned away again; his face was a curious mixture of pain and uncertainty, almost as though he had seen a whole roster of Callie Blankenships. It was as though he knew what she was going to ask and he had no answer. Oddly, also, she felt his pain and knew she had no consolation for either of them.

The captain indicated a stool, and their hostess sat down. Mary moved to sit on a stool beside her, but Ross took her hand and guided her to the short bench where he sat. They were hip to hip and he put his arm around her waist. She knew it was no pretence, to make the Blankenships think they were husband and wife and avoid an awkward situation. The trembling of his arm told her worlds about his own disquiet. It might have been Skowcroft and the vicarage all over again.

'You have not heard from him.' It was a statement and a kind one.

Callie shook her head. 'He was sixteen when he went to sea ten years ago. Mam died when he was a wee babe and I had the raising of Tommy Watts. Crops were poor and times were hard.' She shrugged. 'He thought the navy might be better. Thought he might at least eat regular.'

'He never wrote?'

'None of us can read or write, Captain,' she said, her eyes down. After a moment to command herself, she looked him full in the face. 'How can I find out how he is or where?'

The captain was silent a long time. When a knot popped in the fireplace, he seemed to recall where he was. 'Mrs Blankenship, I can enquire at the Navy Board. Thomas Watts? Has he a middle name? A birth date?'

'No middle name. As for his birthdate, I don't know.' Callie's embarrassment was unmistakable. 'I packed him some bread and turnips one morning and he set off walking south.'

'My dear, do you even know if he reached the seacoast?' Ross asked. His arm behind Mary's back trembled more, so she threw caution to the winds and rested her hand on his leg. He gave her a smile that didn't approach his eyes and only increased her disquiet.

'I do know that,' Callie replied with some triumph. 'He had a friend write a letter. We took it to the vicar and he read it.' She sighed. 'I had the vicar write back, but I never heard anything.' She looked at Ross, expectation in her eyes, as though he held the secret of navy rosters.

'It's been a long war,' Ross said finally. 'I don't even know the number of ships in the navy, and believe me, I am but a small cog in Admiralty machinery.' He grasped her hand. 'I pledge to you that I will ask. You never know, madam. He may just walk back onto your property next week.'

She nodded and rose, the expectation gone from her eyes. 'I've been looking for the past ten years. Not a day goes by...' Her voice trailed off. She dropped a little curtsy and went to her room.

'Do you think she'll see him again?' Mary whispered. 'If I had a brother, I don't think I could bear not knowing here he was.'

'You'd be amazed what you can bear,' he said. 'I failed that woman.' Without another comment, he went outside, answering her question without words.

Uncertain what to do, Mary stood in the front room. Deep cold had already settled in for the night and the captain wasn't wearing his boat cloak. *Why must you take on everyone's woes?* struggled with the realisation that once they arrived in Knaresborough, the journey would be over and none of this would be her business, if it even was her business now. She knew the supreme unlikelihood that any man would take her into his confidence again. For one irrational moment, she hated Mrs Morison for so calmly sending her on an adventure.

'It's war.'

Mary turned around in surprise. She hadn't

heard the door open, but there Ross stood, his expression so bleak that she wasted not a second in going to him with her arms outstretched. He was cold, but he wrapped his arms around her, too.

'You worried me,' she said into his chilly uniform coat.

He chuckled and she thought she heard some mirth this time. 'Mary, you're a looby.' He sighed. 'Or more, I confess. War has ground me down and frazzled me until I am not fit company. I can't lie and cajole our good hostess.'

'She never expected you to,' Mary said softly.

'I think she did, on some level,' he replied. He yawned. 'It's late and I'm cold and tired. Mary, this is so irregular as to be unacceptable, but do you trust me enough to let me just lie down with you?'

'We already did that a few days ago,' she reminded him.

'I suppose we did, *Cuz*,' he said, as if adding a distant relationship made the prospect unexceptionable. He glanced above, where childish voices still chattered, although softly now and with a drowsiness that indicated sleep fast approaching. 'There isn't room above deck. D'ye mind, Mary?'

'I do not,' she replied firmly, then added. 'I will never feel compromised because I trust you.'

'That's a burden,' he said drily, which calmed her.

'And there is the expression "needs must when the devil drives". Just let me prepare for bed first. I'll lie down closest to the wall.'

'No, you won't,' he protested. 'That's the coldest place.'

'That may be, but I'll arrive there first and you daren't dislodge me, or I will cry foul.'

Ross sat down again when she went in the other room, which had no more than a curtain for a door. He contemplated all the Blankenships squeezed into such a small house and wondered that the mother and father ever felt enough privacy to produce so many children. 'Needs must, I suppose,' he murmured out loud, thinking suddenly of his own body's needs. He knew without ever asking that his midshipmen—and probably his lieutenants—could never imagine passion from their captain.

He shouldn't have looked, but he could see Mary's preparations for bed through a slit in the curtain. A gentleman would have looked away, but he was sour and feeling old.

She stood a moment and he wondered if she contemplated disrobing completely or leaving her clothing on, the better to stay warm. He could have told her that so small a bed meant they would warm each other soon, but he was at least wise— or sly—enough to make no commentary through the curtain.

To his pleasure, she decided the dress must go, followed by the petticoat, and what he assumed was a corset. Since it was so cold, she disrobed quickly. When her stockings came off—good God, but she had shapely legs—she hopped from one foot to the other until he nearly laughed. She was down to her chemise now. He suddenly didn't feel old and sour, because she began to stir his body. He tried to summon some immunity, because she did trust him, but failed in the attempt.

I am on a lee shore, he thought miserably, wanting to look away, but unwilling or unable. There she stood in her shimmy. He suspected she had freckles on her shoulders, which he found oddly provocative, he who had bedded women around the globe with skin creamy white, olive, *café au lait* and dark brown.

Look away, you idiot, he told himself, then ignored his own injunction. To his disappointment or his relief—he couldn't decide—she stopped with her shimmy and pulled on her nightgown. She was in bed in a minute. The mattress was straw and noisy, so he knew suddenly that her virtue was safe. This fact should have relieved him, but it did not. He wanted her.

You had better think a little, he scolded himself. Maybe it wasn't Mary he wanted, but just a woman. Aha, that was it. He could defer that particular itch and scratch it when Nathan was back in Mrs Pritchert's care and he had a day or two to visit Plymouth's stews. Hadn't he promised himself that when he was good and certain that Napoleon was gone for good, he would look around for a wife?

He crossed his fingers and hoped Mary would extinguish the candle. He didn't need any highlighting of his current dilemma. Someone would think he was a schoolboy. 'Good Lord, Ross,' he scolded himself, looking down.

She blew out the candle, and he heard the rattle and whoosh as she settled into the straw mattress. Another minute or two rendered him less obvious. He wrapped his boat cloak around himself to be certain, grateful for the shadows.

Mary lay on her side, looking at the wall. He took off his boat cloak and laid it on top of her. 'We might need it if the night grows more frigid,' he said.

He took off his garments except for his small-clothes, then wrestled off his wooden leg, cursing far too fluently when the buckles caught on the string of his underpants. He heard a rustle as Mary turned over and sat up. She released the buckle from the tangled ties, laughing softly, which helped his current frame of mind not at all.

'See here, *Cuz*,' she said, emphasising the word as he had done earlier to her. 'I know you're not related to that brother who was our family's black sheep and I am the daughter of a vicar. Mind your tongue.'

He couldn't help but laugh, which made Mary hush him with her finger to his lips, except that it was dark and she poked his eye. He swore again; she apologised.

He raised his half-leg to remove the wadding, and Mary unrolled it for him without asking. She touched the stitched-over fold of skin as the surgeon used to do, briefly and clinically.

'You've been on it too long,' she whispered.

'I am on it too long most days,' he replied. 'When I get to Dumfries and my sister's house, I intend to stump about for a while on crutches. Her husband is a surgeon and I know he has a pair. Don't tell Admiralty, but I'm an invalid.'

'Oh, you are not,' she replied, her voice as soft as his. 'You just need to take better care of your parts.'

You can't imagine, he thought irreverently. 'Go to sleep, Mary. Cousin.' Great gobs of Boney's phlegm, but he was an idiot.

She lay down again on the noisy straw, wiggled her hips to carve out a nice depression and sighed the sigh of someone as tired as he was. He lay down beside her. True, they had done this very thing the night he drank too much at the vicarage, but something had changed for him. And for her? He knew there wasn't that much foolhardiness in the world for him to ask her.

As the mattress crunched and rustled, Ross composed himself for sleep in the tiny space allotted them. They were decorously back to back, until—horrors—Mary turned over and punched her pillow, as though trying to subdue it. 'Do you suppose those people on the mail coach made it into Knaresborough or are freezing to death on the road?'

He couldn't help himself. He laughed, then put his hand over his mouth when he heard the mattress rustle in the next room. He didn't want to wake the Blankenships and whispered that to his own bed partner.

'I'm sorry,' she whispered back, the contrition evident. She turned over again.

He lay there, knowing he would never sleep, especially when the Blankenships's motions in the straw next door settled into a certain rhythm he was quite familiar with, even though it had been a few years. He couldn't imagine what Mary must be thinking. He hoped devoutly that she was completely in the dark.

She started to shake with laughter, which made him suspect she was a bit more worldly than he imagined. 'Tell me, Ross, have you ever been in a more uncomfortable situation?' she whispered.

You have no idea, he wanted to say, and murmured something—what, he wasn't certain. He chose discretion, which was more than the Blankenships chose, if Callie's low moan was any indication. He felt his face go fiery and his loins began to gather their own heat again.

Davey Blankenship was a study in efficiency, apparently. His own sigh followed Callie's effort and then all was silent in the next room. In a few minutes, Davey started to snore.

'I, uh, deeply regret the education you're getting,' he whispered to Mary, who thumped him.

She shouldn't have done that, in the greater

scheme of things. He couldn't help himself, not with the muted chorus of lovemaking next door on his mind and settling lower via some artery or other. Ross turned over, which meant Mary did, too. She was in his arms in a moment, and God Almighty, wasn't she soft? She had no skill at all, which hardly surprised him, but he could not fault the masterful way she ran her hand so gently down his back.

He weighed the matter a moment, then touched her breast. Her nightgown was heavy flannel, so he unbuttoned it and touched her skin this time. His hand went to her bare shoulder next, because he always liked the way women's shoulders felt—smooth, rounded and fragile. He was mindful this was Mary Rennie and not a white woman, or a brown woman or an olive woman whose names he never knew. She wasn't even Inez, his wife so briefly, and certainly not the lady of his list.

Her hand had strayed down as far as his waist, but no farther. With fingers that shook, he started on the ties to his smallclothes. He had skin, too, and he wanted her hands on him.

'Da?'

He stopped and held his breath. Mary did the same.

'Da?' his son asked again.

Ross was tongue-tied, but Mary was not. She raised up on her elbow. 'Nathan, can't you sleep?' she asked, her voice soft and perfectly normal.

'Mary!' Nathan said, then lowered his voice. 'I'm glad you're here, too. I was feeling lonely up there.'

Mary chuckled. How in the world did she manage to sound so normal? Ross wondered. He relaxed and thought back to his own childhood, when he had done that very thing—crept to his parents' bed. Mirth swelled in him as he wondered just how many times he had interrupted them.

'The loft is full of people,' he murmured. 'How could you be lonely?'

'None of them was you or Mary,' Nathan replied, with the indisputable logic of a child.

He had no proof against that and knew he should not have been fondling Mary, anyway, not after he assured her she could trust him. He lifted the covers. 'In you get,' he said. 'Crawl over me and get in the middle.' *It's safer that way*, he thought. *Maybe between now and tomorrow, I'll think of a way to apologise to Mary.*

Chapter Twenty-One

Filled with remorse, Mary edged as close as she could to the wall. The traitor straw rustled, and she wanted to bury herself so deep that no one would ever find her. *Stupid, stupid,* she berated herself, *You told him you trusted him, but never thought to wonder if you trusted yourself!*

She flinched when Nathan patted her back, then reminded herself that Ross's child was not part of the problem. Somehow between now and tomorrow morning, if the straw hadn't swallowed her, she would have to face Captain Rennie and apologise. The only relief she could see was that surely they would be in Knaresborough tomorrow, the last fruitcake recovered, the ring in hand and both of them heading on their own journeys.

Nathan patted her again. She turned around to face him, grateful that the room was too dark to see his father. 'Yes, Nathan?' she asked, hoping her voice didn't quaver overmuch.

'D'ye mind if I'm here?'

'Heavens, no, Nathan,' she told him, touching his face. 'We're tight as whelks in a basket, but it's a cold night.' She kissed his forehead. 'Besides, I like you. Go to sleep now.'

Mary patted his shoulder, and Ross's hand covered hers. He gave it a little squeeze, then released it. She was so embarrassed that tears started in her eyes. She waited a few minutes until Nathan's breath slowed and became regular. 'I am so ashamed of myself,' she whispered. 'Please... I'll get on the mail coach tomorrow and you and Nathan can continue your own journey. Please.'

'We'll think about it in the morning,' he whispered back. 'Besides, didn't you say that all the people in the mail coach have probably frozen to death?'

She couldn't help smiling a little, until the enormity of what she had done came back like cold water in her face. 'Please, just let me go to Knaresborough,' she pleaded. 'I'm so ashamed.'

Ross was silent. She couldn't possibly see how he could be asleep, but he wasn't talking. She turned towards the wall again and rebuttoned her nightgown, visiting again the feel of his fingers on her breasts. Somewhere deep down, she knew it would never happen again.

The thought had kept Mary awake most of the night. She had discovered there was nothing worse than trying to lie still and breathe evenly in pretence. Maybe she had slept. All she knew was that when morning came, her eyes felt gritty and she was as cross as two sticks.

She prayed Ross would not still be in the bed and he was not. Nathan had curled up close to her, which soothed her heart. It was enough to know that even though she had behaved foolishly last night, Ross's son had no knowledge of the heavy business and still admired her.

That she was going to miss him was obvious to her. She knew that until last night, it wouldn't have been improper of her to ask Ross if he would allow her to write to Nathan in Plymouth. She had no idea what response he would give if she asked now and decided not to put the matter to the test.

She waited quietly until the noises of a small crofter's holding waking up chased away slumber from a tired boy. Nathan opened his eyes, yawned and snuggled close for another minute. Her arm went around him naturally and it was the world's easiest thing to kiss his temple.

'When it's cold out, do you ever just want to stay in bed for ever, Mary?' he asked.

'All the time,' she assured him. *Especially now*, she thought, with equal measures of rue and remorse. *I'd do nearly anything to avoid looking Captain Rennie in the eye.*

The matter couldn't be avoided, especially after the captain glanced in the room and ordered his son to 'get topside and handsomely now'. Funny how he used nautical terms for the commonest event. Funny how he couldn't look her in the eye, either. Maybe he was as embarrassed as she was. She prayed the mail coach remained where she had last seen it.

With the mail coach in mind, she dressed quickly, once Nathan had left the room, and edged out of the house, not looking right or left. The snow had stopped and some enterprising soul had shovelled a path from house to barn. She found both Prestons in the barn, harnessing their horses. They looked surprised when she asked them to stop and let her off, if they happened to pass the mail coach, but they nodded and asked no questions.

When she returned to the cottage, everyone was

sitting down to breakfast and eating out of the pot, sharing spoons. Callie gestured to her and she joined her hostess, taking her turn at the porridge.

No one had much to say, but Callie tried. 'Are ye spending Christmas in Knaresborough?' she asked.

'Edinburgh,' Mary said at the same time Ross said, 'Dumfries.'

Their hostess looked from one to the other, puzzled, but made no comment. Mary felt her face go even redder. She glanced up to see Captain Rennie regarding her with a frown. She blushed all over again to think how eagerly she had found her way into his arms and lodged not one single complaint when he unbuttoned her nightgown. *I am a scandal to the Rennies*, she thought in misery. Reminding herself that Ross was a Rennie, too, did nothing to soothe her mind.

When breakfast ended, she went into the little room to retrieve her travelling case. Ross must have left the nest of coins on the pillow. She added a few of her own, after making certain she had mail-coach fare to Edinburgh. She turned to leave the room and Ross stood in the doorway. Tears of humiliation started in her eyes when he took hold of her shoulder.

'Please don't flagellate yourself over our misdemeanor,' he said quietly after a glance over his shoulder. 'Blame it on close quarters.'

She nodded and pushed past him. After a farewell to the Blankenships, Mary seated herself in the post chaise, dreading more close quarters until they could stop at the mail coach. Nathan bounced inside and sat beside her. He leaned against her, which did nothing to restore her equanimity.

'We're going to find the ring in the fruitcake,' he announced.

'*I* am,' Mary informed him gently. 'You and your father are long overdue in Dumfries. I know I have been saying that over and over, but I never meant it more than now.'

Nathan gave her a look she could only call mutinous, but he kept his peace. Mary knew enough about little boys to reckon that this particular one enjoyed some success in using such an expression on Mrs Pritchert. Such a thought furnished her the only amusement of the morning.

She watched through the window as Captain Rennie spoke with Tom Preston. There appeared to be an argument, which furnished Mary with the opinion that Nathan had inherited the mutinous glance from his father. Preston appeared to be standing his ground, which impressed Mary. In another moment, Ross had turned away and opened the door to the chaise.

'Mary, you are a trial,' was all he said as he sat down and gazed out the window.

She gazed out the other window as they set off. Silence reigned supreme until Nathan nudged her.

'It was something I did, wasn't it?' he asked in a low voice.

Both of them looked at the boy.

'Never!' Mary declared at the same time Ross said, 'Certainly not.'

'I should have stayed in the loft last night,' the boy said with a sigh. 'You didn't like being crowded.'

'I didn't mind,' Mary said and put her arm around Nathan. 'We all stayed warm together. I'm just in the dumps because…because I have to go back to Edinburgh once I find the ring, and England's not so bad.'

Ross chuckled at that. 'A ten-year-old's logic,' he told Mary in a little sidewise comment not meant for Nathan, which made her smile, too, but only a little. 'And I'm in the dumps because I'm tired of travelling,' he told his son.

That's a set down, Mary thought, then tried to assure herself that no one had forced him to follow the trail of the circulating fruitcake.

To her infinite relief, the mail coach came in sight a mile later. All appeared to be well, with the horses prancing a bit and stretching out their necks as if eager for movement. The passengers stood close by, apparently none the worse for wear. A shire road crew from Knaresborough must have smoothed some of yesterday's storm to the side of the highway, because the mail had to get through.

Just as she had asked, the post chaise slowed and came to a stop. Mary got out when the younger Preston opened the door and dropped the step. He took her travelling satchel from the boot and followed her to the mail coach.

'Well, miss! You forfeited a chilly evening huddling with everyone else and listening to one man's story of the Orient, and another's glimpse of Russia,' the coachman of the Royal Mail said, as cheerful as a man would probably be, with a coach full of riders wishing him to the devil and themselves at their delayed destinations.

She handed her luggage to him, and he stowed it and helped her aboard. She steeled herself and did not look behind her.

It hardly mattered. In a moment, Nathan clambered on board, followed by his father, who appeared to have found permanent residence under a thundercloud. 'Nathan,' was all he said, but the delivery was everything. Mary felt her skin tighten.

'I want to ride the mail coach with Mary. She will be alone.' He spoke as firmly as his father.

'The coach is full,' Ross argued, his face reddening. Obviously, his repertory with small boys didn't include reasoning with them without raising his voice in front of perfect strangers. 'She won't be alone. *I* will be alone, if you ride with Mary.'

Nathan only cuddled closer to Mary. 'Mrs Pritchert says captains are always alone, so it shouldn't bother you, Da. I'll see you in Knaresborough.'

Startled, Mary glanced at the captain. His thunderous look had given way to one of infinite sadness. 'Nathan, you should—' she began.

Captain Rennie cut her off. 'No need, Miss Rennie,' he said so formally, trying to maintain dignity even though his son had wounded him. She knew it was unintentional, but Nathan's careless words had struck a nerve. 'I'll see you both soon enough.' He raised his hat to them and stepped away from the mail coach.

She watched, saddened, as he gave the coach-man some money, then returned alone to the post chaise. There was no lift to his shoulders, no pur-pose in his stride. He suddenly looked like what he was—an ageing sea captain with a limp.

'Oh, Nathan,' she said. 'I believe you hurt his feelings.'

'I didn't mean to.' It was a small voice from a small boy. 'Mrs Pritchert does say that about him,' he added in his own defence.

'He wants to spend this holiday with you, not me,' she said as the coachman snapped his whip and they started off.

Let this journey end, Mary thought as she winked back tears. She had no desire to cry in front of one salesmen, a clergyman and a farmer. Her head ached and her heart was sore. She was cured of adventures for ever.

Ross was alone and he didn't care for it one iota. Trust Mrs Pritchert to understand captains. For twenty-four years he had served his royal sover-eign on all seas and in all weathers. His ships had worked death on the enemy from the Baltic to

Chesapeake Bay. He had fought ship-to-ship engagements and killed his share of the enemy face to face. His leg had been detached from him and thrown overboard in the Mediterranean and he had consigned his crew to their own watery ends in all oceans.

This shore leave, which had begun as a chance to visit a dear sister and renew his acquaintance with bone of his bone and flesh of his flesh, had turned into far more than he bargained for. If he was honest—and why not, since he was by himself?—he was ill equipped to handle anything that didn't involve a frigate and a crew. He was as useless as lubbers pressed onto his frigate against their will, because the navy was so desperately short of men in a war that ground on and on.

For years, he had harboured the secret delight of imagining himself married one day and perhaps living a gentrified life on an estate of his own. He had earned enough prize money for just such a scenario. He knew he would marry again because he had planned it out years ago. As he thought about the matter, he became uncomfortably aware that in all the terror of war, the woman with the blonde hair and exotic accent had burned herself into his brain like a brand. 'Go ahead and think it,' he murmured to himself. 'An obsession.' When the horrors of death surrounded him through countless sea battles, he had retreated inside his own head with that lovely lady, thinking of her instead of maimed limbs and bodies thrown overboard during battle, and throat-closing thirst surrounded by the water of distant oceans that no one could drink. She had become his curious retreat from the destruction that would have driven another captain insane; he had seen it happen.

Things had changed after Carlisle. Somewhere in the past week, he had begun to use Mary Rennie as a measuring stick, instead of his blonde lady with the beguiling accent. Some day he would have a wife who was refined, but not rarefied; clever, but not a bluestocking; nice to look at, but not someone who would spend all her time preening in front of a glass; kind to children, but not a pushover; pliable but not a woman to twist in the wind. What had happened to the beautiful lady of his dreams?

For some reason, as disloyal to his dream as it was, Providence had put him in the path of just such a measuring stick. He knew in the deepest part of him that the war was not over yet; it couldn't be. When it was, he might credit Mary with being his inadvertent model as he searched for a wife to make his more mature years comfortable. Inez had been a wife for a man of hot blood. His next wife, whoever she turned out to be, would cause him no grief or anxiety. After a generation of constant war, he had earned such a paragon.

Well and good, but since he was in an examining mood, his plan began to smack of the worst sort of self-serving claptrap. Service in King George's navy had turned him into an efficient killing machine. Beyond urges for women made sharp because men were so long away, it had taught him nothing about daily living on land.

In a way he could not understand, the lady of his list began to mock him. She had always been out of reach because she did not exist. He had clung to her ideal through an entire career at war, almost as though she were real. Was this whole business of war finally driving him mad?

And so he floundered.

Chapter Twenty-Two

Snow notwithstanding, the mail coach dropped them at the Tudor Rose before noon. Mary's head truly ached. In his own way, Nathan had been a comfort, leaning against her and then resting his head in her lap when he dozed. His presence throughout the whole journey from Carlisle had forcibly borne home to her that no one in Edinburgh ever touched her.

All this adventure had done was make her highly dissatisfied with her lot. Mary closed her eyes in weariness, knowing that wasn't entirely true. She had fallen in love with an aggravating man.

She had no particular illusions about men. Unlike Dina, she had never glamourised the male sex into something it was not. Her own innate sense of fair play informed her that men were probably as flighty and foolish as women, possessing no particular abundance of brains that the ladies couldn't own in equal shares. They probably even made just as many stupid decisions. Maybe more; it wasn't the ladies who started wars, except for perhaps poor Helen of Troy and her pretty face.

Somewhere between Cumberland sausage in Carlisle and porridge in the amorous Blankenships' cottage, she had decided that no one would do for her except Ross Rennie. He seemed to find the fruitcake expedition interesting enough to invest time and travel in it. She had wondered if she was in love with him, but had decided, practical woman, that whatever it was she felt would pass, especially after he started offering her advice about Canada. Someone truly interested in her would never suggest she move there.

Until last night—she felt her face grow red in remembrance—she hadn't experienced brains and common sense deserting her body simultaneously. With no urging, she would have given herself to him completely, she who was raised to know better. Thank God Nathan had interrupted them.

What if he hadn't? Without question, she would have been compromised. Perhaps the captain would have offered for her hand out of duty. He had never declared any love for her—far from it.

Several times he had mentioned Our Lady of the List, as he jokingly called her. But was he joking? Likely it would be someone lovely and possessed of her own income. It always came back to money.

'Bother it,' she murmured, which caused the farmer next to her to give her a sidelong glance before returning to his book.

Nathan smiled as the coach guard blew an extra flourish with his yard of tin, maybe because everyone, not just the passengers, was relieved to be in Knaresborough. The captain's post chaise waited at the public house. In fact, Tony Preston helped her from the mail coach.

'God's bones, miss, but the captain is in a foul mood,' he whispered.

'I told him and Nathan to go to Dumfries,' Mary said. 'I'm quite capable of finding Knaresborough by myself.'

As they walked to the chaise, Mary smiled to think of herself at the beginning of the fruitcake adventure, as she intended to call it—unsure of herself, a bit of an old maid. Everything had changed in Carlisle, and she knew she at least owed that to Captain Rennie. Maybe she really would find the courage to cross the ocean herself to North America. The matter would call for some contriving on her part, but she knew she could manage it in a few years, if her little nest egg continued to do well in Uncle Sam's counting house. She could thank Ross for that before they parted company. No, no, Captain Rennie. She probably should no longer think of him as Ross, even if he was a distant cousin dangling from some twig of the Rennie family tree.

'Where to, miss? The captain couldn't remember,' Tom Preston said, as he handed her into the vehicle after Nathan clambered in to greet his father.

'Number Twenty-five Corydon Circle.' She hoped it wasn't far.

It wasn't. The door to Number Twenty-five sported a Christmas wreath, reminding Mary that the festivity was only four days away now. She had not written to her aunt in more than a week. Those particular Rennies were probably wondering where she was. Two days on the mail coach would see her back in Edinburgh.

As Mary tumbled out her story to the butler who answered their summons, he seemed disinclined to interrupt his master somewhere in the bowels of the house until she mentioned Mr Tavish Maxfield of York, the previous owner of the fruitcake.

'Wait here in the hall, please,' he said, holding up one finger.

'He leaves us here in the hall,' Captain Rennie grumbled, the sound of ill usage high in his voice.

'He doesn't know us,' Mary said sensibly, which earned her a glare.

Mr Bartemus Whitney greeted them with a smile. He was dressed to go outdoors, so Mary explained the whole matter to him quickly.

'You have been sent on an expedition to save the world from tainted fruitcake?'

Put that way, Mary laughed. 'Aye, sir!' she told him, which made him smile wider and make some comment about her delightful accent. 'You're a lucky man, Captain,' he said to Ross Rennie, who merely nodded.

Mr Whitney spoke a few quiet words to his butler, who turned on his heel immediately, but did not offer to show them to the sitting room. 'You must forgive me, my dears, but I have an engagement that will not wait. 'Tis the season, after all.'

They exchanged just enough pleasantries—at least Mary did—to tide them over until the butler returned, bearing a familiar box, mailed weeks and weeks ago from Edinburgh. Mary looked closer.

The address had been changed several times, but it was the fruitcake.

The butler handed it to Mary, and she sighed with relief. 'Thank you, Mr Whitney. We'll not take another minute of your time.'

'Happy to help, my dear.' Mr Whitney leaned forwards confidentially. 'Before I received these letters and heard your knock on the door, I was all ready to send the fruitcake to my nephew serving in the army in Belgium. I say, do you think anyone actually *eats* fruitcake?'

To her relief—he had been so silent—Captain Rennie laughed. 'I doubt it supremely, sir,' he told Mr Whitney. 'I never do. Do you, Mary?'

She shook her head. 'I like to help Mrs Morison make it, but that is all. Belgium? That would have extended my adventure most amazingly.'

Mr Whitney gave her a questioning look, but the captain was already bowing and ushering Nathan ahead of him. It was time to leave. Mary thanked him again and clutched the well-travelled fruitcake to her. At the post chaise, she asked Preston to return her to the public house.

'Not so fast, Miss Rennie,' the captain said. 'We've earned a look at that ring, wouldn't you say?'

'I suppose you have,' she replied in what she

thought approximated a cheerful tone. No need for either father or son to know how dreadfully she was going to miss them. The adventure was over. 'Where should we go for what I've taken to calling the exhumation?'

'Mum, we passed a church two streets ago,' the post rider said. 'If you don't mind...I believe it's a Methodist chapel.'

The vestibule was empty, which suited Mary, because there was no need to explain herself to the minister, who must have headed to the rectory for nuncheon. After moving aside a pile of improving tracts, she spread out the handkerchief from her reticule. She took the fruitcake from the wooden box and set it on the handkerchief. Such a lot of trouble this had been, Mary decided, as she explained that she would dismantle it bit by bit, then sift through each handful.

'I'm hungry,' Nathan said.

'If you don't mind crumbs, you can try it,' Mary said as she took a folding knife from her reticule.

'Ready for everything, eh, Mary?' the captain said, eyeing the little penknife.

No. I'm not ready to say goodbye to you, she thought, but nodded. She carefully quartered the dark and dense cake, from which fumes of good Barbados rum rose. 'Now I separate it piece by piece. That's what I've done with the other three. I am ever so careful.'

She invited Nathan to take a handful of crumbs. 'What do you think?' she asked, as he chewed and swallowed. He made a face. 'Oh, is that so?' she teased, as she separated another quarter, searched, and then another quarter.

'This is it, then,' she said, picking up the remaining quarter. Even more careful, she separated the nuts and orange peel and citron and dried cherries, ready to see the little ring with leaves carved into it, the one belonging to Good Queen Bess, if Mr Algernon Page knew what he was talking about.

She searched the last quarter and searched again, as her heart started to pound and her face grew warm. Nothing. Taking a deep breath, she went through each of the other quarters again, sifted and searching. Her face on fire with frustration and embarrassment, she couldn't raise her eyes to either Captain Rennie or Nathan.

'I don't understand...' she said finally. 'This is the fourth and final fruitcake. I searched the others so carefully.'

The silence in the vestibule was so thick she

could have weighed it on a scale. The captain was absolutely silent. All she heard was his breathing as it grew deeper and heavier. She finally raised her eyes to his face, only to see him turn away from her.

'Come, Nathan, we're overdue in Dumfries,' he said and sounded like a stranger. Nathan stared at his father.

'Wait! Surely you don't think I…?' Mary had no idea what he thought. Her words came out pinched and at least half an octave higher than normal. 'I've looked through three other fruitcakes. The ring should be here. It *must* be!'

Captain Rennie glared at her and she felt her heart sink into her shoes. He was a man on the rag-gedy edge of a towering rage, if the mottled red of his face, his narrowing eyes and his quick breath were symptoms. Her heart sank ever lower when she realised what he was thinking.

She tried again, determined that he not think ill of her. 'You can't believe I practised decep—'

To her horror, Captain Rennie took a step to-wards her, fire in his eyes. She stepped back, frightened. When he shouted in what she suspected was his quarterdeck voice, she covered her ears.

'Are you a bored and lonely spinster, Miss Rennie?' he roared, completely out of control. 'What game have you been playing?'

'No game, Captain,' she managed. 'I told you—'

He overrode her relentlessly. 'You tried so hard to send us on our way before Knaresborough,' he said, biting off each word with an intensity she had never heard from anyone in her sheltered life. 'There never was a ring, was there?'

He glanced around the vestibule, as if he suddenly had no idea where he was. He looked as Mary imagined a frigate captain might appear when his ship was under attack. Had he forgotten himself completely?

'What in God's name am I doing in Yorkshire, chasing a…a…damned mythological ring?'

He swore a vicious oath that probably would have shocked the entire French navy, but he spoke only to her, Mary Rennie. She burst into tears, then suddenly found herself in the grip of anger as huge as his own. She dragged a shaking hand across her eyes, trying to calm herself.

'Miss Rennie? Can we help you?'

The captain whirled around to see both Prestons, their eyes wide and faces pale. 'Leave us alone!' he hissed and raised his hand as though to strike them. They retreated to the doorway, but no farther.

He turned back to face her, his hand still raised. Nathan reached for his father's hand, but Ross shook him off. Mary grabbed the boy and thrust him behind her, feeling the greatest sorrow of her life. War had ruined this good man as surely as if he had died in battle.

'Don't you dare.' She said it quietly, with no idea how to calm a man in the grip of something as monstrous as war.

She wanted to run from the church and never look back. Mary took Nathan's hand and turned to pull him from the room with her, since she had no idea what the captain would do. When she turned so quickly, her face connected with the edge of the bookcase holding religious tracts. Pamphlets scattered everywhere, fluttering around Ross Rennie, who stared at his upraised hand as though it belonged to someone else.

'Good God,' he muttered.

Mary staggered against the table as little stars danced in her vision. She blinked her eyes and saw Nathan, ghostly white and staring at them both with his mouth open. Horrified, she willed herself calm, taking so many deep breaths that she felt light headed. With hands that shook, she gathered up the corners of the handkerchief with the fruit-cake and handed it to the boy she loved so much.

'Na-Na-Nathan,' she stammered, 'f-f-find some-where to dispose of this. There's probably a close with an ash-bin behind the church. Please go.'

He snatched the handkerchief from her trembling hand and ran out the door. When he started to wail, Mary covered her ears again. As she turned around to face Captain Rennie, she felt disembodied, as though quiet Mary Rennie had died and left behind a ruined shell. She gathered herself together like the scraps of fruitcake in the handkerchief.

'*That* is what I will regret until I die, Captain,' she said, her voice low and dangerous and completely belonging to someone else. 'He should not have heard us going at each other hammer and tongs. I am ashamed. As for the fruitcake, I saw my cousin put the ring in the batter and I knew where we stored it.'

The look he gave her was so filled with contempt that she closed her eyes in misery. Her cheek was on fire and her left eye was starting to close.

'I don't believe a word out of your mouth,' he said, his voice calmer now, but still filled with anger so deep that she didn't understand where it could possibly come from or why. He seemed almost possessed, as though some dividing line, cob-web thin, between his ship in battle and the two of them standing there in a church vestibule had disappeared. 'Not a damned word.'

His supreme distrust stung. 'Then it doesn't matter what I say. I believe the deception has been practised on *me*. Why, I do not know.' She looked towards the door, where the Prestons still stood, transfixed. 'If you could please take me to the mail-coach posting.'

She put her hand to her cheek. Relieved, she touched no blood, no jagged bone. She felt the captain's eyes on her, and she looked at him, out of ideas, out of hope. What she saw was uncertainty, as though he wondered how she had come by what was probably turning into a black eye of astounding proportions.

'It was an accident. You didn't mean to do that,' she told him, wondering why in heaven's name she felt any urge to excuse him. All she felt was shame that grew and grew as she dragged her mind back to the night at the Blankenships. What a fool she had been. This was a man truly destroyed by war.

'Think what you will, Captain. I am not really a dry twig of a spinster playing games. I am an ordinary woman.' She gulped and swallowed, determined to say what she felt honour bound to say. She turned to the Prestons. 'Go back to the chaise. I will be there in a moment. Please.'

'I don't know, miss.'

'Please.'

She waited until they were gone and only the two of them remaining in the vestibule. 'As for the matter at the Blankenships, I suppose we were both seeking some sort of solace.' He started to say something and she gave him a look so fierce that it was his turn to back away. 'Let me finish! It was solace *any* man or woman could have provided, I suppose. You'll find more reliable and experienced comfort elsewhere, I do not doubt. I don't feel proud admitting that, but there you are, sir. Forgive me.'

Humiliated to her heart's core, Mary managed a glance at his face, surprised to see him wince, as though she had misinterpreted that, too. It scarcely mattered; this journey had reached a terrible conclusion.

'I'm not certain how I feel about that, Mary,' he replied, his voice quiet now, without the cutting edge that she suspected had flayed a generation of midshipmen and young lieutenants.

She turned away, appalled by the reality that war

had ruined what might have been a good man. Astoundingly, she felt sorry for him. 'It doesn't matter, I suppose.'

She heard him step towards her, and she flinched, moving quickly out of his reach. Her action made him take an audible breath.

'Damn this whole affair! I wish I were at sea.'

Mary turned around, her fury replaced by sorrow of the most exquisite sort. 'Is that your answer for all ills?'

'Aye,' he snapped. 'I can manage a ship and men.'

'Then get you to it, sir,' she said softly.

Chapter Twenty-Three

If Ross hadn't already known, one look in Nathan's eyes told him he had made a terrible mistake. Suddenly a stranger to him, his son huddled in a corner of the post chaise, as though he couldn't get far enough away.

Silent, not looking at him, the Prestons had returned to the church after taking Mary Rennie to the mail-coach stop. 'Where now, Captain?' Tom Preston asked, his voice detached and professional, his eyes straight ahead and avoiding Ross's. The companionship they had developed travelling together had vanished like a leaf in a hot furnace.

How dare you condescend to me? he thought, furious all over again and ashamed at the same time. He waited so long that Preston cleared his throat.

'We will take you to the posting house here, Captain,' the post rider said, his voice so studied and neutral. 'Christmas is close and we have been travelling a long time.' He glanced at his son. 'Tony and I would like to head home ourselves. I...I... feel confident you can find other post riders to complete your journey.'

He had been dismissed by the men he had hired to serve him. If Preston had slapped him, Ross could not have felt worse. He nodded, unable to speak.

At the posting house, Ross settled the bill and held out a generous tip to the Prestons. The post rider just shook his head and turned away.

'You know I wouldn't have struck her!' he said to their retreating backs. 'It was you I was angry with.' His words rang hollow, even in his own ears. No reasonable man would have struck his post riders, either. He wasn't even fit company for the people he hired. Never mind; the Prestons left him alone without another comment.

Tom Preston was right; it was easy to find fresh riders. In a matter of an hour, the Rennies, minus Mary, had started out on the journey to Dumfries, where they were overdue. In all this time, Nathan had said nothing to him. When the new post rider climbed into his saddle and they left Knaresbor-ough, Nathan closed his eyes and turned away, pretending to sleep.

'Son, please,' Ross said. 'Oh, please! You know I would never have hurt Mary. She ran into the bookcase. It was an accident. Even…even *she* said it was.'

'You should have seen your face, Da. You fright-ened me, too.' His face crumpled and he began to weep. 'And Mary even more! Da, I love her and you chased her away.'

Wordless, Ross opened his arms, nearly in de-spair at the length of time it took his child to ac-cept his embrace. Nathan cried himself to sleep.

Ross had stared out the window until dawn came hours later, wondering what demon had possessed him in the church vestibule.

In fairness to Mary, now that his ferocious anger had dissipated, she had seemed as surprised as he was that she could not find the ring in the final fruitcake. Perhaps someone *had* practised a decep-tion on her. And even if no one had done such a thing, there was no explanation for his irrational anger. She was a woman, after all, and not a battle-hardened sailor used to harsh treatment. Perhaps he was truly not fit for land.

The idea chilled him, but he could not deny it. For twenty-four years, he had truly been in the service of Napoleon the puppetmaster. On the other side of the Channel from France, instant obedience was expected of him by his royal sovereign, King George, his other puppetmaster. In turn, Ross ruled his own watery kingdom, meting out harsh punishment when required, starving or thirsting with the men who looked to him in all things and obeyed without question. He had fought alongside his people in ship-to-ship engagements throughout the oceans of the world. To call his life anything but hard would be a great error.

As they rode along in the dark, the other side of his conscience reminded him that women like Mary led hard lives, too. She had known heartache and disappointment. How arrogant he was to think his was worse. If some of his hopes were disappointed, so were hers. Shame on him.

On the second day, Nathan and Ross started talking about inconsequential matters, each avoiding anything that might bring back a memory of Mary or the church vestibule. He could have stopped at a few more public houses or inns where wardroom officers had written down their favourite foods on that list that was starting to haunt him. Somewhere in that honest part of his heart, he knew he did not stop because the food would always remind him of fine days with Mary Rennie, his gentle travelling companion, humouring him by sampling lemon-curd pudding and Cumberland sausage.

He revised his opinion of her gentleness. Aye, she was sweet and bonny, but she was also a strong woman who did not flinch to handle his peg-leg or save his worthless hide in Ovenshine when his former purser was bent on ruining him. And in bed with her at the Blankenships, when Nathan interrupted what Ross knew in his bones would have been a coupling of prodigious proportions, she had that same fire he remembered from Inez. With Mary, he would never want for anything.

For the final time, he thought of the lovely lady of his dreams, appalled that he had actually de-scribed her to Mary. How could he have been so stupid? The sweetest woman in his life had trav-elled with him for glorious days, and he hadn't the wit to acknowledge it. He could not imagine a big-ger fool that the man who glared at him through the window's reflection.

One bad moment came when they passed a mail coach bowling along and swaying from side to side. Nathan sucked in his breath and stared out the window, his eyes searching for Mary. He began to cry and only shook his head with some vehemence when Ross reached for him.

They arrived in Dumfries two days before Christmas. It pained Ross that Nathan was still wary of him. His wariness went unnoticed when his sister scooped them both into her generous embrace and they began Yuletide celebrations. If Nathan was more quiet than usual, Alice Mae didn't know, because she seldom saw either of them. Perhaps after a few days of eating, merriment and gifts, Nathan would forget the quiet woman who had such a sure touch.

Mary discovered something useful about travel on the Royal Mail with a black eye: people generally felt no inclination to pry. The coach was cold, too, so it was easy to keep the hood of her cloak around her face. If she could scamper aboard first and seat herself on the left side of the coach, she could turn her face towards the window and no one was any the wiser. It didn't matter that she knew her black eye had been an accident. No one who saw her ravaged face would know the whole story, one she knew she would never tell.

She had no particular problem remaining aboard during stops when the horses were changed. Beyond a quick visit to the necessary and a drink of water at the ice-rimed bucket left there for impecunious travellers, she could resume her place in the coach as they travelled north. She had money for food, but she was not hungry. She was defeated.

If there had been any place to go except Wapping Street in Edinburgh, she would have gone there. For a small moment, a day earlier, she almost asked the coachman to let her off near the village closest to Skowcroft. She knew the Everetts would take her in, but it would mean explanation and she was too upset to explain anything.

By the time Mary arrived in Edinburgh, she had concocted a serviceable lie to explain her black eye that was even now turning a mottled purple. She took her travelling case and found a hackney. She had hoped that saying 'Number Fifty-six Wapping Street, please' to the jehu would change her misgivings to relief, but it did not. The Rennies' home had been a refuge when her parents' died, but it was just an address now. No, it was something worse: Wapping Street was the final stop on her life's journey that had begun with promise, twenty-seven years ago.

The jehu let her off, looking at her with some sympathy because she had been unable to hide her face from him. 'I can take you somewhere else, if you wish, mum,' he had said in a low voice, perhaps interpreting her reluctance to enter the house because she feared for her treatment there. It was kindly meant, and she smiled at him with what she hoped was reassurance. His glance remained sceptical, so she wished him Merry Christmas, squared her shoulders and knocked on the door.

The butler opened the door, smiled to see her, then gasped as he looked closer. Mary laughed and handed him her travelling case. 'Jackson, you know how Mrs Morison wanted me to have an adventure.'

'Aye, lass, but…' he said, dubious, concerned.

She pointed to her eye. 'This is the consequence of icy highways and a sudden stop.'

And then everyone was in the vestibule—her aunt and uncle, Dina and a plump fellow with two-and-a-half chins who must be Mr Page. Their concern turned to smiles when she described how she crashed into a skinny vicar with an amazingly sharp elbow, after the coach skidded sideways near Knaresborough. 'What a joke on me,' she said, then took a cautious look around.

Everyone seemed to believe her. It was the one good moment she could recall in the past days of solitary travelling. Better have them smiling before she admitted defeat. 'Alas, for all my obvious pains, no ring,' she said. 'I fear I have failed you.'

To her astonishment, everyone laughed. Dina came forwards, tugging Mr Page with her. She held out her hand and waved it in front of Mary's one good eye. Mary gasped. The last time she had seen that insignificant little ring was just before it sank into the fruitcake batter.

'Fooled you, fooled you!' Dina crowed as she danced around.

Mary sank down on one of the hall chairs and put her head in her hands. When she looked up, feeling despair settle around her shoulders like wet laundry, the others grew silent.

'Mrs Morison wanted you to have an adventure, silly. You were turning into such an old stick. That's what she told me when she handed me the ring after you left,' Dina said, when no one else spoke. 'You'll have to go downstairs and tell her everything.' She clapped her hands. 'Better yet, we'll get the old dear upstairs and you can tell us what happened when you chased fruitcake all over Scotland and northern England. I have explained it all to Mr Page. We were amazed to get your note from Carlisle with word of York.' She glanced at the butler hovering nearby, a frown on his face. 'Get Mrs Morison.'

'No!' With all the dignity she could muster, Mary picked up her travelling case and went to the stairs. The treads looked tall enough to require a stepstool and the stairway landing so far away. Child's play. With a sob she could not hide, she left them standing in the hallway.

Ross did not protest when his sister insisted they drive to Kirkbean to visit the estate she had mentioned in more letters to him than he cared to admit. He put on an interested face as Alice Mae described the six bedchambers, two sitting rooms—'One small and dainty for a wife, should you ever choose to marry, Brother'—efficiently drawing fireplaces, panelled bookroom, library and billiards room.

He couldn't deny that it was a lovely estate, with well-tended lawns and a postage-stamp view of the sea that Alice Mae had promised. The trees were bare of leaves and the little burn frozen in place until spring. 'It will look so much more lovely by April,' she assured him, and he could not deny that either.

He stood a long time at the upstairs window in what was the largest bedchamber and probably destined to become his, if Alice Mae badgered him enough. He didn't really care any more; everyone probably needed a house. Damn the matter, but the view of the ocean was too paltry to please him. All it made him want to do was start walking until he reached the ocean and found a coasting vessel to take him south to English ports and warships.

'What do you think, Brother?' Alice asked after the tour.

I think I am God's fool, he told himself. *I am a wicked man.*

'Brother?'

'It's lovely, dear lassie. I don't know that I am much in the mood to buy property, though.'

He waited for her pout—ah, there it was. 'I have all but promised the agent...' she began.

'Then unpromise him!' he declared, probably more sharply than he intended, but not nearly with the vehemence that had lacerated Mary Rennie right down to her bone marrow. 'I'm sorry. Just give me time. The war's not over yet, despite what everyone thinks.'

That was his problem, or one of them, he had decided in the week after Christmas when he began his solitary walks that took him farther and farther from his sister's home. Nathan seemed content to play with his cousins and their Christmas toys. He certainly never asked to accompany his father.

Ross's stump always ached, but he couldn't help himself; he had to walk. It was as though he were trying to distance himself from himself, an impossibility. He started taking along his pistol, tucking it in the inside pocket of his boat cloak. On the third day, he sat on a boulder in sight of the ocean and took out the pistol. It was a spoil of war, taken from the body of a French captain after a sharp engagement near Hawaii. The firing accuracy amazed him, but he had scant use for it in close combat, preferring his hanger, because he never had to reload a cutlass. Still, he had turned down plenty of offers for the little beauty.

It would be so easy. He put it back in his pocket.

* * *

The next day, Nathan came to him, defiance in his eyes, and said he was writing to Mary.

'I think you should, Son,' Ross said simply. 'Do you know her direction?'

Nathan stared at him in surprise, and Ross wondered how long his boy had nerved himself to announce his intention to correspond. *I have become an unpredictable ogre to my child*, he thought in perfect misery.

'Wapping Street is all I know,' Nathan said, his demeanour less reserved, probably because his father hadn't forbidden him.

'Try it. We know the family name is Rennie.'

Nathan gave him the first genuine smile in days. 'I really like her, Da.'

'What is it you like about Mary?' He had to know. Ross knew what he liked about Mary, not the least of which was the softness of her breasts. She was smart and lively in a quiet sort of way—even if that did seem contradictory—resourceful and courageous. As he waited for an answer, Ross looked down the long corridor of years ahead. If the war was really over and his life wasn't in so much danger any more—discounting the usual dangers at sea—he wondered how he would manage without Mary.

'I like the way she looks at me and touches me, and listens to me,' his son said.

'I do those things, too,' Ross reminded him, feeling sorry for himself and suddenly envious of Mary.

'I know, Da, but you have to,' his boy told him with that logic of children. 'Mary doesn't have to do any of those things, but she does, because I'm special to her.'

He couldn't help but smile. 'How do you know that, Son?'

'I just do,' Nathan replied simply. 'I don't need words.'

Snow was falling the next day. The sky was Scotland grey, the wind a tumult. They were leaving next morning for Plymouth. To further placate his son, Ross had told him they could travel by mail coach if he wanted. A shadow had passed over Nathan's face and he shook his head.

'Why not? You know you love the mail coach.'

'No, Da.' Nathan sighed. 'I'd just be looking for Mary at every stop.'

And so Ross walked again to the headland, pistol

in his pocket. He knew Nathan enjoyed his cousins. He could live here with them. After a sleepless night, he had risen early to write an amendment to his will and testament that would probably stand up in probate. Years ago, he had signed over everything to his son, with his sister as guardian. This codicil would mean a handy competence to Mary Rennie of Wapping Street, Edinburgh, that would get her to Canada or the United States. He folded it, put Alice's name on it, and left it on the desk in his room.

He took out his pistol, loaded now. For the last time, he flagellated himself for the folly of using war as an excuse never to find a wife, or to moon over a mythological lady. What nonsense that was, considering how many of his lieutenants and friends had found wives to marry and worry about and miss. Some of his friends had died in service to their sovereign, leaving widows and children behind. For years he had secretly thought them foolish. *They* had been the brave ones, to love and marry and get children on those odd moments they were in port, as though their lives were normal and the world was not at war.

As each year passed and his senses became more dulled by violence and death, he had turned into the worst kind of man, a man without hope. Until he died, which likely would be within the next few minutes, he would see the stricken look on Mary's face as he accused her of deception. Perhaps she *had* fooled him. Did it matter, really? He loved her. He had never told her and she was gone.

With a steady breath, Ross put the pistol into his ear. The cold barrel made him wince. He pulled back the hammer, then stopped. He pulled away the pistol. Shooting himself in the head would be unsuccessful, he reasoned with a wry smile. The events in Knaresborough had proved to everyone in the Methodist Church vestibule that he had no brains. Shooting himself there would do no damage at all.

He reflected on the matter and unbuttoned his uniform jacket. He edged the barrel through his shirt opening and held the pistol against his heart. This would be fast. Lord, no, it would not do. 'I have no heart, either,' he whispered to the wind. 'What good would it do to shoot myself there?'

He took the pistol off full cock and threw it over the cliff. He would jump to his death. That would work. If he landed on his feet, his leg bones would ram through his body and kill him quickly. If he landed on his head, his neck would snap. He knew the descent would be unpleasant. He had seen fore-topmen fall from the yardarm, screaming all the way down. Still, in the greater scheme of things, it was a quick death, preferable to gangrene from a gunshot wound in the heat and stink of the Malay Peninsula, dying by degrees in terrible pain, as Dale Everett had died.

That was another thing to chastise himself about. Was he a coward to lie to the Everetts and tell them their son had wasted away from a fever, sinking into a merciful coma? He could not bring himself to write the truth, even to a vicar who dealt only in truth. Pray God no one would ever check the co-ordinates he had given them to carve on Dale Everett's tombstone in the church's holy ground. Few had died as painfully as his midshipman.

Ross took off his boat cloak and set it on the rock. He felt in his pockets for a scrap of paper and a pencil stub. Perhaps he should put his name on the paper, in case the leap rendered him unrecognisable. But that was folly; his peg would identify him. He took his hand from his pocket and brought with it the list, the pernicious list that had guided him to Mary in Carlisle. If there hadn't been a list, he would never have met the woman. He opened it for a last look and stopped.

Nathan had written an entry—*Mrs Pritchert's kitchen, burgoo for my da and cod and leeks for me.*

Furious with himself and humbled in a maddening way, he ripped the list into shreds and tossed them after the pistol. They blew back into his face instead like an indictment.

'You have a son, you blockhead,' he roared in his loudest quarterdeck voice. Ross put on his boat cloak again, wishing he hadn't tossed away a perfectly good pistol. It was time to return to Plymouth, cod and leeks and burgoo.

Chapter Twenty-Four

Because children were charitable and kinder than adults, Nathan had sat closer to Ross on the ride to the West Country and Plymouth. He had seemed in good humour again, laughing and teasing with his father. The nights were different. On the last night before Plymouth, Ross woke to Nathan in tears.

'Oh, laddie, what?' he asked, holding him close in the bed they shared.

Maybe Nathan was still asleep, because Ross doubted he would have been so blunt, had he been awake. 'Da, you did a fearsome bad thing,' he said, drowsy.

'I know. Please forgive me.'

'What about Mary?' Nathan yawned and returned to sleep.

* * *

In the morning, there was no indication that he remembered his question. Ross knew he would never forget it. What *about* Mary?

Mrs Pritchert greeted them both in her arms-open way, scolding Nathan for leaving his collar unbuttoned in this raw wind and not tying his muffler tighter. Ross watched them, a smile on his face, listening to a good woman scold. The smile left his face. In a coup d'état that he never quite understood, Mary had taken over the duty of seeing that Nathan was buttoned and warm, but she never sounded like Mrs Pritchert. He supposed it was possible for two women who both loved his son to use different tactics. He decided he preferred Mary's gentle admonition to Mrs Pritchert's rough-and-tumble justice: same result, but maybe easier on the heart.

Loathe to leave his son in Plymouth, he sat in the kitchen, blinking his eyes against his own weariness. Now that Nathan was deposited again, Ross knew he had to pour himself back into the post chaise for a quick trip to London and Admiralty House. He had sailed often under Special Orders, but surely the orders in January of 1815 wouldn't have much teeth to them, now that Napoleon was on Elba. Maybe his duty would allow him more frequent trips to Plymouth, where he could attempt to repair his faulty credit with his son. A captain could hope.

Admiralty House seemed to be sleeping, so maybe the long war really was over. His orders included nothing more strenuous than cruising the Channel at his own discretion—ah, the reward for being a well-seasoned post captain—and popping into port now and then, if the mood was on him. These orders were a far cry from desperate days when only his Britannic Majesty's Sovereign Navy stood between Napoleon and defeat. If this was what peace was going to look like—dull—he wasn't sanguine about his prospects.

Ross returned to Plymouth, argued with himself for a few fruitless moments at the posting house, then visited a discreet house far enough from the docks to cater only to officers. The whores were as pretty as he remembered them, but he picked out one new to him this time. His regulars pouted and he couldn't quite understand his impulsive choice, either, until he took a closer look at the sprinkling of freckles across her nose that she had tried to disguise with powder. *I have to stop seeing Mary everywhere I look, especially here*, he thought with disgust, as he followed her upstairs. *She'd slap my chops into next Tuesday if I ever mentioned this.* The reality that he would never see her again turned him glum.

After closing the door and kissing him, Belinda—Good God, she reeked of roses—asked him what he wanted her to do. He was about to list his particular favourites, when he surprised himself. 'Would you remove my peg first? It's paining me a bit.'

Belinda—or was it Marcella?—stared at him and gulped. She backed away, eyeing his wooden leg with revulsion.

'You're probably better at that than I am,' she temporised. She came closer, unbuttoned his uniform jacket and started edging her hand down his trousers, maybe thinking to distract him so he'd pull off his own leg.

Mary didn't mind removing it, he thought, as he backed away from whoever she was. He couldn't recall that Mary had looked on his peg with anything but curiosity, at first. There had been no disgust on her face when she touched his stump and remarked that it felt hot. Following that first experience, he couldn't recall that she ever said anything about it.

'I should be about my business,' he told the astonished whore. He left a small sum on the bed—after all, he had occupied ten minutes of her working day. 'Time and tide won't wait.' He was down the stairs and out the door in mere moments, but not before he heard his winsome, mid-morning choice lean over the banister and tell one of the other parlour girls about the cove who wanted her to 'tyke orf his bleedin' laig'.

Unrefreshed and ashamed of himself, he returned to Flora Street to say goodbye to Nathan. He was hoping his son would greet him with his former enthusiasm and he did, except this time he waved a letter and the enthusiasm wasn't for him.

'She wrote, Da, she wrote!' Nathan said as he hurtled into his father's arms. He wrinkled his nose. 'You smell like roses.'

'Imagine,' was all Ross could think to say, as he blushed and hoped Mrs Pritchert wouldn't notice. 'How did Mary know to write you here?'

'Aunt Alice said I should give her this address, or else her reply would end up in Dumfries. Roses, Da?'

Forgetting him, Nathan wandered into the

kitchen, where Mrs Pritchert was flouring veal cutlets. He sat cross-legged on the bench, nodding at what he read, then handed the letter to his father.

Ross opened his mouth to object. He closed it, not wanting to protest that it wasn't good manners for him to read a letter meant for someone else, when he was desperate to know what she had to tell his son. Any crumb from Mary was surely better than all of Belinda's dubious talents.

"'Dear Nathan,'" he read to himself, "'imagine my surprise or chagrin—ask your father what it means—when I arrived in Edinburgh to see Dina wearing the little ring. It seems Mrs Morison, the cook, had retrieved it from the batter when I was out of the room. She sent me on my errand because she wanted me to have an adventure. Perhaps she feared that if she had left the ring in the batter, I might have not found the dratted thing. Ah, well. I still haven't been below stairs to talk to her and perhaps I won't go.'"

Ross looked up at his son. '*I* would have left the ring in the fruitcake and let Mary find it.' *And then Mary wouldn't have been humiliated by a bully who didn't believe her*, he thought with remorse.

'I would have, too.'

He returned to his son's letter. "'My journey

wasn't for nothing and I give your father the credit."'

Ross nodded to Nathan. 'I did something good? It's nice to hope.'

'Keep reading, Da.' Nathan cleared his throat as though it was his announcement, and not Mary's.

Ross read, "'I informed my uncle Sam that I was going to work in his counting house and he would pay me. He wouldn't hear of it, but I sat in his lobby in his counting house for one week until he changed his mind."'

Bravo, Mary, Ross thought with admiration as he continued reading. The smile left his face. "'I intend to save my earnings until I have enough to emigrate to the United States. I might go to Savannah or Charleston where it is warm. I have decided it is too damp and chilly in Edinburgh."'

She's leaving and I can't blame her. Besides, it was my idea! I doubt there is a bigger fool on this entire island, he thought, discouraged beyond words.

'May I write her back, Da?' Nathan asked.

'What? What? Aye, lad. And…and tell her hello from me.'

Ross handed back the letter and his son immediately started to read it over.

'I'm leaving now for the Channel,' he said.

Nathan merely nodded, his eyes on the letter. He walked slowly from the room and upstairs. Mrs Pritchert gave Ross a look full of sympathy, something he did not want. He told her goodbye and left the house.

He stood outside, looking up at Nathan's bedroom window, waiting for his son to wave and blow him kisses, as he usually did. The window remained empty. He waited a long while, then walked slowly to the harbour.

The matter of employment in her uncle's counting house had not been as easily accomplished as Mary had suggested in her letter to Nathan. She couldn't bring herself to go below stairs to see Mrs Morison. She blamed it on utter exhaustion for keeping up the cheerful pretence that her accident was a chance encounter with an elbow on the mail coach. The little tale made the rounds of Wapping Street, nobody questioning her. If she never saw Mrs Morison again, Mary knew she would not mind greatly.

'What am I going to do with my life?' she asked herself over and over during the days when she hid upstairs as the black eye faded. There were no avenues for well-bred women except marriage. She even dared to wonder what would happen if someone ever did propose. She knew that she loved Ross Rennie: one-legged, experienced at sea, a well-off post captain, and a man dogged by demons she couldn't imagine. The war had ruined him and she knew no cure. Even with all that, if someone else proposed, she would turn down this mythical suitor. Mary Rennie wasn't a woman to deceive a husband into thinking she loved him, when her heart belonged to the most inappropriate man on the planet.

That resolved, although not pleasantly, Mary remembered a conversation of theirs, when he had said he might marry some day when the war ended, and she wondered what she would do. He had suggested she emigrate to Canada or even the United States. The idea had struck her as funny then, but as January dragged out in her comfortable room on Wapping Street, she changed her mind. That was precisely what she would do.

She puzzled about how to take such a shocking step. She knew her aunt and uncle had the money to oblige her, but she knew they would never agree to it. She had a modest competence slowly growing in sensible funds. What she needed was employment. When her answer came the next morning, she interrupted Uncle Sam over breakfast. They always ate together, even though he spent most of the time behind his newspaper.

When he was finished and enjoying that final cup of tea, she announced, 'Uncle, I have decided to work for you in your counting house.'

He sprayed the newspaper with tea and stared at her.

'I am very good with figures. I need to earn enough money to move to the United States of America.'

That wasn't so hard. Mary felt no fear because she had made up her mind. She smiled back when he continued to glare at her.

'It's out of the question,' he said finally.

'No, it isn't. Just because you do not currently employ any females doesn't mean that it is not a wonderful idea, Uncle. I prefer to keep my little inheritance gathering interest. When I am ready to leave I will withdraw it. I plan to earn my passage working for you. In your counting house. Starting tomorrow.'

'Over my corpse,' he said, his thin lips even thinner.

'It won't come to that,' Mary told him just as firmly.

Feeling competent, wise and brave, she gave him a day to think about her declaration. When he left for work the next morning, she followed him right out the door and down the street. He said nothing to her, trying to hurry ahead as though she were a stray dog nipping at his heels. Eyes ahead, she marched right behind him. She followed him into Rennie and Son Counting House, past the astounded receptionist and into the office waiting room, where he ignored her for an entire week.

At the beginning of the next week, he silently cleared off a desk, placed a stack of ledgers with columns on them and told her to add them and make no mistakes. Mary did, finishing sooner than any of the other clerks. By Thursday of week two she was figuring percentages. On Friday he paid her. That night, she knelt by her bed and thanked the Lord. She had been neglecting Him for a year or more and knew how much she owed Divine Providence.

She wrote about the whole experience to Nathan, who became her regular correspondent, as January stepped aside for February. She was a little surprised to learn in one of his letters that he shared her correspondence with his father, who came into port more often than usual. If Captain Rennie found some amusement in her efforts, that was all right with Mary. Maybe he even remembered that emigrating was his idea.

Mary had to chuckle when Nathan wrote back that Da had grumbled and said something that made Mrs Pritchert gasp, when he read him that part about emigrating to the United States. 'You see, Mary, he still smarts over the time a Yankee privateer with a letter of marque and reprisal cut a cargo ship right out of a convoy he was guarding towards Spain,' Nathan wrote, which made her laugh, not a frequent occurrence at either Wapping Street or in the counting house.

She never went below stairs to see Mrs Morison. Aunt Martha had begged her to say something to the old cook, but Mary knew she was not ready to forgive her for the horrible scene in Knaresborough, which no one knew about anyway, because she never explained. Maybe some day before Mary sailed for Baltimore, Maryland, she would see Mrs Morison. The war with America had ended and perhaps someone in that city needed a counting-house clerk. She could have chosen any city, but Mary liked the sound of Baltimore. Since Ross and

Nathan were never to be part of her life, it probably didn't matter which city, really.

She discovered one true pleasure in being a woman on her own: all decisions were hers. She had no need to consult a husband or children. And if she decided that Charleston might suit her better than Baltimore, or that Delaware was more to her taste, so be it; she could move there just as easily, without a by your leave. That was something to smile about, except the emotion that inevitably followed all this independence was the pain of losing Ross Rennie, he who had never been hers in the first place. Heart and soul, he belonged to his Britannic Majesty's Navy, a monolith she could not fight, any more than she had a say in war. She was powerless, but so was he. And if he ever found Our Lady of the List, Mary wouldn't have wagered much success for either of them since he was a ruined man.

She had spoken 'I will love you until I die' into her window that overlooked Wapping Street until she almost felt the sentence was etched there. Mary knew she would say it into the wind as she crossed the Atlantic and then into other windows and vistas. It would be her heart's refrain until she finally breathed her last and proved the statement true. What folly was love.

* * *

On February the twenty-sixth, the day that Napoleon bolted from Elba and began his journey to Paris, gathering old veterans as he marched, Cousin Dina married Mr Algernon Page. In a burst of romantic feeling—Mary was surprised—Mr Page had arranged for a wedding journey to Paris. Dina had had to settle for the Highlands, because That Beast Napoleon had ruined her plans. She came home with chilblains and a putrid sore throat. Mr Page came home with the look of a man who could see his future spooling out before him in a way too bleak to contemplate. Poor Mr Page.

Mary discovered that she had not even begun to get over Captain Rennie. Her heart surprisingly tender, Mary continued her days in the counting house, where all the talk among the clerks was of renewed war. There were some moments during her breaks and luncheon when she retreated to the broom closet and wept, praying for Ross Rennie's safety. No one knew except Nathan, who expressed exactly the same fears to her in his letters. She wrote to him daily now and they comforted each other through the penny post. With every fibre of her bruised heart, Mary Rennie longed to see Nathan. She made the mistake of telling him that in one unguarded moment, when all England waited for news of a battle in Belgium.

Both of them knew better than to think Captain Rennie was anywhere other than at sea and probably twiddling his thumbs with a tedious escort service to transport troops and war materiel. They also knew, because they had told each other in more than one letter, how tired they were of war.

And then she heard no more.

Chapter Twenty-Five

In late June, the frantic note from Mrs Pritchert caught up with Captain Rennie in London celebrating the Duke of Wellington's victory over Napoleon in a Belgian wheat field. Already the newspapers were combining Liège, Quatre Bras and Mont Saint Jean into the all-inclusive Waterloo. His frigate had sailed into Portsmouth with the wounded and he knew the whole dirty business was finally over.

Since he still sailed under Special Orders, Ross went to London and checked into his favourite hotel, before taking his post chaise to Admiralty House. Mrs Pritchert's note had been sent to Standish House, but with all the excitement in a city mad with joy, the note was overlooked when he arrived and signed the register.

Ross hurried to Admiralty House with his logs,

but prepared to begin the paperwork that would lead to the resignation of his commission. He was under no illusion that he could just walk away right now, not when there were more wounded to transport. Soon there would be troops to escort home as well, as Europe turned from Napoleon's playing field to independent quarrelling nations. Perhaps by the end of summer he would be a free man.

When he returned to Plymouth to inform his son, he would have leisure to scout about for a tailor. He still liked navy blue, but maybe a dark-green coat with a paisley waistcoat would suit. Maybe the agent in Kirkbean had not entirely given up on him. Or he could ask Nathan where he wanted to live. He knew he wouldn't really mind Plymouth because he knew he would miss the ocean.

The overworked porter in Admiralty had just indicated an open door down the hall when his counterpart from the hotel pounded up to the high desk and demanded to see Captain Rennie.

'Right here, lad. What have you?'

'Sorry, Captain, but we've been busy.'

Still out of breath, the man handed Ross the letter and accepted the coin tossed his way. 'Thank'ee,' he said, but Ross had already turned away, letter in hand, to stare for a second at Mrs Pritchert's crabbed handwriting—she rarely wrote to him—and to feel dread weigh him down more than duty.

He ducked into an empty office and ripped open the letter. 'Good God,' he whispered, and read it again and once more, until a bare smile played about his lips. 'You scamp, Nathan', was all he said. Duty still called, so he continued down the hall to the door the porter had indicated.

Lord Melville himself sat there. Ross doffed his bicorn and made a proper bow. 'My lord, I have logs and papers for your secretary and a sudden burning urge to travel to Edinburgh, rather than back to Belgium.'

'You do? How singular, Captain Rennie.'

Ross knew they stood on some degree of friendship, after all these years and Special Orders that took him here and there at the First Lords' whim and the exigencies of war. 'My lord, I know you have sons.' He handed over the letter from Mrs Pritchert.

Lord Melville read it through and his lips began to twitch, which relieved Ross.

'Do you think, my lord, that I could, uh…hotfoot it to Edinburgh? My first luff is entirely capable of returning *Abukir* to Europe's shores for more escort and transport duty.' He paused. 'I have but one son to your four, my lord.'

The First Lord nodded and handed back the letter. 'You may.' He glanced out the window. 'London has gone mad and we can spare you. But why Edinburgh? I saw no mention of that city in the letter.'

Ross unfolded the letter. 'These are Mrs Pritchert's words: "All he said was Mary needed him."'

'And Mary is…'

Ross swallowed. 'In Edinburgh. She's the woman I plan to marry, if she'll have me. The matter hangs in some doubt, my lord, and I am not sanguine.'

'I shouldn't wonder at that!' Lord Melville looked him in the eye. 'The war has not been kind to you and men like you, Captain Rennie.' He waved a hand to dismiss Ross. 'But do try. When you have retrieved your boy and had whatever success you might find with, uh…Mary, return here.'

'Aye, my lord. Good day.' Ross bowed again and started from the office. He stopped and asked another question, which made Lord Melville laugh out loud and refer him to the Inns of Court.

By late afternoon and after shelling out an amazing amount of money—he who seldom was in port long enough to spend any—Ross had been on the

Great North Road. Forty hours later, his mud-spattered post chaise pulled up to Fifty-six Wapping Street.

Call it vanity. He knew he was not, in himself, much out of the ordinary in appearance, but the uniform, even travel-stained, was as effective as ever. An elderly butler showed him into the sitting room immediately. 'Come on, Mary, receive me,' he muttered and then started pacing as though on his quarterdeck. Old habits were going to die hard, apparently.

Two people met him instead, a woman in tears and a man with a preoccupied air, looking supremely uncomfortable. They introduced themselves as Martha and Samuel Rennie, aunt and uncle to Mary Rennie.

He bowed to them both and introduced himself, even though he could tell they already knew who he was. 'Mary?' he asked. 'My son?'

'Sit down, Captain.'

'I've been sitting for the past two days! Kindly produce at least my son!' He hadn't meant to shout, not really.

The woman burst into tears and Mr Rennie glared at her. Even with his own brief experience with Mary Rennie, Ross could have told Mr Rennie that was a technique not destined to prosper.

'Captain, she resigned from my counting house a few days ago upon the receipt of this letter from your son and departed for points unknown.' He handed Ross the letter.

'Damned secretive of her,' he muttered, as Mrs Rennie gasped. He opened the letter to see Nathan's familiar handwriting. It was a short letter.

Mary, I'm coming to see you. I don't have much money, but I should at least make York. Your friend, Nathan

'So they are in York,' he said, handing back the letter. 'Well, well.'

'We have no idea where!'

'I do. Good day to you both.'

This impromptu trip north was turning into the sort of travelling he used to do during the worst days of the Great War, when desperate doings and secret messages meant trips to London from Plymouth or Portsmouth. He had been hungry and tired then, and sometimes wounded—his leg was paining him now—but he had also been younger.

He stopped for the night in Galashiels, a small city of some pretension he remembered vaguely from the infamous list. His tired brain eventually spat out the Horse and Rider, and something do to with cheddar. He ate cheese and slept hard and was on the road by daybreak.

A day later, he arrived in Apollo Street. His eyes felt like fried eggs and his stump was fiery and painful as though he had been walking on it. He looked down to realise he had been pushing and pushing against the floorboards, as if to make the chaise go faster.

A strange butler ushered him into the house, saw him to the sitting room and said he would fetch the mister and mistress. Ross looked around, startled. There had been no mistress in December when they stopped here. Was he in the wrong house?

When the door opened, he winced and rose to his feet to see Tavish Maxfield and a lovely lady of equally advanced years. He stared, then he understood. He bowed, rejuvenated despite his utter exhaustion. 'Well, my dears. You must be—let me guess—the former Miss Ella Bruce. My congratulations to you both!'

He must have looked hungry as well as tired, because the conversation continued immediately over the dinner he had obviously interrupted. Before he tucked into a welcome meal that hadn't come from a posting house, he had to ask, 'My son and Mary Rennie?' Obviously they were not there. He who could make anchorage in strange ports through fog was beginning to doubt his ability to find a gentle lady with a kind face and a boy with handsome Portuguese features.

'They have been here and gone,' Mr Maxfield said.

Ross groaned. 'Then I am stymied and bludgeoned.'

The couple smiled at each other. 'You'll figure it out as soon as you've had dinner, Captain,' the new Mrs Maxfield said. 'Eat and let us thank you, too, for the fruitcake.'

He did just that, eating everything within easy reach and listening to a lovely tale of an old fellow working up the nerve to travel to Stirling, precisely as Miss Bruce's nephew in Carlisle had wished.

'More potatoes, Captain? I screwed up my courage and proposed on the spot. Love, hand the dear captain the gravy,' Mr Maxfield said with a blush that belied his years. 'We have been married upwards of six months now and we owe it all to Mary Rennie.' Mr Maxfield leaned closer. 'We think you should marry that lovely lady.' He giggled. 'She told us that you were all Rennies, but not spliced.'

Ross absorbed all this without a blush as he ate. 'I am so tired and my brain is not working, sir. I *want* to do precisely as you wish, but damn me, I am out of ideas.'

'No, you're not, Captain,' Mrs Maxfield said, her eyes so kind. 'We think it best that you have dessert somewhere else.'

'I'd rather have Mary and Nathan.' He thought a moment, than slapped the table so hard that the jam jar jumped. 'Lemon-curd pudding, eh?'

'I told you he was smart man, Ella,' Mr Maxfield said. 'Will you have a nap before you…oh, well, Captain. Good day!'

When they pulled into Skowcroft a day and a half later, Ross could barely sit up. The pain in his stump was as bad as if he had stood on it through storms and battles, but the pain in his heart was worse. He directed the post rider to the Everetts' parish, but hadn't the energy to move when the post let down the step. He just sat there, his head on his knees.

He heard a door open, then felt gentle hands on his arm. 'Mary?' he said without looking up.

'The same, Captain. Nathan, you take his other arm.'

The pain was so great he collapsed on the walkway and they were not strong enough to heave him to his feet again. To his embarrassment, the post rider helped him up, Mary leading the way, the Everetts concerned, but smiling, too.

'Everyone is so damned cheerful here,' he muttered, then closed his eyes.

When he woke, he wore a nightshirt and his leg was blissfully unencumbered with the peg, which he saw propped against a chair across the room.

Mary sat in a chair by the bed, her stockinged feet on the coverlet, reading, Nathan seated beside her. She put down the book and chuckled when he tickled the sole of her foot.

'You're among the living?' she asked. 'Nathan, better bring up the lemon-curd pudding.' When Nathan ran down the stairs, she moved from the chair to the bed. 'You've been mumbling about lemon-curd pudding for an hour or more.'

'Kiss me,' he ordered, and she did. She had no more skill than in the crofter's cottage, but she had something more important, an intensity of purpose that began to stir his worn-out body.

He held her off then. 'Mary, I owe you more apologies than exist.'

She shook her head, then returned to the chair

when she heard Nathan on the stairs. With a flourish that reminded Ross of Inez just a little, Nathan set the bowl of pudding on his father's lap. There were three spoons, so they all gathered close. While they ate, Nathan apologised for stealing Mrs Pritchert's household money.

Ross thought it was an apology, but he couldn't be certain, because Nathan ended with, 'Da, I really think you should leave more household money with Mrs Pritchert. Suppose I need to run away to Edinburgh again?'

Mary gasped and grabbed his son, rubbing his head until he squealed. 'That's no apology!' she declared. 'You are a rascal and a scamp!' They grinned at each other.

Her arms around Nathan, Mary picked up the thread of the adventure. 'As you know now, I found him in York. We came here because it's on the way to Edinburgh. We figured you were headed there, too.'

He nodded and felt his eyes close. 'Won't you both come south to Plymouth with me?'

There was a long pause. 'Nathan will.'

Chapter Twenty-Six

She didn't change her mind through a day of pleading, but did suggest that the tide was running more in his favour. Ross knew better than to accuse her of toying with him, because he knew her well enough to know that she was genuinely unsure. Could he blame her? He knew he had been ruined by war and he knew she knew it, too.

Still, he was a leader of men used to having his way. He told her he had a special licence in his pocket and wanted more than anything for Mr Everett to marry them right away. She merely nodded and told him to hang on to it just a little longer.

'Say now, are you doing this to get me back for what was assuredly a nasty piece of meanness in Knaresborough?' he finally asked, exasperated, as he let her ease him into his peg again.

'I would never be so petty,' she assured him.

'Do you at least love me?'

'More than I could possibly express in words,' she told him. 'The only thing left is to *show* you how much I love you. You'll have to wait a bit, though. I have to apologise to a cook in Edinburgh and settle a few affairs.' She hesitated then, and looked away.

'Is it still Baltimore?' he asked quietly.

'I truly haven't decided,' she replied, and left the room so he could finish dressing. She paused at the doorway, her eyes so tender. 'You are *not* totally ruined. Trust me on that.'

She left for Edinburgh early in the morning, before he and Nathan had finished packing. He watched her spend a long moment with his son, the two of them forehead to forehead, as she talked to him. He took heart, because he reckoned Nathan was her son now. They had forged a bond during their helter-skelter trip following a fruitcake— Good God, a fruitcake—from address to address. Lonely boy and lonely woman, they had written to each other while he was at sea—probably at sea in more ways than one, if he wanted to be honest.

'You are not totally ruined. Trust me on that,' was the last thing she said to him before the post rider handed her into the chaise for the short ride to the nearest mail-coach stop. He told her he could arrange a post chaise for her, too, but she wouldn't hear of it. Mary Rennie wasn't a Scot for nothing.

Not wanting to embarrass themselves in front of his son, and post riders and the Everetts, too, he had kissed her goodbye in the upstairs hallway. Only an idiot couldn't have noticed how much improved they both were. Of course they had practised the evening before, when she kindly helped him out of his peg, and before breakfast, when she had helped him into it. No matter how the whole affair fell out, he had no intention of telling her that he hadn't needed assistance in years.

Before the post rider could close the door, Nathan jumped inside. He clung to Mary and she to him, then she wrenched herself away, her face a mask of pain, and told him goodbye. Tears came to her eyes as she looked over Nathan's head to Ross.

'I have had enough of hails and farewells!' he couldn't help shouting in that quarterdeck voice of his as the chaise rolled away.

Their summertime return to Plymouth reminded Ross forcefully of their trip in December to Dumfries. Father and son needed to reintroduce themselves to each other. By the second night, they were easy with each other again, with one exception: both of them felt the lack of Mary Rennie. If he lived to be an old, old man, Ross knew he would never understand the pull of such a quiet lady. Strangely, he thought of the Napoleon he had watched nearly a year ago on the deck of Tom Ussher's frigate. Napoleon Bonaparte, a little man filled with ambition and cunning and genius, had ruled Europe for a generation. One man like that could change the course of history. One Mary Rennie would change nothing beyond the reach of her modest sphere. The world would never forget Napoleon. One man and one boy would never forget Mary Rennie. He knew, for the first time since the war began, which mattered more.

On the third day, Ross gave his son the scold he deserved for running away and frightening Mrs Pritchert, but he did it while the boy was close in his arms in the post chaise. He told his son everything he remembered about his beautiful Portuguese mother and told him he could ask anything he wanted about her. Nathan nodded and sighed. 'I never knew her, though.'

'No. She was a fine lady, Son. I loved her.' He

pulled his son closer, overwhelmed with his own uncertainty. 'I love Mary Rennie now.'

'What if Mary won't come to you?'

He had no answer.

When they arrived in London, he took Nathan to Admiralty House with him. They waited in the antechamber until Lord Melville summoned him.

'You'll sit here quietly, Nathan?' he asked.

His son nodded. 'My running days are over,' he assured his father, who turned away to hide his smile, because he sounded so dramatic.

Ross was not surprised when the First Lord offered him a desk job at Admiralty, an occupation with considerable responsibility, and coming with an increase in pay far exceeding his captain's salary. 'Of course, this will mean swallowing the anchor, Captain Rennie,' Melville told him. 'Your sailing days are over, but you'll stay in the navy.'

Ross could not deny that the position flattered him, but he had considerable wealth increasing in volume under the careful management of Brustein and Carter in Plymouth. London was far grander than Plymouth, but he had never cared for London. And why would he want to continue in thrall to the Royal Navy that had ruined him?

'I think not, my lord,' he said, after not overmuch consideration. 'I am mindful of the honour, but I really stopped here to resign my commission. My war is over, but I do not know if I have won or lost.'

Lord Melville gave him a strange look. Ross knew that every post captain still standing at the end of this world war would understand precisely what he meant, even if the First Lord did not.

'You could give it more thought, Captain,' Lord Melville suggested.

'I could, my lord, but the answer would be the same.' He bowed and started from the room.

To Ross's surprise and no little gratification, Lord Melville walked him to the door. 'As we speak, Captain Maitland's *Billy Ruffian* is shepherding Boney to St Helena.'

'Good God Almighty. That is a miserable rock in the middle of nowhere,' Ross exclaimed.

'Precisely. Goodbye, Captain. Fair winds and following seas to you.'

He had counted the miles to Plymouth, mainly because every mile took him farther from Mary Rennie. When the seaport was nearly in sight, he asked Nathan, 'What would you think if we were to move to Baltimore? It is in Maryland, at the head of Chesapeake Bay.'

'Da, that's enemy territory,' Nathan said. He thought a moment. 'Mary's thinking about going there, so it can't be all bad.'

'Aye, lad, and the American war is over, too. It's just a thought.'

Ross paid off the post chaise a few streets from Flora Street, because he still liked the walk. Whatever Mary had done to him in Skowcroft, his stump barely pained him.

'Do you think Mrs Pritchert will ever forgive me?' Nathan asked.

'She probably already has, laddie, but be prepared for the scolding that you richly deserve.'

They sauntered along slowly, Ross's hand on his son's shoulder. He never had to leave his boy again, but the whole thing hadn't settled in yet. Maybe a few days of peace would remedy the strangeness he felt.

When they arrived at Flora Street, Ross looked up to Nathan's bedroom window out of habit. A little embarrassed, he glanced at his son. 'Lad, I know you're beside me, but old habits die h—'

'Look.'

He looked again and drew in a shaking breath. Mary Rennie stood there, gazing down at them. He blinked. She was gone. He had imagined her.

Transfixed, he stood there as he heard light footsteps on the stairs. Nathan stepped away from him. When the door opened, Mary stood still for only a moment before she flung wide her arms and pulled him into her embrace.

'Did you change your mind?' he asked her breathlessly when he could speak.

'No. I told you somewhere or other while looking for fruitcake that I would love you until I die.'

Plymouth, one week later

'I trust I have met some expectations, madam wife,' he whispered into Mary's bare shoulder. 'You certainly have.' He eased his arm round her and kissed her sweaty hair. 'We'll have to do that a few more times to make certain.'

'Only a few more?'

No one would ever hear it from him, but his wife's mouth wasn't working so well. He thought her eyes had a glazed expression, too. Mary had told him earlier that her mother had never warned her about sailors, so he decided not to shoulder any of the blame—his first executive decision as a husband, after saying 'I will' to the vicar.

'Perhaps more than a few times,' he amended.

They lay so peacefully in a back room at Mrs Pritchert's house, the one he had bought to provide a home for his infant son and to expiate some of the guilt he had felt when Mr Pritchert had perished in battle. He and Mary had wanted Mr Everett to marry them, but neither wanted to climb into yet-another post chaise for a trip anywhere. Thank goodness the Everetts had no objection to travelling to Plymouth. Even now, Nathan and Mrs Pritchert were escorting the Everetts around the pretty little town their son Dale had known so briefly. Mary had blushed most becomingly when Nathan suggested she come along, too, since she didn't know the town too well, but Ross had overruled his son.

'She can do that later. I'll just show her around the house here while you're gone for an hour or two.'

'I'm certain she has seen a house, Da.'

'Not this one.'

'Well done there, husband,' Mary had told him later, after the tour which ended rather quickly in that back bedroom.

'I thought so.' Ross raised up on his elbow and ran his hand down Mary's breasts and stomach. When she moved his hand lower, he knew she was the perfect sailor's wife.

He had a question, though, and moved his hand back to her stomach. Even a year ago, he had never thought he would have his hand on a wife's belly and begin to dream about more children. Anything was possible now.

'I have to know something, Mary Rennie. Ah, I like the sound of your new name. Mary Rennie—there's such a ring to it.'

Mary thumped him in a tender spot.

'Maybe I will call you Mary Rennie Squared.'

'Maybe you will ask your question, so we can get back to business,' she said, sounding amazingly wifely after only their first tour of the house. How did women *do* that?

'Is it to be Baltimore?'

'I believe it is,' she said after a lengthy pause that told him she had just decided. 'I want a fresh start in a new country.'

'I thought you might, but be honest with me, wife: Is it your fresh start or mine?'

'Yours,' she said softly and kissed him. 'Do you mind?'

He turned onto his back, crossing his stump over his other upraised knee and waggling it at her. She laughed and rested her head on his chest. His hand went naturally to her head, and he caressed her hair, humbled to know that he never had to leave this woman for war.

'I've been thinking about Baltimore, too. I hate to admit this, but Yankee schooners and frigates ran rings around us in the Second American War. I can't tell you how I envied those clean lines. Damn, but Yankees can sail! I want to build a shipyard in Baltimore, or maybe Annapolis, and design yachts. With some assistance from former enemies, I don't doubt.'

'My goodness. Can we afford that?'

'Aye, lass. You married a reasonably well-off man.' He could spring the whole amount on her later. 'I'll design yachts, hire Yankee builders and encourage future customers to forget that we burned their plaguey capital. Maybe I'll start to drawl in that amusing way Marylanders do. Yes, I've known a few. Captured some. To make you happy, we'll save money if you are my clerk. At least, until you have other matters to keep you busy.'

He fingered her breast, noting a mole. She was

going to be great fun to explore. 'One thing, though: absolutely no fruitcake. I will not be moved on this matter, no matter how you beg.'

She thumped him again.

He turned on his side, and she did the same, running her hand gently and a bit timidly down his ribs and hip, pausing at a scar he might explain some day, if she wanted to hear more of his war stories. He just looked at her, amazed at his good fortune in finding a wife. 'Mostly, though, I will love you until I die.'

'I thought you might,' she said softly and kissed him.

* * * * *

MILLS & BOON®

Why shop at millsandboon.co.uk?

Each year, thousands of romance readers find their perfect read at millsandboon.co.uk. That's because we're passionate about bringing you the very best romantic fiction. Here are some of the advantages of shopping at www.millsandboon.co.uk:

* **Get new books first**—you'll be able to buy your favourite books one month before they hit the shops

* **Get exclusive discounts**—you'll also be able to buy our specially created monthly collections, with up to 50% off the RRP

* **Find your favourite authors**—latest news, interviews and new releases for all your favourite authors and series on our website, plus ideas for what to try next

* **Join in**—once you've bought your favourite books, don't forget to register with us to rate, review and join in the discussions

Visit **www.millsandboon.co.uk**
for all this and more today!